Something Surprising
By Paul Hart

Printed in the United States of America

First Printing

ISBN: 978-1-092-82743-0

Email: twopdhart@yahoo.com

There! I've Said It Again
By Redd Evans and Dave Mann
© MUSIC SALES CORPORATION

Cover
Max Guillory

For Vicki

*"In the morning sow thy seed, and in the evening
withhold not thine hand:
for thou knowest not whether shall prosper, either
this or that,
or whether they both shall be alike good."*—
Ecclesiastes 11:5-6

Chapter 1
Leaving Home

"Careful, Pop."

Tom grimaced as he planted his cane on the edge of the porch and took a slow first step down. Oh, that beautiful cane: His pride and joy! His grandson, Chad, made it as a Boy Scout project. Pecan wood, perfectly sanded and stained, it went everywhere with him. Ask him and he'd tell you all about it.

In the same way, he'd tell you what a fine young man Chad is, and how gifted his really smart sister, Hannah, up at Mizzou is. And, what a fine husband and father Tom Junior is, and how Judy is just the perfect daughter-in-law an old fellow could have.

A guy his age couldn't ask for better.

"My kids," he called them.

That cane had become as much a part of Tom Bentley as his gray moustache, his thin gray hair, the wire-rim glasses that made him look slightly bug-eyed, and his shuffling gait.

Tom Junior's grip on his arm helped—but his father didn't want to admit that. After all, he had been going down these steps for eighty years, thousands of times.

What was one more trip down them, even if it was to be his last?

He was leaving home.

One, two, three, steps, then down the narrow sidewalk and through the gate in the wrought-iron fence that circled the immaculate yard.

Tom knew what to do.

And what of this kid telling tell him how to go down them? Hadn't Tom been the one who carried seven-and-a-half pounds of newborn son up them for the first time? Well, yes, he had, nearly fifty years ago.

"Kid" is relative but a son is always a son—even when a son has a son. And furthermore, his father, Tom Junior's grandfather, had carried Thomas J. Bentley Sr. up these steps the first time just over eighty years ago.

Home.

The Victorian wonder towered behind father and son as they ambled toward the gate. He could walk down this sidewalk blindfolded, Tom thought, even if walking anywhere caused problems nowadays.

Not many men can say they lived in the same house for their entire lives but Tom Bentley could, even if he hadn't been able to safely go upstairs in months.

"Just a minute," he mumbled, as he stopped and turned around for a last, longing look at the gables, turrets and gingerbread.

"This is hard," the old man said with a sigh.

"I know," Tom Junior agreed. "Remember, I grew up here too."

Their old house towered above father and son, as beautiful as ever, mustard yellow trimmed in dark green with that ornate, stained-glass transom above the oversize front door. Gauzy curtains hung in the windows of the big turret on the southwest corner, with a fancy, pressed-tin pinnacle at its peak.

The Bentleys had money and they lavished proper maintenance and upkeep on the place—and it showed. Family heirlooms and collected antiques complemented the interior. One of those cable TV home-improvement shows sent a video crew up from Dallas several years ago, they gave Tom a DVD of the episode.

The house, his house, their house, was an absolute showpiece.

What a gem.

Tourists loved it—the most popular stop during Randall, Missouri's annual Pioneer Days. Frumpy, middle-aged ladies from the historical society, dolled-up in corsets and bustles, showed them around.

There was that one year that, unbeknownst to Tom, the historical society women served the tourists mint juleps in the parlor.

Scandal!

It made the locals aghast that Tom—Imagine! Tom Bentley of all people!—allowed liquor to be served in his home. Who would'a thought it?

Only he didn't know and he put a stop to it. No booze in his home—enough whispering and gossip. Next year the ladies went back to lemonade.

Oh, the memories: cleaning and tidying up the big house for hundreds of strangers to troop through. It finally turned into too much work for one old widower, even with volunteer help.

Coming down the hill from Randall's east end, if you veered left on Ninth Street in front of the Bentley place, 902 Poplar, the neighborhood changed from residential to commercial—doctors' offices, a law firm, things like that. If you veered right through the S-curve, the parade of Victorian castles continued on down the hill to the edge of Randall's nice—but dying—downtown.

A couple of the other old gems down Poplar became bed and breakfasts, catering to tourists headed to or from that tourist trap over in Branson, or Eureka Springs down in Arkansas.

Such a transition zone, where Ninth and Poplar converged, would lend itself to change, maybe more doctors' offices, a coffee shop or a Zumba studio?

The land might be worth more than the house. Tom didn't want to think about bulldozers and rubble.

He let out a sigh, shook his head and turned back to the street.

"Hmph, nursing home," he muttered sadly.

"Look, Pop, you're the guy who claims to be an optimist, who's always looking for the good in life," Tom Junior said cheerfully. "What's that old hymn you like to sing, *Something good is going to happen to you?*"

"I guess so."

"See? You don't know what lies ahead, this could be the start of something big," the son added.

"Maybe," his father replied flatly, unconvinced.

Tom Junior's Lexus sat just beyond the gate underneath the big oaks. More memories: At that same spot once sat Tom's father's brand-new '36 LaSalle. The memory still glowed in his mind: A barefoot five-year-old running down the sidewalk to see daddy's new car.

It had been sixty years since he ran anywhere.

Tom Junior opened the passenger door and helped his old man in, buckled his seatbelt and shut the door. The son went around to the driver's side, buckled up, pushed the start button and the motor sprung to life.

10

"And what will you do with the house?" Tom asked, staring ahead at the red mailbox with "902 BENTLEY" painted on its side, just above the flag. Both men, as boys, had stood on tippy toes to reach into it.

"We have the cleaning service coming tomorrow to tidy everything up," Tom Junior replied as he put the car in drive. "We may have to do a little painting and fix-up; one thing at a time. I'd like to get it on the market as soon as we can, fall isn't a good time to put a house up for sale.

"Who knows what will happen? Someone may want to make it into a bed and breakfast or, well, they may just want the lot. It's hard to say."

That made Tom shudder.

"Did you get all my stuff?" the father asked.

"As much as we could we moved over to your room. The rest, well, maybe, we still have some things to go in the tra—, uh, sort out. Judy's working on that.

"Some of grandma's antiques are worth a lot, we have appraisers in town, we could make money."

In his mind's eye, Tom saw a thirty-yard dumpster in the side yard, in front of the stable that had housed more cars in its lifetime than horses—with scrapes on its door frame to prove it.

Stuff, lots of stuff, memories, matériel from four generations, thrown in a big metal box and hauled off to the dump.

And he was getting dumped too.

"Let's do one last drive through town," Tom suggested. He loved Randall.

"Sure," the son replied as he flipped the turn signal on and headed off through a swirl of autumn leaves down

11

Poplar. Randall still had its picturesque Midwestern town square with the big Limestone County Courthouse, built of red granite, in the middle. A weather vane that may, or may not, swing into the wind topped its clock tower, but the clock still showed the right time.

Nearby First Presbyterian's tall steeple with the gold cross on top provided a soaring counterpoint to the courthouse spire.

Otherwise, downtown didn't amount to much anymore.

Once-bustling Koppel's Department Store had disappeared, along with Kinnard's Shoes, Draper Furniture and Wiesen's Jewelry, all choked to death. Blame that gargantuan, big-box supercenter out on the bypass around the north side, surrounded by chain motels and fast-food joints.

The chic-as-Randall-ever-got A La Mode ladies' fashions had gone away too and a peeling, hand-lettered plywood sign reading RESAIL hung over a dusty, padlocked door, surrounded by empty wine bottles.

The historic First Baptist Church building next door now housed Helping Hands Ministry for the homeless, and a clutch of scruffy transients sat around it most days. The church itself had moved into an impressive, hangar-sized building out on the bypass, and changed its name to Family Fellowship. A gigantic billboard flashed Bible verses at motorists speeding past on the four lane.

Likewise, TV had killed the Rialto Theater a half-block up from the square. Paint peeled off its ornate, two-story sign, and the marquee had been set for years:

TONGUES OF LIVING FIRE
TABERNACLE 9AM SUN

The stately Merchants & Planters Bank building with its big limestone pillars remained the tallest building in town—eight stories—but now had a backlit sign over the revolving front door advertising MissouriTomorrow Bank.

Oh, and what about The Malt Shop? Who could forget?

Tom and all other faithful Randall High Rams huddled there. To this day, anytime the old man smelled hamburgers and French fries he thought of the joint. Macho football players wore their gray and white letterman's jackets with the big blue R on the front to The Malt Shop to impress the gals, even in summer heat.

But now, Tom saw a neon sign reading Rio Bravo—Comidas Mexicanas flashing busily in red, white and green above the familiar door.

The old man sighed as they drove past.

"When did The Malt Shop close? It was the place to be back when, all the kids went there."

"It's been gone, what, a decade or more?" Tom Junior replied. "Nowadays Rio Bravo is the happenin' place in beautiful downtown Randall. It goes nuts Friday and Saturday nights, hour-long waits for a No. 3 dinner and mariachis. Some travel magazine rated it 'worth a stop' in a big cover story on the Ozarks. I come at lunch, the crowd's not too bad.

"Then there's Bea's Hen House, that all-you-can eat fried chicken joint, over there, across from the courthouse," Tom Junior added, pointing out the windshield. "It's where the furniture store used to be.

13

"Fried chicken? Yes, Bea's. I remember we went there once, I think for Judy's birthday? Your kids were little and I had them convinced an old tank car parked down on the railroad track had a load of gravy for the mashed potatoes," Tom laughed.

"I remember that!" his son replied, joining the laughter. "Salesman that you are, you really had them goin'.

"Randall has become the dining hub of South Missouri. You come down here on weekends, you can't find a place to park. People drive over here from Springfield and Rolla."

Tom shook his head and grunted.

"Things change, alright, but I do like crunchy tacos and fried chicken. I'm glad I still have all my teeth, not everyone my age can say that."

Father and son enjoyed another laugh as they idled down the street.

These weren't empty and rundown buildings for Tom, they were people. People owned them, worked in them, shopped in them, worshiped in them. The people were gone, leaving empty brick and stone skeletons.

Every street, every building, every door held memories. His eyes watered and he braced his cane between his knees as he stuck a finger behind his wire rims and brushed a tear.

"They're gone and now I am too," he mumbled.

"No Pop, c'mon, that's not true, things just change," the son replied. "You know, some developer wants to convert one of the old buildings into loft apartments. Will that work in Randall? Who knows? But it might perk up downtown to have twentysomethings living down here."

"Hey, uh, go out by the old depot and the high school," Tom said, pointing ahead.

"Sure," his son answered as they waited at a stoplight for no one.

The light turned green, and they slowly made their way around the grand courthouse. They rode on a couple more blocks, past where the old Carnegie Library once stood—long since replaced by a modernistic travesty Tom complained "looks like a wrecked airplane" with its swooping roof. They passed empty warehouses and the weedy lot where a tidy brick railroad station once served as the town's transportation hub.

But the big, yellow-brick warehouse with the red-and-white Bentley Hardware sign on its roof remained, "thanks, Tom Junior" the father thought as they drove by.

They rumbled over the tracks and rode past the high school, one place that looked much as the old man remembered it, except for new windows. His eyes caught CLASS OF 1949 carved on one corner and he thought back to that May evening with his classmates, when some politician from President Truman's cabinet made a speech about leaving home and chasing your dreams.

The school buzzed, a counterpoint to the empty downtown. Cars and buses filled the parking lot, many hung with blue and white balloons, streamers and banners that proclaimed victory at that night's football game with Lebanon.

Fat chance.

Area teams regarded playing Randall as the next best thing to an open date.

"Seen enough?" Tom Junior asked, "Or, do you want to swing by the cemetery?"

Tom sighed, licked the corner of his gray moustache and pushed his glasses back on his nose. He thought for a moment, sighed, and answered, "No, it'll make me miss your dear mother all the more, maybe some other time."

The son turned and drove out from town, past the country club and its golf course that rolled along Quartz Creek, down a little state highway that heads off through beautiful countryside, where the Missouri prairie melts into the Arkansas Ozarks.

"Did you let your sister know I'm moving?" Tom asked.

"I tried. I called the last phone number I have and it wasn't working; no email. I mailed a letter to the last street address she gave me, someplace in California. It came back yesterday, return to sender," Tom Junior said with a sigh.

"I really don't know where she is."

The old man sadly shook his head.

They passed the first cow pasture out of town, and there it sat on the right, behind a big sign:

Hickory Bough
Solutions For Senior Living

A low building made of cream-colored stone framed a parking lot that held a handful of cars, a big van and an ambulance. A helipad sat to one side with a limp windsock lazily rocking back and forth.

16

The turn signal came on and the Lexus turned in, then slowed to a stop underneath the covered driveway at the main door.

"Hickory Bough sounds so much better than 'nursing home," Tom complained, "Except your grandfather used a hickory stick on my behind."

Tom Junior hung his head and let out a loud sigh as he pushed the button and shut off the engine.

"Look, Pop, remember: Be positive!

"We've been over this, you simply cannot continue to live alone," his son replied firmly. "You have those fainting spells, you black out. You've been in the hospital once, the emergency room twice, you've broken bones."

"Isn't there something better? They have those nice senior apartments at that assisted-living place down in Bella Vista, Concordia?, over in Arkansas," the old man complained.

"That's true, they are nice, but that's a two-hour drive—if Springfield traffic's not too bad. There are options in Springfield too," Tom Junior said.

"But I thought we agreed we want something nearby. If anything happens, I want to get here as soon as I can. This is the best there is in Randall, you'll like it."

"But what about the house?" the father replied, almost pleading. "We could get someone to check on me."

"Hey, we did, and it didn't work. You still fell and hurt yourself when she wasn't there," Tom Junior said. "You know you can't live alone anymore. Stop and think, Pop: How did you feel last time you fell, there in the kitchen?"

The boy had a point.

17

After the pleasant memories this morning, Tom didn't want to dwell on that awful day.

It was another one of those weird things that came on suddenly, when least expected. The floor began to spin, his eyes went dark and he passed out as he went off into some strange place of dreams, hallucinations, flashbacks and nightmares.

And more than once, as Tom Junior noted, he fell and hurt something before he managed to sit down or grab a table.

"Why?" Tom wanted to know. What caused it, low blood pressure, a tumor, some hormone imbalance?

There had been all sorts of tests, including that big MRI thing at that hospital over in Springfield. His ears rang for days after they stuck him in that big donut hole.

The doctors, always, scratched their chins, looked at the test results, then said they weren't sure: "Here, take this prescription, maybe that'll help."

The result?

He could make a meal out of his daily pills—blue, pink, white and yellow; oval, round and square. And that didn't count all the vitamins and mineral supplements Judy made him take.

"We want to keep you around!" she'd tell him cheerfully whenever she brought Tom another sack filled with bottles of pills and powders she bought at that vitamin store out on the bypass.

The grandson's beautiful cane didn't help with that fall in the kitchen. That was the worst one. How long was he out, several hours?

An agonizing pain throbbed in his ankle when he came around. Of course, he didn't have his phone in his pocket and he had been flat on the floor, moaning, in blinding pain, for ever so long.

Lucky for him it happened the one day a week Missouri Maids came to clean house and the two ladies found him, sprawled in front of the kitchen sink. The ambulance came screaming up Poplar and took him to Randall's little hospital. X-rays showed a bad break to his ankle, he went home in a cast.

A doctor cautioned, "Next time it'll be your hip or a concussion. Be careful, take precautions!"

That's when Tom Junior started pushing the issue: It's time. Your eightieth birthday is here, get in some sort of assisted-living place. You can be comfortable and when something happens—and it will—they can take care of you.

That, of course, meant "nursing home," to Tom. He spit the words out in multiple arguments.

But the family won, he would move.

"Dad, this is a nice place, it's fairly new. You'll have your own little apartment and make new friends," Tom Junior said. "Great things could happen here!"

"Not likely."

Here they went, around and around, as in other conversations and arguments.

The son didn't want to go through it again—not now, not by the front door with strangers walking past and staring through the windshield.

And the father knew the son, his dearest friend, the boy he adored, was right.

19

By your ninth decade, a person knows things don't always work out like you want. But Tom Junior was sharp, and "my kids" really cared about him.

The old man would adjust, somehow.

Chapter 2
The Big Board

The son opened his door and came around to help his father out. The pair walked up to Hickory Bough's double door and a hostess welcomed them, exchanged pleasantries and pointed them to the office.

They meet Mrs. Stevens, the middle-aged, plump and mostly pleasant—but all business—Hickory Bough manager. She wore her usual forced smile. She had streaks of gray in her short, black hair and reading glasses she kept half-way down her nose.

"It's so nice to see you. Now let's see, 'Thomas J. Bentley,' here it is," she said as she pulled a big file folder off her credenza. She had Tom and son sign a blizzard of forms, then the trio headed through the big lobby and dayroom toward what she smilingly called "a suite" and Tom called "a room" when he saw it.

"We have four hallways—A, B, C and D. Your new home will be suite B 9," she explained cheerily as they matched the slow pace of Hickory Bough's newest resident and his cane. Sure enough, at a door with "B 9" on a little sign to one side, a freshly printed card announced "Tom Bentley."

Home?

Never!

"Nice touch for a cell," Tom thought to himself.

He found Mrs. Stevens's "suite" optimistic for one, fair-sized room, painted light gray, with a divider. It had a small conversation area with a sofa and chair, next to a tiny kitchen with a little refrigerator scarcely big enough to hold a six pack, a small sink and a microwave. A modest-sized television sat atop an empty bookshelf.

A stack of unopened boxes sat on the floor beside the shelf.

Behind the divider Tom saw a bed, a recliner and an oversize door to a bathroom with grab rails around the toilet and tub/shower. A surprisingly large closet already held Tom's clothes, thanks to Judy.

Dark blue drapes covered big windows on the far wall.

Not bad, but a far cry from the big Victorian house. Four-thousand square feet to two-hundred square feet, Tom estimated.

"Well, I guess that's all for now," Tom Junior said with a sigh as they stood, surveying his father's "suite."

The pair shuffled back to Hickory Bough's front door.

"I'll be back out in a day or two with Judy to check on you. Once you get settled I know you'll like it here; nice place," Tom Junior said, forcing a grin.

He hugged his father tightly, knocking the old man's glasses askew. He held him for a moment with that certain tenderness adult children save for aging parents, then gave him a wave as he headed out to his car.

Tom waved back as he silently watched the Lexus drive off. He stood there for a moment alone, then turned and went back inside where the manager waited.

"Would you like to look around?" Mrs. Stevens asked.

"I guess so, but what is there to see?" Tom asked as he pushed his glasses straight with his thumb.

"Oh! We have a beautiful facility! I'll show you the lounge, the library, the dining room—we even have an exercise facility and a swimming pool," she replied.

A pool? A swimming pool? That was like running barefoot. Tom couldn't remember the last time he had been in water, even in a bathtub. He did showers. Could he still swim? He wasn't so sure if he could. One of those boxes by his TV held his Scout uniform sash with a swimming merit badge, but he couldn't remember any strokes.

The exercise room had all sorts of dark-gray gadgets with pulleys, levers and stuff. Together, they looked like some complex Rube Goldberg machine, Tom thought. A little old lady rode a stationary bicycle at the room's far end.

Now that might be doable, he noted, although he hadn't ridden a bike in years.

They went on at Tom's usual slow shuffle, the cane clicking on the floor, until they came to a large open lounge.

"And this is our beautiful dayroom," the manager said with a practiced wave of her hand.

It horrified Tom.

The room and its furnishings were nice enough but, ugh, the people—if that's what they were.

It was a freak show: Ragged, sleeping, unkempt; some drooled, some were tied in their wheelchairs so they wouldn't fall out.

"Good Lord, it's the bar scene from *Star Wars*!" Tom thought to himself.

And the smell, yuck! It reminded him of the bathroom back home, years ago, toilet training Tom Junior and Brenda.

Again, what was *he* doing here?

Did he look like that bad?

Did he smell that bad?

Maybe Tom Bentley was in worse shape than he knew.

No, no he wasn't!

He could walk, he could go to the bathroom by himself. He should not be here.

Hang it, maybe he would move down to Bella Vista anyway—and the kids could just drive!

But he said nothing and followed Mrs. Stevens as she continued her well-practiced tour. They went through the airy dining room with big windows that spilled sunshine across the tables. Lunch wasn't far off and some sort of industrial-grade, food-type odor enveloped the place.

This time it wasn't potty training, rather Army mess halls in Korea that came to mind.

Mrs. Stevens didn't seem to notice Tom's silence and went on smiling and chirping about "nice" this and "excellent" that. He had decided to just walk along and nod from time to time.

Eventually they ended up back at B 9. She smilingly said to let her "know if you need anything!" and the hallway nurse would be by to introduce herself.

Ugh.

Surely there must be something modestly pleasant or enjoyable about Hickory Bough.

Tom knew, more than ever, nothing good could come out of this dreadful place.

He turned and looked at himself in a big mirror.

Behold, Tom Bentley: The brown hair had long-since disappeared and what little hair he had turned gray. The moustache trailed behind his head a few years but now it too was gray.

Wrinkles, lots of wrinkles, and crow's feet flowed back from the lenses of his glasses like flames painted on a dragster's fenders.

Still, he looked better than the other Hickory Bough residents he'd seen.

Definitely! The smile remained.

But what happened to that good-looking boy in his pep club sweater? Or, that proud teen-ager with his hand up, giving the Scout pledge at his Eagle Scout Court of Honor? What became of the track team member holding a (rare) trophy with his teammates? Where did the handsome lad in a suit getting inducted into the National Honor Society go?

And certainly, what about that sharp-looking guy waltzing at the senior prom as classmates cheered?

The photos in the boxes and the memories in his head—the popular, friend-of-everyone guy, the one girls giggled over, the above-average student, the class president—did not match the bent, shuffling little man in front of him, leaning on a cane, a grandpa getting thrown away.

He sighed, then decided to investigate his "suite." Phooey with that: room. There must be big windows behind those curtains. Hickory Bough sat out of town, getting into the hills. That might not be so bad! Southern Missouri's hills and woods can be beautiful, especially in the fall, and this far out he should have a nice view.

Tom shuffled over to the far end of the drapes and pulled the cord. Sunlight flooded the room.

He gasped. Instead of lovely trees and hills, his windows offered a magnificent view of the building's big air conditioner, an emergency generator, an alley dumpster and the greasy kitchen loading dock.

No, it was too much, just too depressing.

He slumped down in the room's big chair, sat his cane against an end table and cupped his face in his gnarled hands. His eyes watered, he took off his glasses.

He had lived for eighty years to end up in this? A successful businessman, a decorated Army veteran, a devoted husband and widowed father, thrown here? Tom Bentley, who maintained the family business, who served as a Baptist deacon—in this?

Tom Bentley made Randall, and maybe the world, a better place. And this is what he gets?

He sat silently as tears wetted his hands; depressed.

Then he noticed it: the incessant drone of multiple televisions down the hall, all playing at once, loudly and on different channels: audio chaos.

Tom felt a kick of anger. Televisions have off switches and they should be used, except maybe for baseball games and *Jeopardy!*

Thankfully, he had a door. Tom sat back, grabbed a Kleenex from a box on the nightstand and wiped his eyes with a loud sigh.

This was going to be hard.

The brooding suddenly ended with two loud, sharp knocks at that open door and, seemingly, a gigantic bowling ball rolled into his room.

What on earth?

His jaw dropped, could it be another dizzy spell? The floor didn't spin, he didn't black out—but could he be hallucinating?

"Helloooo! You must be Tom Bentley!" the bowling ball sang out.

No, wait, the gigantic ball had stubby little legs, puffy little hands and big, round glasses. It must be human.

He realized he saw a short, obese, middle-aged woman wearing, of all things, a clerical collar. It—she— must be some kind of priest or nun or something.

"I am so glad to see *you*!" the bowling ball sang out cheerily.

"Uh, hello," Tom replied carefully, looking at her sideways. "And you are?"

"Oh! I'm Gaylene Gillogly! I'm the Hickory Bough chaplain!" she chirped as she clapped fat little hands. "I am the *Reverend* Gaylene Gillogly! Welcome to your new home at Hickory Bough!

"This is *not* my home," Tom thought to himself.

The priest had a puffy round face framed by curly, salt-and-pepper hair cut short. The round glasses and toothy smile gave her sort of a Teddy Roosevelt look.

She spoke in exclamations.

She bounced.

This woman must be real, no hallucination here.

Gaylene had gone on chirping away for some time about "wonderful" this and "exciting" that as Tom carefully studied her. Her voice made him think of a canary twittering.

"There are so many nice people here! There are so many things to do! Why, just yesterday I told your neighbors you were coming to join us! They are so excited!"

On and on she went.

Tom stared at the carpet and thought: How could anyone be so bouncy, upbeat and joyful about a ghastly hole like Hickory Bough? What had he missed? Could he find some joy there?

Not likely.

Gaylene didn't notice his pensive look and went on talking at top speed.

"I know we are going to be great friends! I'm so looking forward to helping you settle in! I know you have questions!" Gaylene said, finally pausing.

"Yes, I have one," Tom said, coughing. "You are a full-time chaplain *here*?"

"Oh no! I have a parish too! I'm rector at St. Aidan's Episcopal over in Hartville! What an honor! They are just the sweetest people! But I just love to spend time here! I get to help all the wonderful Hickory Bough people—like you!—who make their home here! It is such an honor!"

Hartville, oh yes, east of town, Bentley Hardware had a dealer there for years. Take the highway a few miles east, on out Poplar, not much to it. The town had some Civil War battle or something; roadside historical marker.

"Well! I have to run along! You take care of yourself, Tom! I'll be back soon! Good-bye and God bless you! We are all so glad to have you! You are beginning a wonderful new life journey!"

With that, the ball rolled out his door.

Tom sat, speechless.

"… *Wonderful new life journey*," now that sounded like something a preacher might say. But what an odd person, her bounce made up for some of the coma-like characters he had seen.

"Further proof I'm in *Star Wars* with things like that running around," he mumbled.

Tom reached in his pocket to check the time on his phone: 12:01. No wonder he felt hungry. Breakfast had been sparse, the dregs of a box of bran flakes shared with Tom Junior. The emptied kitchen had little to eat, they had just barely enough milk for their cereal as the son finished cleaning out Tom's refrigerator.

Let's see, where did he see the dining room? That industrial chow odor had now drifted into his, uh, suite so it must be nearby.

He took his cane, stood up and headed for the door. Just as he came out in the hall a wheelchair, going backwards, stopped at his door.

Another dizzy spell? A swarthy, gray-haired man with bushy eyebrows reached out his hand.

"So you're the new guy?" the wheelchair's occupant asked.

"Yes, I guess I am, Tom Bentley," he said as he reached out to shake. "And you?"

"The name's Tony, properly Antonio Di Burlone, been here a coupl'a years now. Yes, a few of us are sane."

Tom laughed. "You read my mind."

"I figured as much," Tony replied as he glanced in Tom's room. "I'm the resident manager of snarky remarks. Pleased to see your interior design consultant recommended the charming, dishwater gray décor. Hickory Bough also features moose brown, fungus green and dirty-diaper yellow options for residents with differing tastes."

The pair enjoyed a good laugh.

"I'm glad to meet someone else," Tom said. "I've only met the manager and the chaplain."

"Oh, the rev, Gillogly," Tony replied with an eye roll. "Whee! She's off in her own world—welcome to Pluto! But I'll say she means well, she wants to help folks, just kinda' kooky."

"So what happened to you?" asked Tom as he joined his backwards-moving friend and they slowly made their way toward lunch.

"Stroke, bad one. I can speak and think, but I can't walk, read or do much of anything else. In fact, the best way for me to get around is pushing myself along in this thing.

"Can you imagine? I'm tryin' to figure out how to live my life backwards. Maybe a few more years of this and I could be that hunky young Italian guy again with the slicked-back hair, the one the girls went crazy for. Back when, I had a couple of 'em convinced Frankie Avalon and me were cousins."

"I hope you figure this life-backwards thing out, and if you do let me know your trick," Tom answered. "There are several things back there I'd do differently if I had the chance."

"Ain't that the truth!" Tony added. "Most of us do, but hey, we have it better than some people around here, let's be pals," he said as he slowly pushed his chair with a foot. "You might stick to the B and C halls, A and D are the three-hots-and-a-cot people."

"The what?" Tom asked, puzzled.

"Medicaid: three meals and a bed, minimal things to keep an indigent alive, your taxes at work," Tony explained. "Their rooms are half the size of ours and they share. Very sad, you don't know how good you have it."

"Maybe not," Tom said, mulling the remark.

They turned the corner and Tom's new friend motioned up at a big whiteboard on the wall. "Look, you're famous!"

Tom somehow missed it earlier but handwritten in blue Magic Marker were life's basics for Hickory Bough's often confused residents:

- Today is: Friday
- Weather: Partly cloudy, turning colder
- Lunch: Corned beef & cabbage
- Dinner: Fish fry
- Activities: Card night
- Greet our new resident: Tom Bentley

Corned beef and cabbage? "Gag me with a spoon," Tom thought. So that's what he smelled.

He hated cooked cabbage. It made him think of kimchi, and that make him think of Korea. He wasn't getting off to a good start with the kitchen.

"Not my favorite meal but I'm hungry," Tom said, nodding at Tony.

"Understood. Make it a point to check the big board after breakfast every morning and you can plan ahead. Cheese and crackers in your easy chair beats the dining room sometimes," Tony explained.

Hickory Bough's residents, at least those who could walk, were in the dining room but Tom noticed the quiet. An odd assortment of slurping and gurgling sounds played as the wait staff hustled around.

"Come sit at my table," Tony offered. Tom sat down next to Tony's spot with no chair and a waitress brought them their meals. Tom ate the corned beef and took a few bites of the cabbage, just to be polite.

Tony had a challenge trying to eat, leaning backwards, but the two new friends had a good conversation.

"Are you from Randall? I don't remember meeting you and you look about my age," Tom asked.

"Oh no, I'm from Wop Hill, Little Italy in St. Louis," Tony explained. "I grew up down the street from Harry Caray's home, life-long Cardinals fan."

"So how did you end up here?"

"My daughter and son-in-law retired five years ago, they lived out in the County, Woodson Terrace, near the airport. They bought a little place in the mountains, just over the line in Arkansas. Hickory Bough's the nearest nursing home, so they moved me here," Tony said.

"Ah! You said 'nursing home!' I gather that it is not allowed in a center dedicated to solutions for senior living?" Tom said with a laugh.

"You are quite right, my friend," Tony said seriously. "Don't ever say those two words in front of Mrs.

Stevens. That's one thing that will make that plastic smile turn into something mean and ugly. Trust me, I know.

"And you, may I ask what made you choose Hickory Bough as your senior living solution?"

The question made Tom laugh.

"Oh, I'm a native, lived in Randall my whole life, same house as a matter of fact, except in the war. My son and his family live here in town and they want me close by. I couldn't live alone anymore, even though I'm in pretty good shape for a guy my age.

"I stopped driving a couple years ago, gave my creampuff Oldsmobile to our church. Hey, they stopped making those things. My son runs the family business. My kids are really sweet and try to take care of good ol' grandpa."

"Now what war would that be?" asked Tony, staring intently at Tom. "You look a little young for War Two, I'm guessin' Korea?"

"You guess right," said Tom. "I enrolled in Army ROTC in college up at Missouri. The whole mess started right after my freshman year. I came home for the summer of '50 to work for my dad and suddenly, Bam!, just like that I got jerked into Officer Candidate School.

"I did a lot of drill, fired a lot of artillery, took a lot of tests and presto: instant Army officer!

"I was the classic ninety-day wonder, a shave tail. I got my lieutenant's commission that fall and off I went. I may have been the youngest officer in the U.S. military."

"So, I guess you watched every episode of *M*A*S*H*?" Tony asked brightly.

"Hardly," Tom answered grimly. "The good Army doctors and nurses saved my life. I watched it a couple times, found it tacky."

"Well, I didn't make it to Korea," answered Tony. "I got outta' high school, spring of '53. My best friend's older brother came home in a box, great guy, we all loved him, their mom cried her eyes out.

"That really upset me. I decided when I graduated I'd enlist, then go over there and kick me some commie butt to even the score. I enlisted two days after I graduated."

"Let's see, June of 1953, that cut it close," Tom said. "So did you ship out?"

"Too close, they signed the truce while I did basic at Fort Sam in San Antonio. When I finished, the Army gave me this extended leave while they tried to figure out what to do with me. I got ordered to Fort Polk, Louisiana, as a cook's assistant in a mess hall for two years. I stirred enough soup to make PFC and I went home.

"A kitchen in a Louisiana summer is not the place you want to be, that's my memory of the Army. Did you see combat?"

Tom sighed, "Yes and no. The Army put me in the Quartermaster Corps and I officially served behind the lines. But the Korean War was a mess the first year or so, there were no lines. I got hit and have a nasty scar to prove it on my leg, haven't walked right since. For God-knows-what reason, I made it."

The two old veterans sat silently.

"Korea was a hell hole, awful place," Tom continued. "I couldn't understand why we were fighting

34

over this depressing, rocky country with dreadful weather populated by people living just this side of the Stone Age. They ate dogs. Who would want it?

"I thought they should just let Kim have it, then we could all go home. Believe me, weeks and months of that, lying in your bunk listening to artillery in the middle of the night, and Randall, Missouri, and the people here looked like heaven.

"The worst part for a QM officer came with ordering caskets. I ordered a lot of caskets. Some of them were for guys who couldn't take it anymore and, well, you know. An M1 shoots any way you point it.

"From what I saw the Koreans would just keep shooting at each other and we'd never hear from them again once we left," he added.

"Oh yeah?" Tony said, laughing.

"Ha! You know how that turned out!" Tom replied. "I have a Samsung TV in my room and I bet the kitchen back there has a bunch of LG refrigerators. They unload shipping containers at the family warehouse with 'Hyundai' painted on their sides. Nowadays the Koreans pop up everywhere, they even send us baseball players. Our church had a Korean evangelist speak during last spring's revival."

"You're right, my daughter drives a Kia," added Tony. "It's the same thing that happened with the Japs. They lost the big war but won, sort of: Toyota, Sony, Nikon, you name it. Sometimes the best thing that can happen to you is to lose."

"It just goes to show you can be wrong about things," Tom said with a chuckle as he finished off a slice of cake and wiped his mouth.

"That's for certain," Tony said. "Sometimes we don't know as much as we think we do."

The dining room had emptied and the friends left their table and began the slow trip back to their suites. They rounded the corner into B Hall as a little woman came toward them holding tightly onto a walker. She stopped and waved at Tony with a shaky "Hello!"

"Oh, Nancy, this is Tom Bentley, the new guy. Tom, this is Nancy."

Tom nodded, the bent-over little woman smiled at him and shuffled on. A few steps later and there suddenly came a thunderclap of a belch. Tom jumped and looked back.

"What was that?" he asked.

"Not what, who—don't be rude," Tony said. "Her name's Nancy Reagan but we call her 'Noisy' for obvious reasons."

"Nancy Reagan? Really?" Tom asked.

"Yep, you can't make that up. I guess she has some kinda' intestinal or bowel problem and, well, some bricks dropped off her load, if you know what I mean," Tony explained.

"But she's a sweet little lady, very sweet. Nancy's just the nicest person. She'll just show up and sit down and smile at you, then, well, bodily function stuff happens that you want to avoid. But she's a good friend."

Tom turned into B 9 as Tony continued his backwards scoot down the hall with a wave.

He dug around in a box to find the iPad Hannah and Chad bought him. What a lucky guy to have such thoughtful grandkids.

They loaded it up with Stephen Ambrose books and Shelby Foote's civil war history, stuff they knew he liked.

They also set him up with one of those email account things on the web, mostly so they could send him jokes, videos of piano-playing cats, and other funny stuff to brighten an old fellow's day. He also got a Cardinals baseball update every day; great stuff.

He opened up *Undaunted Courage* but reading didn't last long as he dozed off.

The old man was well into a good afternoon nap when a knock on his door woke him. He raised his head to see a broadly smiling young lady of color in a nurse's uniform.

"Monsieur Bentley? May I come in?" the nurse asked with a thick accent.

"Oh sure," Tom replied, "You must be the hall nurse."

"Oh non, ce n'est pas moi!" she answered, "Excuse me, I am sorry, I am Clémence, I am just the assistant. I need to check the vitals."

She spoke with an accent so thick it took sleepy Tom a moment to figure out what "vee-DOLLS" were. But he sat up on the edge of the bed and obliged while she checked his temperature, pulse and blood pressure. No surprises.

"Uh, you must be new to Randall, young lady," Tom said politely as he rolled down his sleeve, trying to make small talk.

"Oui, I am from Cote d'Ivoire. Have a nice day," the nurse said, still smiling all the while as she scurried out his door.

Tony joined him for dinner with lots of St. Louis Cardinals talk. They were starting dessert, peach pie a la mode, when Noisy Nancy scooted slowly to their table. She greeted them with a mumbled "hello boys," sat down and let out a sneeze that shook the room. The men went on talking baseball as Nancy sat and smiled without eating.

His first week proved uneventful. He met Josefina, a young Hispanic, who alternated shifts with Clémence. Both liked Tom.

Tom Junior and Judy came by the next weekend. His daughter-in-law busied herself emptying the rest of the boxes into Tom's shelves and drawers as he and the boy talked.

Tom watched her busily sorting things, he appreciated her so much. Judy was the daughter he had always wanted.

Tom tried to be as upbeat as he could. It helped that things were comparatively festive right then by Hickory Bough standards with Thanksgiving coming. There were paper turkeys going up on the walls, Indian corn ears on the dining tables and more bustle than usual.

They were back with Hannah and Chad on Thanksgiving Day for, what else?, turkey and dressing. They had the standard holiday conversation that included Tom's usual question: "Have you heard from your sister?"

Tom Junior, as always, answered "No."

Tony vaporized over the holiday but reappeared at dinner Sunday night. Tom had started work on a club sandwich when his companion backed in.

"So how about the fam?" his buddy asked.

"Oh, fine, good to see them, had hoped to introduce you," Tom answered.

"Didn't want to get in the way, you don't know how lucky you are," Tony said.

"Oh? I thought you had family nearby."

"I do, but I don't see 'em much. They'll make their semiannual appearance Christmas Day; Easter and Christmas."

"I hope they come more often than that," Tom replied with a note concern. "Is there, maybe, an issue between you?"

"Oh no, not at all. You're new, you don't know how it works. Someone moves in here and the family and friends have intentions to come out every week. And they do, for a while. Then the visits come less and less often. You'll see," Tony said.

"Speaking of Christmas, have your kid bring you some ear plugs next time he drives out," Tony volunteered as they watched the staff hang Christmas ornaments as they took down the turkeys.

"Whatever for?" Tom asked, puzzled.

"For all of the kids and choirs and stuff," his friend answered. "Every do-gooder church, school, ladies' guild, barbershop quartet and service club in town will be out here between now and Christmas to sing for the geezers. They post whoever's singing that day on the big board."

"I bet Gaylene has something to do with this," Tom added.

"Of course! She books 'em and probably hands out the same music to all: 'Here, sing this!' Well, I know her heart's in the right place.

"Turn off your hearing aids, you wear hearing aids?" Tony said.

"Well yes, I do, thanks for the tip."

Tony proved correct. For three weeks before the big day there were children's choirs, various adult groups, an Elvis impersonator, even a kazoo band, all making the trip to Hickory Bough. The buddies avoided most.

Just for kicks they sat in on a performance by the Randall High School honor chorale that did a pretty good job with some classical music. The sharp-dressed teens, sporting blue blazers and gray slacks or skirts, finished a carol with a loud "Alleluia!" and in the short silence that followed there was suddenly a loud "Ha-ha-ha-ha-ha!" followed by a loud burp and hacking cough.

Nancy.

Tony looked at Tom with an eye roll and Tom nodded back.

Christmas Day proved nice. "My kids" came out to have lunch with the old man. Tom saw Tony talking to a sixtyish couple he surmised to be family.

Then came New Year's, and the solutions for senior living settled into a dull routine. The weather remained bad and a scheduled trip to the doctor in Hickory Bough's oversize van had to be postponed due to snow.

February came, and there were groundhog decorations in the dining room for a couple days that brought out some particularly snarky remarks from Tony that left Tom laughing so hard he dropped his fork at dinner one night.

Noisy Nancy would join them sometimes but rarely said anything, just smiling as she ate, interrupted too often by violent coughs, or worse. She would come by Tom's room from time to time, stop and lean on her walker to look in as Tom read or watched a movie.

He would look up, nod, Nancy would smile, wave weakly and move along.

She didn't say a lot, she just seemed to care. That meant a lot.

Nancy never had visitors, although she had lots of family photos in her room.

Sunday lunch always proved the best meal of the week, followed by Gaylene's insightful—and typically energetic—sermons. Together, Sundays usually were a high point, and most weeks a visit from Tom Junior and Judy made the day still better.

Rarely, Chad and Hannah tagged along. You didn't see many teenagers around Hickory Bough.

One Sunday after a big snow the grandkids showed up too, snuck around back as the parents yakked, then starting lobbing snowballs at Tom's windows as they laughed.

Grandpa Tom loved it and made faces at them.

A week later, Tom had gone back to his room to contemplate Gaylene's sermon, "What is God's grace?" and take a nap when the fam strolled in.

"Hi, Pop!" Tom Junior said as he came in with Judy and the grandson. Hannah had gone back to Mizzou for the semester. The usual conversation began about this and that and Tom hinted broadly that "Gee, wish I could get out of here more often."

"Not right now," Tom Junior replied. "The weather's been pretty bad, it's been a rough winter." He promised to take his father for a drive sometime.

His kids said good-bye after hugging the old man and Tom decided to take a stroll and walk off lunch. He could nap later.

Tom found his cane and ambled out his door and down the hall. He came to Nancy's room and the door, oddly, was closed. He tapped on it with his cane and pushed to open it but found the door locked. He was thinking that unusual when Josefina scampered quickly down the hall.

"Mister Tom, do *not* go in!" she said sharply.

He nodded and shuffled on toward Tony's place at the far end of the hall. His best friend sat watching a basketball game on TV.

"How 'ya doin'?" Tony called out as Tom had a seat.

"Oh, fine, the family came by, good visit," Tom replied. "Say, I just went by Noisy Nancy's and her door was locked."

Tony hung his head and mumbled "Oh no."

"What's wrong?" Tom asked.

"She died," Tony said with a sigh. "Poor Nancy."

That stunned Tom. Okay, he was in a nursing home, true, but the reality that some of his neighbors would not be here long had not hit.

"You sure?" he asked.

"Locked door, that's how you know. They'll quietly move the body out with a sheet over it when no one's looking," Tony explained. "You better get ready for that sort of thing."

"So will they put something on the big board?"

"Oh no way! Only the names of those coming in, never going out," Tony added.

Tom held his cane and rubbed his face, thinking about the loss of his friend. Noisy Nancy was such a sweet little thing, and they had become friends, of a sort, in the brief time he had known her.

It hurt.

"So we're in a roach motel, you can check in but you can't check out?" Tom asked, shaking his head.

"That's about the size of it, pal," Tony replied. "I guess that'll happen to all of us, and there's not much for us to look forward to until then."

"Thanks for being here," Tom said as he got up.

"Likewise."

He shuffled back to his room and avoided looking at Nancy's locked door.

What a depressing place, even for an optimist.

Gray skies and a couple days' worth of snow didn't help. The sun finally came out Wednesday morning, which perked him up. He got around early and headed for the

43

dining room, enjoying the sunshine streaming through his windows.

Breakfast wasn't bad for once. Tom had a second cup of coffee, stared across the dining room for a while, then pushed his chair back, picked up the cane and headed for his suite.

He shambled out of the dining room, leaning over to look out the window. The sun had disappeared and leaden clouds had started to spit snow again. The red arrow on the big thermometer on the far side of the courtyard pointed around twenty.

A few birds pecked at seeds on the big platter the staff had set out as a bird feeder. He wished he could see it from his room, he liked the birds.

Tom shook off a chill and pulled his sweater tighter. Well, here we go with another exciting Hickory Bough day. Maybe he and Tony would get together and talk baseball, or he had the iPad and real books to read. Maybe he'd go ride a bike in the exercise room?

Well, he'd find something to do.

As always, Tom stopped on his way out of the dining room after breakfast to check the big board:

- Today is: Wednesday
- Weather: Cold, snow showers
- Lunch: Mac & cheese or tuna salad
- Dinner: Italian night
- Activities: Movie night, *The Godfather*

Then a shock. It hit as he read the last line: dizzy, tunnel vision. Tom jerked, something powerful went through him, lightning bolted across his brain, the floor began to spin and his eyes went black.

Oh no! A blackout, bad one! Tom shook, he gasped, grabbed his chest and his cane fell to the floor as he dropped back, luckily slumping onto a sofa behind him, as he read the line:

- Greet our new resident: Claire Dearborn.

Chapter 3
Good Chemistry

Tom walked out of a dark tunnel: Where was he? What was happening?

The mental fog cleared: Fall 1945—the war's over! Japan surrendered just as school started and his brothers would be home from Europe!

What a great way to turn fourteen and start your freshman year at Randall High! Tom had looked forward to high school all through eighth grade and all this made it even better!

Yes sir, he saw good times ahead!

A beautiful fall afternoon found him stuck in weird, ol' Mr. Ross's chemistry class. Freshman chemistry was sixth hour, the end of the school day. No track team practice today, he could go straight home, or by The Malt Shop, or he could go to Dearborn Park with his buddies and throw a football around.

Time to relax and enjoy yourself, life was good.

Wait! What did Mr. Ross have the class doing?

The teacher divided the students into lab groups to do experiments on the big counter underneath the windows. The teacher outlined the assignment: Each team would heat some kind of crystals or something in a test tube over a Bunsen burner. Then, someone should light a little sliver of wood but blow out the flame. A team member then would stick the glowing stick in the test tube.

If they did things right, the glowing embers on the wood would snap, crackle, pop—or possibly flame briefly.

What caused this and what did it prove? What chemicals were involved? Each four-person team would write a detailed report about their experiment and turn it in the next day.

And as usual, as the class went to work Mr. Ross quietly eased out to the teacher's lounge next door to have a Lucky.

Tom and his team had not used great precision in setting things up. It took a couple tries just to get the Bunsen burner lit.

Oh sure, Tom's team did as instructed—burner lit, test tube mounted and pointed off to one side, crystals inserted, wait a few seconds, somebody light and blow out the flame on the stick, then poke it in the test tube.

Except, something went wrong—very badly wrong.

Instead of a barely audible snap or crackle, his team's test tube turned into a roaring blowtorch. A couple feet of yellow flame blasted out of the glass tube with a loud whoosh and flashed across a window shade above the counter. Students shrieked and screamed, some fell to the floor as the flame roared. Tom ducked, then reached over and turned the Bunsen burner off.

End of problem, except for a curl of smoke that lazily rose from the tube. Everyone started talking at once.

What happened? What would Mr. Ross do? Were they in trouble?

Except Mr. Ross wasn't there.

Speaking of flames, his Zippo had just lit another Lucky.

Maybe they wouldn't get in trouble after all.

First: Cover your tracks!

Tom's team huddled to figure out what to do as the other teams stared, chattered and laughed. Destroy the evidence: the scorched shade. Someone rolled it up and sunlight spilled in through the window, ending that problem.

What next?

The nervous chatter, laughter, giggles and gasps continued. The shade seemed the only visible damage. Perhaps they could avoid getting in trouble?

Some guy on his team volunteered, "But, I guess we have to put this in the report!"

More laughter, then someone quietly added, "Maybe."

Who said that?

It struck the whole class as laugh-out-loud funny. Tom found the riposte hilarious too and looked around; pretty clever. It was a girl's voice, and there was only one girl on his lab team, standing across from him. He glanced at her.

Time stopped.

The sun rose.

Did he hear a choir sing?

Tom Bentley plunged into absolutely unfathomable awe.

She was the most beautiful thing he had ever seen.

He stared at her for—how long?—seconds, minutes, hours? He didn't know, but he could not get enough of her angelic face.

The girl was tall, slender, very feminine, and Tom noted he looked up slightly at her. That's not unusual, of course, lots of ninth grade girls tower over ninth grade boys who haven't hit growth spurts. But looking up added to his feeling of unspeakable wonder.

She had a flawless, fair, complexion with high cheekbones, complemented by very long, fine yellow-blonde hair that ran down over her shoulders from a simple part in the middle of her head. Except, there were wisps of that glorious hair falling over the right side of her oval face, hiding her right cheek and eye.

She had a slender neck and a long waist that made her look still taller.

And those eyes! Oh goodness, her eyes! She had crisp, clear deep-set blue eyes that looked right back at him.

Ohmigosh, she was pretty! Tom could scarcely breathe.

He recalled some movie actress with hair like that. This girl looked sort of like her, what was her name?

Wait a minute, he had seen one of her movies, oh, the one about the nurses in the war. Let's see, *So Proudly We Hail*, yes, that's the one: Like Veronica Lake!

The hair, that long, straight, fine hair, made for the grabber.

This was 1945 and girls wore their hair bobbed, chopped, clipped, permed, frizzed, bleached, dyed and pinned above their ears—short.

Not her.

You just did not see girls with hair like that around Randall High.

She had a straight nose that perfectly accented her face, in front of those beautiful, sparkling blue eyes beneath equally blonde, narrow eyebrows. She had a small mouth with slightly pouty lips turned to silently say "bored," an odd half smile, above a square chin.

She was intense.

Tom stared on. Whoever she was, she dressed better than other girls; mature. The mystery girl stood against a desk with her arms crossed and long, thin legs extended below a stylish skirt. She wore pumps and hose, not bobby socks and loafers.

Tom was smitten, Cupid's arrow had hit home.

But who was she?

Hey, popular, everybody's pal Tom Bentley knew every kid in Randall High—or so he thought. Maybe she was new?

Yeah, that's it, she must be new to the school. That other little school district merged with the Randall last year. It had just a hundred or so kids in twelve grades, she must be from over there.

Quiet through the whole scare, the girl stood right there across from him with that slight, half smile. She may, just may, have been looking back at him.

Could she be staring at him? Tom wasn't sure. He stared on.

She captivated him, he looked on at what was absolutely just the most beautiful thing a boy of fourteen had ever seen.

Mona Lisa.

The Sistine Chapel.

An Easter lily.

Birds flying at dawn.

The northern lights glowing.

A Grand Canyon sunset.

And yes, no doubt about it, she definitely looked back.

At him.

Tom slowly looked her up and down. She looked him up and down.

He remained lost in space and time. Another one of those atom bomb things like the Army Air Force dropped could have gone off outside and Tom would not have noticed.

His eyes locked on hers. Her eyes locked on him.

Mr. Ross finally came through the door with a loud, "What's goin' on?" as he stuffed a cigarette pack in his shirt pocket.

Back to class.

Tom snapped out of his trance and realized everyone around the two of them continued to chatter away.

There were mumbled comments about the experiment and the team reports but no one said a thing about the blazing flamethrower.

"Okay, fine," the teacher replied. "Class is almost over, finish your reports tomorrow, now clean up, get your books and stuff. The bell's about to ring."

Tom leaned forward from the counter as other students, including her, walked back and sat down. He tried to be nonchalant as he walked past her desk. She hunched over, looking at a book, and that beautiful yellow hair ran most of the way down the back of her dress.

Maybe he would see her name?

He peeked down and there at the top of a piece of notebook paper was "Claire," but long thin fingers, accented by perfectly done nails with clear-pinkish polish, covered her last name.

Claire who?

Now let's see, yeah, he did vaguely remember a Claire Something-or-other, a skinny, awkward girl, quiet, a real wallflower. He never paid her any attention but recalled she had blonde hair.

When Tom got home he bounced upstairs to his bedroom and pulled eight years' worth of Randall School *Rampart* yearbooks off a shelf onto his bed with a thump. If she were a local, she would be in there.

He grabbed last year's annual, *Rampart, Answering The Call, Randall Public Schools, 1944-45*, his eighth-grade yearbook, and thumbed through it. Honor students like Tom would take chemistry as a freshman with other students taking it as a sophomore. He flipped through the eighth-grade section. Claire … Claire … Claire ….

And there she was: Claire Dearborn.

Oh, her.

The photo showed the bland, plain-Jane girl he remembered, but she did have the same blonde hair and that odd smile.

But this could not *possibly* be the beautiful young woman who captivated him in chemistry.

Could it?

Maybe there's another Claire?

He fanned through all of the hundred-odd photos in his class. Nope, only one. He looked through last year's ninth grade section—this year's sophomores.

Nope, no Claire there.

My oh my, had she changed in one year. Wow!

53

He backtracked—seventh grade, sixth grade, on down to first grade, younger every year, and always with that yellow hair and that bored, indifferent expression. Fifth grade she had a ponytail, in third grade she wore braids, and he could make out freckles across her nose.

She had been there, just a few seats back in how many classes? A, B, C, D: Most teachers seated classes by the alphabet, so a few C-named students separated them all those years. He remembered her as quiet, one of those kids who's just sort of there, but you never notice 'em.

But look at her now! How could he *not* know her?

Had *she* changed, or had *he* changed?

Check the index! What did she do?

Tom flopped last year's annual over to the back, past all the merchants' ads, and thumbed down the list of the names: Dearborn, Claire—band, Latin Club, library assistants.

Nope, nothing that Tom did, so their paths never crossed outside class.

He flipped back to the organization pages, first to the bands. She sat up front in the eighth-grade band photo, holding up a flute with a piccolo in her lap. The other group shots were on risers in the gym but, again and again, there was that tall, kind of skinny, gangly girl in the back row.

"Are you coming to eat or not?" his mom called sharply up the stairs.

Obviously it wasn't the first time she had yelled but Tom had missed it.

"Okay, just a minute!" he answered as he dropped the yearbooks back on his bed and hurried downstairs.

54

He ate dinner, did his homework, then got the fidgets. He had spent a lot of time in his room. It was dark by now and too late for a walk or playing with the dog.

He went downstairs to the living room where his parents sat in front of the family radio. *Songs By Sinatra* came on, one of his dad's favorite shows, and Tom's train of thought switched to music. After the usual commercial for Old Gold cigarettes, Sinatra crooned his way through his latest big hit. The studio audience applauded and show comedian and emcee Bill Goodwin started his usual monologue with a chirpy, "Thanks, blue eyes!"

Oh no! Why did he have to say *that*?

Claire came back. He had for a few minutes thought about something else. He bounced up from the floor and let out a loud sigh, which startled his dad, looking up from his newspaper.

"Are you all right?" he asked.

"Oh sure, uh, well, got some more, uh, homework; good night." He turned and did two-at-a-times up the stairs as his parents stared.

Tom took a shower and went to bed, like every other night, but sleep didn't come for a long time. But when it did, he dreamed of her. He didn't remember it well when mom woke him the next morning but it shimmered in his mind—vivid, real.

Claire wore a white gown and floated above him with that long, blonde hair framing her face. She came so close he could feel her fingertips touching his outstretched hands. He called her name and the pouty lips briefly smiled at him. Then she slowly disappeared, evaporating into the night.

He was in love.

Well, okay, maybe he had a really bad crush.

Did she care? Would she laugh at him if he spoke to her? After all, that bored look in chemistry did not look welcoming. And he had stood there and stared at her for he didn't know how long; embarrassing.

She had stared back, true, maybe she looked because she thought him stupid or weird or dumb.

Sure, big-man-on-campus Tom had gal pals but, hey, this was different. He wished he had a sister like other guys to give him pointers on how to talk to good lookin' girls and stuff.

The school day blurred by—algebra, English, history—then as he walked to the cafeteria he saw her coming the other way in the hall. As she passed, he managed a weak "Hi!"

Claire stopped, looked at him, stunned, and mumbled "Lookin' good!" and walked on.

Now what did that mean?

If you told someone "Hi!" in the hall they answered "Hi!," that's the way it worked in high school, right?

Tom stopped in the middle of the hall and looked back at her as the river of students flowed past. He watched her walk away until a burly football player in a letterman's jacket ran over him, scattering Tom's books in the floor.

"Watch it, plebe!" the big kid warned.

"Sorry," he replied as he picked up his things.

Sixth hour finally came and tension tied his stomach in knots. He wondered how he would handle things. The experiment report turned out mechanical. One of the other guys did the writing as the team finished its review. Tom kept his head down but glanced over at Claire once as his huddled team discussed what to write—without mentioning the blowtorch.

She caught his gaze sideways, blinked, then quickly looked down.

Well obviously, she didn't care. This was all in his head, just some stupid crush, nothing to get excited about. C'mon, Tom.

But what if….

They passed in the hall a couple days later and on impulse he said "Hi!" again. This time she nervously smiled back and answered "Hi!"

Saturday morning found Tom doing homework at Randall's Carnegie Library, referring to atlases for a map he had to draw for history. It was kinda' fun, he enjoyed the class, but it didn't take long to get what he needed. He put the big map books back on the shelf and looked around.

Let's see, anything else to read? Somebody else was thumbing through the latest issue of *The Sporting News*. Nope.

Wait! He flashed back to that fourth-grade Cub Scout library tour and how the little old, gray-haired librarian made a big deal about the genealogy section over in the corner; boring.

But just maybe, it might tell him something about Claire?

He ambled over to check. The ladies from Randall's Mormon ward published a genealogy of Limestone County pioneers and he thumbed through it. The big book included a section on his own Bentleys and their trek west from North Carolina and Tennessee in the 1800s. Supplying picks and shovels to the new, westbound railroads and the area's developing lead and zinc mines turned into a family business.

Fascinating, but was it okay for a Baptist kid to look at Mormon books?

Well, no one would know, he'd be sneaky.

Tom slowly pieced things together as morning turned to noon.

Another search of the genealogy shelf found a recently published *History of Limestone County* put out by the historical society. Oh yeah, his mom had helped with that, Junior League project.

He took out his notebook and jotted down what he had learned.

Claire Elaine Dearborn was the banker's daughter.

She was born one week after him in September 1931. Her great-grandfather, Wallace Dearborn, came west from New England, the son of Scottish immigrants, to seek his fortune in St. Louis before the Civil War.

A devout and outspoken abolitionist, he had been unpopular with the city's slave traders and pro-Southern businessmen. But St. Louis thrived and he found lots of business in products other than slaves.

The city proved dangerous as the war began. Pro-slavery rioters torched houses in the weeks surrounding Lincoln's inauguration. Wallace had to go. He quietly took a westbound train one night, his hat low over his face, to the end of track at Rolla. He guessed, correctly, that out here in the pro-Union Ozarks business should boom when "the current unpleasantness" ended.

He would bide his time.

Wallace provided quiet support to the Union army for the Battle of Hartville and received a citation from the War Department. A nearby trading post, Randall's Crossing, had been named seat of the newly created Limestone County. He decided to put down roots there.

Wallace had a knack for making money—lots and lots of money. And as far as anyone could tell he did it honestly. The fellow was sharp.

Claire's great-grandfather organized one bank, then another, until "Dearborn" became synonymous with banking in Missouri and Arkansas as the Nineteenth Century rolled into the Twentieth.

If your business needed a loan, or you wanted a safe place to deposit your savings, Randall's Merchants & Planters Bank, or Dearborn-owned banks in other towns, were as dependable as any financial institution could be in those days.

Oh yes, there had been whispers in saloons that Wallace had a secret deal with outlaws and that he and Jesse James were pals. That would seem far-fetched, one writer noted, since Jesse and his brothers got their start as outlaw Confederate raiders.

But somehow, Merchants & Planters never had a robbery. A secret deal? Luck? Good business procedures? No one knew. The luck held through the Great Depression.

Son Alban and grandson Campbell proved as successful as Wallace. Besides banks, the Dearborn name became attached to other businesses.

Campbell, being an orderly sort, named his children alphabetically: sons Angus (or Gus) and Bruce, followed by the baby of the family, Claire.

The Dearborns enjoyed a lifestyle unknown even to the prosperous Bentleys. Tom stumbled across a paragraph in the *Randall Ledger's* society section from last summer noting "The Dearborns have returned from their monthly summer retreat at The Broadmoor in Colo. Springs, reporting a good time and pleasant weather."

He got tired. Tom tried to pick up his research, he found something about a fire, but he couldn't concentrate.

Oh well, better get home.

He carefully shelved all the genealogy books, slipped out the front door, skipped down the front steps and headed over to The Malt Shop for a late lunch of French fries and a cherry Coke.

The afternoon shadows stretched across Poplar as he walked up the hill and around the curve toward home. A full stomach made it easier to think.

It dawned on Tom the Dearborns were the other rich family in Randall:

The Bentleys owned hardware stores, the Dearborns owned banks.

The Bentleys were Baptists, the Dearborns were Presbyterians.

The Bentley men were Kiwanis, the Dearborn men were Rotary.

The Bentleys lived well, the Dearborns lived very well.

For a teenage boy who would need to start shaving soon and whose voice was just beginning to croak and drop, who thought mostly about sports and cars—and now a girl—all that meant little.

A beam of sunlight hit Tom as he sat on the sofa, bringing his mind slowly from the blackout. How long had it been since that day at the library?

He rubbed his face, then reached down for his cane on the floor. But thoughts of that long-ago autumn continued.

Chapter 4
Double Up!

He recalled how the next days proved awkward. Always watching for her, Tom would see Claire coming in the hall or in chemistry class, then say "Hi!" or give her a smile and a nod as they passed. He usually received that half smile, sometimes a blank "Hi!"

Tom absent-mindedly came around a shelf in the school library one day and there she stood, reading. He bumped into her and managed a weak "Sorry!" as she dropped her book.

"It's okay, I was in the way," she said as they both bent over. She got the book, stood up, and added, "I guess I should go sit down if I'm going to read." Claire made a nervous glance at him with an apologetic smile—oh, those blue eyes!

She never said anything in class, it was the most Tom had ever heard her say, and Claire's smooth, low voice made all of his romantic thoughts flow again.

A few days later the office invited Tom to an all-morning meeting with other freshmen deemed "leaders" by school administrators to discuss how to make Randall High a better school. It broke up at the start of third hour after a rousing pep talk by the principal, so he went to lunch early.

Did he see a blonde at the front of the cafeteria line? Could it be? Tom had no idea when Claire ate.

He took his plate, a dessert and a carton of milk and swung around in line to the cashier. He spied Claire just then sitting down at a table off to one side of the lunchroom, by herself.

Could he sit with her? Did he dare? He hung in deep what-to-do thought as the cafeteria lady at the cash register repeated "ten cents please" again.

He dug out a dime, stepped out into the lunchroom and stopped. Some of his usual pals sat at the back of the lunchroom, laughing and talking loudly.

No, he had a chance: Do it.

Tom took a deep breath and headed toward her, the plates on his tray nervously wobbling. He set his tray on the table in front of her as she looked at her plate, eating.

He spoke a perky "Hi!" It startled her and Claire looked up, surprised.

"Oh! I didn't know you ate now," she said nervously.

"No, I went to that meeting this morning. I usually eat in the last shift," Tom said as he sat down.

"So, how was it?"

"Very interesting, not sure how I got invited," Tom replied with a chuckle.

"Oh, that's not a surprise at all," Claire answered flatly.

It was chit-chat. We play Marshfield this week? It's supposed to get cold tonight. The leaves have been pretty. Did you have family in the war?

Of course chemistry class came up but nothing about the experiment that went bad. Mr. Ross is an odd duck, kids don't like him. What do you think? Did you do the homework for this afternoon?

Nothing exciting.

Oh, how Tom wanted to say so much more. He wanted to jump on the table and yell "You are the most beautiful girl in the world!" Then Claire would leap into his arms as the other kids cheered.

Right.

But he just couldn't. It was just all he could do to nervously hold up half a conversation. He treasured the gift of sitting there and looking at her.

Oh my, she was so pretty. Wallflowers can bloom.

Claire paused to get a drink and he managed to mumble "that's a nice dress you have on."

Claire stopped, took the straw out of her mouth, tilted her head and said, "Why, thank you!"

Then more chit-chat. She finally wiped her mouth with a napkin and mumbled "I guess I better get to class, see you this afternoon." She stood, picked up her tray and walked off.

Now what good did that do?

Nothing that he could tell. Tom shook his head as he watched her walk away. One of his weekly English spelling words came to mind: Perfunctory.

"Stop it!" he told himself as she put her tray and dirty dishes on the belt back to the kitchen and walked into the hall. It's obvious she doesn't care. She's just tolerating you, so why torture yourself? She's always so cold.

Focus on other things, like your grades.

A week later he got stumped on chemistry homework one night. He should call one of his buddies, one of them might know the answer.

Or, he could call Claire.

Ohmigosh, he couldn't do that! What if she hung up on him? What if she laughed at him?

But then she had not said anything tacky when he sat down with her at lunch. He dug around in his notebook for the student directory and looked her number up.

Okay, maybe.

He trudged downstairs to the family phone in the hall, picked up the receiver and waited for the operator:

"Number, please."

Tom froze but finally mumbled "8935."

"Thank you."

The phone rang twice and the low, feminine voice answered, "Hello?"

"Hi, this is Tom, have a minute?"

"Oh, uh, um, sure."

And off he went on chemistry. Claire wasn't much help but they talked about the class for a few minutes, more chit-chat. Tom stuttered, "Uh, well, I better go."

"You're welcome, 'bye," and Claire hung up.

"Perfunctory" came to mind again—but she didn't hang up on him, she didn't laugh at him. Everything went okay; friendly. But no more.

Forget her, he had other stuff to do, like earning a slot on the track team. Or, he had the one school activity he really enjoyed: the new Rowdy Rams boys' pep club.

He and his buddies tried to whip up memberships to match the long-established Roarin' Rams girls pep club. All the swell gals were Roarin' Rams, the boys sat next to them at games, and right in front of the cheerleaders!

Frankly, Randall's struggling varsity needed all the help it could get.

A month had gone by since that bright afternoon in chemistry and the last football game of the season was on the road at Springfield.

Springfield! Who put Springfield on the schedule?

Much-bigger Springfield always had a good team and it had been quite the surprise last summer when the 1945 football posters went up in downtown shop windows that Springfield would be the last game of the season.

Tom and other boys lobbied to let the Rowdy Rams go. The principal said fine. Problem was, it'd take every school bus the district had to haul the team, the band, the cheerleaders and both pep clubs. Some rather doubtful, seldom-used, dusty and long-in-the-barn vehicles got backed out and gassed up.

A motorcade of buses and cars formed to move a surprisingly large group of students, teachers and parents. The pep club boys got the job of lining everyone up, hanging blue and white decorations on the buses and generally directing things.

It fell on Tom to direct the whole thing, and he showed exemplary organizational skills.

Off the parade went with streamers and bunting flying, and the visitors had a surprisingly big crowd on hand that Friday night for a chilly kickoff.

Randall got the ball but the Rams' shaky offense went three-and-out. Randall managed to pin Springfield behind its five-yard line on the punt when Springfield's receiver lined up out of position. The ball plopped on the field, took a wild bounce, then rolled and rolled toward the end zone.

On Springfield's first play, a lucky Ram linebacker blew through and got a clean hit on the quarterback, who fumbled backwards. The ball rolled and rolled—out the back of the end zone.

Randall scored a safety!

Tom and the rest of the Randall crowd didn't know what to do. They were ahead, 2-0! Puzzled silence turned into cheers, the band came to attention. The director raised his hands and the band roared into the fight song as Randall partisans sang and clapped along:

"Go Rams, win team,
Fight for our blue and gray!
When our Rams go marching…"

Caught up in the excitement, Tom glanced around at the equally surprised band and there she sat, playing her flute. For one busy afternoon he had forgotten her.

Well, of course Claire would be there, she was in the band!

Tom watched her arms wag back and forth in time with the rest of the band as it charged through the fight song again.

He stood there, staring, and forget to sing. Her baggy blue and white uniform did nothing for her but that long, beautiful blonde hair fell down her back, making up for the uniform in Tom's mind. Some guy in the pep club finally slapped him on the back and yelled, "You okay?"

"Yeah, sure," Tom replied.

Back to the game.

Halftime came and went and clouds rolled in, then misty rain started in the fourth quarter. Boy, it was cold!

The Rams outplayed themselves as the clock ticked down. With a minute left, Springfield led 14-12 but the Rams had the ball and managed, amazingly, a couple first downs after some good runs to reach Springfield's fifteen.

The clock ticked down.

Tom and the crowd yelled themselves hoarse. If only Randall could manage a field goal. The coach called timeout and sent in the team's kicker.

Hoo boy.

Okay, the kid did manage to make the point-after for Randall's lone touchdown in the second quarter, but the ball hit the crossbar and bounced through; dumb luck. And, the Rams' third-quarter field goal sailed through easily but that was on fourth down from the two-yard line—a yard closer than a routine point-after.

The kicker set up, the center snapped the ball, the quarterback teed it up and off the ball flew through the dark, wet mist. It cleared by an inch and the refs stuck their arms up: Randall 15, Springfield 14.

The clock stopped at four seconds as the visitors went wild.

Do you believe in miracles? Yes!

The Rams were gonna' win!

Randall lined up for the kickoff, Springfield's receiver caught the ball but managed just a yard or two before an excited Ram, with enough adrenaline in his veins to power an army, hit him for a tackle.

Time expired. Randall—unbelievably—had won.

The band roared through the fight song again as shouts and cheers continued while the crowd shuffled through the chilly mist toward the parking lot. The Rowdy

Rams clambered aboard the bus that had a hand-lettered BOYS PEP sign taped to the windshield and Tom found a seat toward the back, exhausted.

Loud chatter continued as the boys sat down and waited, and waited, under the weak dome lights.

Excitement slowly turned to irritation, why the wait? But none of the Randall buses moved.

Mr. Ross was the boys' chaperone, seated behind the driver, and the two excitedly talked about the finer points of the Rams' tremendous victory. Suddenly, Mr. Ross got up, went out in the dark, came back in, did a head count, then went down the steps and out the door again.

Now what?

He finally came back in and called out a loud, "Hey!"

Silence.

"One of the buses won't start so we're gonna' have to double up! We're gonna' put some band members in here so you boys hop up and let the ladies have your seats!"

He had to be kidding.

It was late, everyone was damp, the boys drained. They slowly got up with a low murmur and milled around in the dim light.

A couple of band members stepped up through the door and stood behind him, so Mr. Ross sat back down in the seat behind the driver to let them pass. The pair immediately returned to their lively game critique.

Other band members slowly tromped up the steps and, to Tom's surprise, the first one in line was her: a soggy Claire, standing with a jacket over her band uniform.

Wow, the object of his every affection actually stood in his bus!

Claire came forward a row past Mr. Ross, stopped, then barked out new orders, waving her flute case for emphasis: "C'mon, you boys sit down and we can double up!"

More grumbling.

Well, okay, if that's what you want. The boys sat back down, expecting Mr. Ross to jump up and overrule her. But he didn't. The chaperone and the driver, absorbed in the thrill of victory, went right on talkin' football.

Tom leaned against his window and watched as a short, fat girl in a gray, Roarin' Rams uniform made her way back to the chubby kid seated next to him, immediately plopping down next to him with a big smile. Three people stuffed in a seat meant for two.

Several band members came in the now warm, sticky bus, then a couple of cheerleaders carrying their blue and white pom-poms.

He watched as Claire's blonde hair swished back and forth as she pointed to empty spots here and there as the kids behind her, all girls, hunted for places. Every row had been filled.

What was she doing?

Last of all, Claire herself threaded her way over and through the legs hanging out in the aisle.

There was nothing left, would she have to stand?

She worked her way back, stopping even with Tom's seat, as he watched. She looked at the short girl and her plump boyfriend and ordered, "Move!"

The rotund pair slowly stood up in the aisle and Claire turned and backed into Tom's seat, climbing past them, then sat herself down squarely in Tom's lap, upright against the bus wall and window. She bent down and placed her flute case in the floor under her feet and looked at him with those piercing blue eyes as their seatmates sat down, engrossed in each other.

It struck Tom dumb.

He could not have been more shocked if President Truman himself had marched in and sat down in his lap.

Claire looked at him for a moment and finally managed a nervous "Hi."

His throat dry, he moved his mouth but said nothing. He swallowed hard and managed a raspy, "Hello."

"Hello," she replied with a raised eyebrow and just a little more than her usual half smile.

What just happened?

Tom could not believe it, this must be some kind of joke, a set-up. Surely Mr. Ross would jump up and order her to move. But the driver started the engine, swung the door shut and turned off the dome lights. The overloaded bus turned dark except for the glow of streetlights and headlights shining through its steamed windows. It groaned under its heavy load as it slowly took its place in the line of Ram faithful finally headed home.

Tom tried to be nonchalant, or maybe he was so scared he didn't know what to do. He glanced out the window to see what was going on, but there was nothing to see through the foggy glass. The bus lurched and turned left, then picked up speed as it bounced and swayed along dark, wet streets on its way out of town.

No, this could not be happening.

Claire slowly leaned against Tom's shoulder in the dark and nuzzled his face. He felt his stomach heave, he would vomit. No, no, that would not be good right now, hold on.

He stuck his hand over his mouth and held his breath for a moment, then turned his head so they were cheek to cheek, moving his face up and under that blonde wisp over her cheek.

He smelled cinnamon, or some kind of spice. What kind of perfume is that? He had never smelled it before.

His lips lightly kissed her earlobe, more or less by accident, as the bus bumped along.

Claire jerked back instantly.

"Uh-oh!" he thought, expecting a face slap.

But instead, she turned straight toward him, nervously cupped his cheeks in her jittery hands and planted a wet kiss straight on his unsuspecting lips—and held it, and held it, and held it.

Shimmers of light from passing streetlights dimly lit her out-of-focus blue eyes, just an inch across his nose. Hey, he had just turned fourteen and he had never kissed a girl. He didn't know what to do, he didn't close his eyes.

But neither had edgy Claire.

Tom shook—hard—but finally pulled back and gasped for breath with a faint "Whoa!"

Claire leaned back and flashed a big smile in the passing headlights. It was the first time he had ever seen her really smile.

"Did you like that?" she whispered nervously.

No, no, he thought, something is seriously wrong here. Mr. Ross will be back any second, yelling at him, or Claire will scream, or something really bad will happen.

He glanced sideways, were they being watched? But the chubby kid next to him had his hand up the skirt of his round girlfriend as they passionately kissed.

Maybe not, maybe this was really happening.

He didn't answer but instead wrapped his arms inside her jacket, around her damp uniform, pulled her close and kissed her again, closing his eyes.

Go for it, guy.

And Claire kissed back, oh my, did she kiss back.

He savored the moment, this special moment, holding the girl of his dreams in his arms. The kiss lingered. This time Claire pulled back with a sigh.

"You don't know! You don't know!" she gasped, then leaned back against him.

What did that mean?

Tom certainly did not know, but he did know he was going to enjoy every minute of the trip home. Just as long as Mr. Ross could talk football up front, he could have a good time with this stunning vision of loveliness in his lap.

They wrapped themselves around each other with a mutual giggle and nuzzled as the swaying bus bounced along in the rain. Car lights flashed by, playing over her damp hair and face. He slowly moved his hand up and down her side under her jacket but didn't dare get too close, too intimate, or go too far like his toady seatmate.

Tom was a gentleman.

He also was scared to death.

It took about an hour to drive to Randall in good weather and on a sloppy night like this it took longer. A couple of times the groaning bus fishtailed and there were gasps and screams as its passengers braced.

He grabbed Claire and she grabbed him, smiling at each other.

But even kissing the girl of your dreams gets old. What next?

The two of them sat there cheek to cheek, warm in the glow of their special moment, both breathless.

What to say to let her know how much he cared? To say a clunky "I love you" would just not work.

Then it came to him: Dummy, sing! She's a musician, she loves music. Hey, she's sitting here in a band uniform, for heaven's sake. Sing to her!

But what?

Oh, wait a minute, there's that song that all the radio stations played last summer, the one Vaughn Monroe crooned on *Your Hit Parade*. Hey, he knew the words to that one, would it work? Would she think it corny?

Maybe, but he didn't know what else to do.

Tom nuzzled back up under her hair and whispered quietly in her ear, just loud enough for Claire to hear over the groaning bus:

"I love you, there's nothing to hide
It's better than burning inside,
I love you, no use to pretend
There! I've said it again!"

He felt Claire gasp and jerk back as the thought flashed through his mind: "Finally, something's gone wrong!"

She leaned back, raised her hand, but said nothing. She sat there for a moment, squinted at Tom, then leaned back on him. He continued where he left off:

"I've said it, what more can I say?
Believe me, there's no other way,
I love you, I will to the end,
There! I've said it again!"

Claire let out a giggle and Tom nearly died: He had blown it. Then she nuzzled his cheek again and whispered, "I *love* that song!"

"Oh, do you know the bridge?" Tom asked.

"Of course I do!" and they whispered an impromptu duet to each other:

"I try to drum up,
A phrase that will sum up,
All that I feel for you.
But what good are phrases?
The thought that amazes,
Is you love me,
And it's heavenly."

Claire paused, a car light flashed by and she leaned back on Tom as she sang the last verse:

"Forgive me for wanting you so
But one thing I want you to know,
I've loved you since heaven knows when
There! I've said it again!"

He had never heard her sing and had hardly heard her speak. That soft, feminine voice, and to have it singing to him—to him!—whispering in his ear, was more than a teen-age boy could wish for.

Without thinking he blurted out, "Let's stick together."

"Of course we will!" Claire replied instantly with a big, inviting smile.

They sat there, quietly cuddling, just enjoying being close, Claire's head on his shoulder.

The bus lumbered and bounced on through steady rain toward the end of its overloaded journey. The stops and turns became familiar, streetlights began to cut the dark and shortly the bus turned into the high school parking lot as dozens of headlights played across the misty windows. Midnight had passed and irritated parents had been waiting a long time.

"We're here," Tom mumbled.

"I know," Claire answered sadly, then she leaned over and they shared a final peck just as the dome lights came on.

The bus creaked to a stop, the driver opened the door and the passengers untangled themselves, slowly got up and shuffled down the aisle. Claire reached down, grabbed her flute, then slid into the aisle in front of him. Tom held her other hand as they scooted past Mr. Ross, still seated up front, watching the students shuffle by.

"Hey you two, none of that!" the teacher snapped, looking down at their joined hands.

They jerked apart. They went down the stairs, through the door and stepped out onto the soggy gravel. The rain had stopped. Now both of them had to find their waiting parents in the swirling crowd of tired students and grumpy adults.

"Will there be more?" Tom asked hopefully as they separated.

"Wait and see," Claire answered flatly with her odd smile as she dissolved into the dark.

Now what did that mean? He thought he saw a wink in the dim car lights and it sounded like a promise, but a promise of what?

Just then his father walked up.

"There you are! What took so long?" his dad asked.

"Busted bus, we had to double up and that took a while."

"Well I hear you won, I guess that's why you look so happy."

"Yeah, yeah, it has been quite a night," Tom answered, smiling, knowing his father would miss the double entendre as they found his dad's idling DeSoto.

"Let's get home, I've had the heater on, cold out here," the father said, as they got in and slowly inched around the crowd and into the street.

"So tell me all about it, must have been quite a game. Hey, what's that funny odor? You smell like you've been eating cinnamon rolls or something."

Caught!

What to say? Sure dad, your fourteen-year-old son has been making out with a girl who wears cinnamon perfume.

"Uh, oh, who knows?" Tom replied. "It was so crowded on that bus, I got mashed up against a whole bunch of people."

Tom thought to himself "one in particular."

Change the subject, quick.

"Let me tell you, that field goal at the end was something!" Tom went on about the game as it came to him there might be more evidence—evidence he needed to destroy, and fast. He felt of his face for lipstick—he didn't think she had any on. Do girls wear that stuff all the time? Powder? Don't they wear that too?

No, her face was damp from the rain, probably had washed off or something, he hoped anyway. He wiped his face with the damp sleeve of his blue pep club sweater several times. Maybe that would be enough.

Chapter 5
The Christmas Tree

Saturday, Sunday, then Monday: Tom worried some of the pep club guys would tease him about the bus trip, but not a peep. Every boy on that bus either had a story about a gal, or wished he had one.

He knew he would see Claire in sixth-hour chemistry. But how would it go? He caught her watching the door as he came in. He winked at her, mouthed "Hi," and Claire gave him a wink back with a knowing, broad smile.

Nothing was said and she left immediately when the bell rang, which disappointed him. Aloof again, he thought.

But he came out the classroom door to find Claire waiting for him in the hall. "Did you understand what he was talking about?" she asked.

"Not really, can I call you tonight and we can discuss it?" he asked.

"Of course, hey, I better go."

Tom called after dinner and they talked for more than an hour, which got awkward with him standing in the hall. They even discussed a little chemistry.

Nothing the next day, it was Tuesday afternoon after he ate when he stopped by his locker. He spotted an envelope lying on top of the pile of books, dirty sneakers and his gym bag at the bottom of the locker. It had a simple "Tom" written on it. He started to open it when the bell rang—time to get to class. He stuffed the envelope in a book, went through his afternoon classes, including chemistry. Claire was looking down as he walked in. Mr. Ross droned on for the whole hour.

Claire glanced at him as class ended, he smiled at her and she smiled back, then she left. Was she avoiding him?

Oh well, Tom had a pep club meeting that afternoon to discuss the basketball season. Then the usual walk home, dinner and upstairs to his room and his homework.

Wednesday came and went. Claire gave him a half smile and a "Hi" in the hall but seemed cool when he walked into class.

Was it over already?

That night when he started his homework Tom opened a textbook and the envelope fell out.

Dummy! How could you forget that?

He opened the envelope and unfolded the page, catching the slightest whiff of cinnamon. He thought so. The penmanship was perfect cursive, black ink on cream paper:

My dearest Tom,

You cannot know what Friday night meant for me, it was a very special moment I have looked forward to and I will treasure it forever. Please forgive me if I was too forward. But trust me, I was sincere, I know you to be a very special boy. I don't play around, all my kisses are saved for you.

You have made my life so rich and full, I hope we can spend so much more time together in the future. I am devoted to you, I want to be your girl!

Love,

Claire

Tom fell back on his bed, he couldn't breathe. Wow, just wow!

The words just went off into a dizzy spiral in his head—*I am devoted to you, I want to be your girl.* He held in his hand the most beautiful thing he had ever read. Shakespeare could learn from it. Quiet Claire had sprung another surprise when she slipped the note through one of the vents of his locker door.

But how did she know which locker was his?

Thursday morning he saw her coming down the hall between second and third hour so he cut over toward her through the packed hallway.

"Thank you for the note," he said as she passed. "That meant a lot."

"You're welcome," she said with her half smile.

And that was that.

Their lives changed.

All of the busy-ness of school now included how and when to see each other. It wasn't if I see him or if I see her, but when.

They both felt it.

They stopped to chat in the hall after chemistry every day, lab team projects had a whole different vibe— even if there were no blowtorches to worry about.

One particularly nice afternoon Tom didn't have track practice so they talked longer than usual as they slowly worked their way toward the school door. Tom blurted out, "Wanna' go by The Malt Shop?"

Claire stopped and looked at him seriously.

"Is this a date? Daddy says I can't date until I'm sixteen," she said firmly.

"Well, then no, we're just doing homework. Correct?" Tom said with a wink.

"Great!"

The burger joint's big Wurlitzer played Perry Como and The Satisfiers' *Till the End of Time*, flashing every color of the rainbow, as Tom opened the door for her and they walked in. They wound their way through the usual clutch of people loitering in front of Randall's only newsstand. A hand-lettered THIS IS NOT A LIBRARY sign hung above yesterday's editions of the *Tulsa World*, *St. Louis Post-Dispatch* and *Kansas City Star*, plus the latest *Saturday Evening Post*, *Collier's*, *Life* and more.

Your parents came here to cash a check after the bank closed. And if you caught the right waitress working the cash register, she might sell you a pack of Camels "for my dad."

Right.

Loud students filled most of the tables, counter stools and booths. Claire led and they wove their way through the crowd to the empty back booth.

They just had drinks, Tom paid. He had a cherry Coke and she had a strawberry shake. The chit-chat continued.

"You know, we're being watched," Claire said solemnly as she swirled her straw through the lumpy pink liquid in her glass. "Who's that with Tom? You know what I mean."

"Well, then, I guess we better get our chemistry books out. We're only doing homework, right? We don't want people to talk!" Tom answered, smiling.

Claire covered her mouth and giggled.

They opened their books on the table, then went on talking about what teachers they liked, the pep club, the band, *Your Hit Parade*—and each other.

He is such a fascinating boy, great sense of humor, knows everybody, smiles a lot, handsome, and he likes me.

She is such an intelligent girl, thinks through stuff, sharp dresser, poised, really pretty, and she likes me.

Tom called her a few more times and they talked forever—without mentioning chemistry. But the personal chemistry worked fine. He finally pulled a chair out of the dining room so he could sit in the hall.

They got their big packets of School Days freshman-year photos one afternoon. Tom used his pocketknife and a ruler to carefully cut out one big photo in each packet and they swapped. He took Claire's photo home and stuck it on a mirror in his bedroom and figured, correctly he found out, she did the same.

He could lie there on his bed and look across the room at her anytime. Oh wow, what a swell girl, and she was *his* girl!

Having a girlfriend/boyfriend proved new and exciting.

Thanksgiving came and went, the first snow of the season came and went, and the Bentley household caught itself in greater-than-usual holiday excitement as telegrams came from his brothers: Both were on their way home!

There were the first couple of basketball games of the season and Tom helped the pep club cheer. But the band didn't play basketball games.

His brothers, Chuck and Phil, made it home the week before Christmas, amid the promise of the first normal holiday in five years.

Tom got caught up in the excitement as the family reunited on a chilly night with hugs and handshakes at the train station. Then there were shopping trips to Koppel's and over to the big Heer's Department Store in Springfield.

Christmas 1945: What a wonderful time to be alive!

The long war nightmare had ended. Stuff returned to store shelves to buy without ration stamps, and dad could fill up the DeSoto's gas tank whenever he wanted. He was out in the stable-turned-garage with a scraper to take his B Ration sticker off the windshield as soon as he could.

The holiday loomed. It was the Saturday before the big day and Tom had gone downtown with mom to do more shopping, grab a sandwich at The Malt Shop and then head home.

He tromped up to his room for a quick nap, maybe he and his brothers would go to a show at the Rialto—if they ever came home from visiting their buddies. He just dozed off when he heard the phone ring downstairs, then his mother called out "Tom! Telephone!"

Huh?

Since school was out it couldn't be pep club or track stuff, maybe something at church, or maybe dad needed him at the warehouse?

He climbed out of bed and went down the stairs, rubbing his sleepy eyes, to the hallway phone, where mom stood holding her hand over the receiver with a puzzled look on her face.

"It's some girl," she whispered.

Now, who could that be, maybe his Sunday School teacher?

Or maybe?

Nah, gals don't call guys.

Tom shrugged an "I dunno'" as he took the phone and managed a flat "hello?"

"It's me," was the reply.

Claire!

"We're decorating our Christmas tree this afternoon, uh, would you like to come over and help? Mom's making some of her special stew for tonight since the maid's off today."

Would he! Tom jerked but managed to mutter a dull " just a minute."

He placed his hand over the receiver and looked at his mom, standing there in the hall, thinking all sorts of things about her little boy growing up.

"Uh, it's a girl from school. Could, um, you or dad run me over to her house?"

"I guess so," mom replied, "Where does she live?"

"Not far, I think."

Tom turned back to the phone, "What's your address?"

"We're on out Poplar from you, 1572."

"Sure, see you in a few minutes, 'bye."

Claire said "bye" and he hung up. Now came the question:

"Who is she?" mom demanded with wide-eyed expectation.

"Claire, Claire Dearborn, they want me to come over and help decorate their Christmas tree, then stay for dinner."

"Claire? Claire Dearborn? The Dearborns' girl?" she gushed. "Well! Well! Well! You are moving in the right circles, young man! Let me get your dad, he knows where they live, up the street, I think.

"Isn't that a photo of her in your room?"

Tom nodded, "Yeah."

Mom smiled knowingly.

"She certainly has turned into a pretty thing."

Tom appreciated the ride although it would be an easy walk, it was cold. He recognized the house as they pulled through the gate—the one really different house on the street. After blocks of towering, ornate Victorian and Queen Anne palaces built in the last century, here sat a modern, low-slung place made of decorated concrete blocks, stamped on one side with an Art Deco zig-zag design, and glass-brick windows. A clerestory jutted above a flat roof.

How did it get there? Oh yes, the fire he read about at the library. Then came a faint memory of himself as a little boy, standing on his toes, looking out his bedroom window as firetrucks screamed by in the night.

And in its place went up this ultra-modern, Frank Lloyd Wright original, something only the Dearborns could afford.

Somehow he'd never connected that people actually lived there, it looked more like a doctor's office or a

National Guard armory. Tom's dad idled around the circle drive, stopping at the front door.

"I don't know how long I'll be, I'll call," Tom said as he got out. His father waved as he drove off and Tom turned to the front door, excited to see Claire. School had been out a few days, he missed her.

He rang the doorbell and the door opened immediately—to her parents. Oh no! Claire's dad stuck out a big palm to shake hands and in a perfect radio voice welcomed him with "You must be Tom."

"Yes sir."

"We're glad you're here, come in," the father added as they shook. "I'm Campbell, this is Claire's mother, Jewel."

Tom glanced at the middle-aged couple as he took off his jacket and hat and handed them to the mom. He sensed they were checking him out and, in his teenager way, he did the same. What kind of parents could produce such a fabulous girl?

Campbell was tall with a thin build, but sported a midlife paunch. He had receding, reddish-brown hair. His wife was petite, just a little chubby, with fine blonde hair cut short.

Dad's height, mom's hair—these were her parents alright.

"We're so excited to meet you, Claire talks about you all the time!" Jewel Dearborn gushed. That comment jangled Tom's nerves.

What did she have to talk about? What did she tell them?

Jittery, he wanted to know but didn't dare ask. Claire scarcely talks to anyone at school, he thought, did she make up for it chattering at home?

And what's this "all the time" business? It had been scarcely two months since that afternoon in chemistry class, plus one lunch, some "homework" at The Malt Shop and a few phone calls.

Tom was pretty certain Mr. and Mrs. Dearborn didn't know details of the bus ride.

So what did she have to say about Tom Bentley?

The mom started off explaining that the Dearborn Christmas tree would go up late this year, very busy this time around, but they wanted it decorated before Claire's two brothers made it home on tomorrow night's train. They met in New York and were coming home together.

"I hope you don't mind coming over, Claire thought you might help. I know your family is busy also!" she said with a motherly smile.

"Mind?" flashed through Tom's head.

An invitation to spend an afternoon with the girl of my dreams, who has been in my thoughts every waking minute for two months? Do I mind? A girl who is the most beautiful thing I ever laid eyes on, and more than that likes me?

Tom thought to himself, "Lady, I'd pay you every cent I will ever have in my life to be here."

He looked around the room, a low-ceilinged, wood-paneled, tile-floored living room with modern furniture. To a kid who had lived his life in a turreted Victorian castle with 15-foot papered ceilings, creaky hardwood floors, overstuffed divans and big chandeliers that had once been lit with gas, it looked very odd. The ceiling was so low that six-foot-plus Mr. Dearborn could touch it with an up-stretched hand.

They were standing in a living room, with a dining room to the left, and some kind of family room or den beyond. The den, noticeably brighter, must have the clerestory, Tom thought.

"Clerestory," now that was a word he'd never used. He remembered it from a study of European cathedrals in a history of Christianity course for Sunday School.

Neat!

They walked into the den, more wood paneling and recessed, indirect lights around the outside of the room. A modernistic fireplace filled one wall and a well-stocked bookshelf covered the wall across from it. The far wall was wood paneled, on which hung two large oil paintings of Claire's brothers, probably done about the time they graduated from high school. Floor-to-ceiling glass brick made up the exterior wall, framed by two conventional windows.

A bare Christmas tree stood between them.

Oddly, the house otherwise had few photos, mementos or other family kitsch, a marked contrast to the antiques and family photos that filled the Bentley home.

Past that room a hallway led to the bedrooms and whatever else in the back of the house. He could see a grand piano in some kind of music room. At the far end were double doors to a covered porch that overlooked a big backyard.

Way at the rear of the backyard stood an old-fashioned, white gazebo with a copper roof.

"Claire, darling, Tom's here!" her mother called liltingly down the hall.

Tom heard a door open and then around a corner here she came, pulling a baggy, navy blue sweatshirt over her head, briefly exposing a trim, pale midriff and navel. She smoothed the sweatshirt over the top of her jeans, revealing "Cottey College" in bright yellow across its front.

The dark blue sweatshirt accentuated her blonde hair all the more. Claire shook her head as she pulled a long pony tail up and out of the neck and laid it down her back.

Once again time stood still. Was it the sight of a little skin, or that he had never seen her in anything besides fashionable dresses—never mind that lumpy band uniform?

Whatever, he felt his jaw drop as Claire came toward them.

"Hi," she quietly said as she walked up to the three of them.

"Uh, Merry Christmas," Tom managed to reply.

"And Merry Christmas to you," Claire answered with her usual slight smile. "Are you ready to get to work?"

"Sure."

Claire's dad hauled out boxes of lights and ornaments from a hallway closet. The work went fast as her parents opened the boxes and handed the decorations and light strings to Claire and Tom. They shifted around the tree, working up, under and around each other. Tom warmly thought they hadn't been this close since, oh, never mind....

"This is always is such a special time of year, and this Christmas will be the best ever with Gus and Bruce coming home!" Jewel said cheerfully.

"We're excited too," Tom replied, "The last four Christmases have been rough for everyone. My brothers got home a few days ago."

The afternoon sun quickly disappeared and twinkling lights lit up the room as Claire's mother placed various ornaments and pictures on a bare fireplace mantel and several tables. Tom helped Campbell move the empty boxes back into the closet.

Done.

"Let me get something for everyone to eat. Claire, not to disappoint you, darling, but I decided not to fix that stew you like," her mom said. "Bruce sent me that cookbook he got in Italy and I decided to try a recipe for 'pizza.' Hope you like it, it's kind of a meat pie thing."

Wow! Things get exotic with the Dearborns, thought Tom. They live in an avant-garde house, and Italian food.

Mom hurried off to the kitchen. Tom, Claire and her father sat and listened to a choir on the radio, quietly admiring their twinkling handiwork as they made small talk.

"You have a nice house," Tom said. "It's quite new."

"Ten years," Claire's father replied.

"Didn't you build it after a fire or something?"

Both Claire and Mr. Dearborn suddenly squirmed and sat up. Tom sensed he had said something wrong, or brought up something they didn't want to talk about.

"I'll, well, uh, sometime. Oh, isn't that Christmas tree nice!" Claire said, awkwardly changing the subject.

Mrs. Dearborn yelled a cheery "Come and eat!" and the three of them walked around to the dining room. Campbell sat down at the head of the table and motioned to the chairs on his left for his daughter and Tom. Mom had set sodas at four places. Then she brought in a big, flat pan with the sliced pizza and set it down in middle of the table.

"I hope this works, how he found a cookbook in Italy written in English, I have no idea. I had to convert grams to ounces and Centigrade to Fahrenheit, I may have ruined it."

The three Dearborns put their arms up on the table and held out their hands. They knew the drill, Tom didn't.

"It is a custom in our home to always ask the Lord's blessing before we eat," Campbell explained as he took the hands of his wife and daughter. Well okay, if that's what you do, Tom thought, as he reached across the table to take Mrs. Dearborn's outstretched hand, then Claire's hand at his side.

"Our dear heavenly Father...." Mr. Dearborn began and Tom lost him. Here he sat, holding Claire's hand, right in front of her parents, and it was okay!

The girl's hand was warm and soft and she slowly wrapped her long fingers around his palm. Tom gave her hand a squeeze. Claire squeezed back.

"Amen," the prayer concluded. Mrs. Dearborn served each of them a wedge of meaty pizza. Tom took his fork and cut off a bite and chewed.

"Not bad," he mumbled.

"If you really want to be authentic, fold it up and eat it with your hands," Mrs. Dearborn explained, and she did just that. The plump woman biting off the end of a pizza slice struck him as funny but he didn't dare laugh.

"This is going to catch on," Claire's father stated firmly between chews. "Outside of New York or Chicago most people have never heard of pizza. You just watch, in a few years there'll be restaurants serving this stuff all over the place."

Yeah, right, thought Tom.

That sounded far-fetched, but Claire's dad seemed to have a knack at business. Maybe he knew something?

"So tell me about your dad's outfit, how are hardware sales?" the father continued.

"Dad says they're swell, we're making up ground we lost during the war, but some of the old-timers have cautioned that a recession's coming, like after the First World War. He doesn't know what to do, order more merchandise or pull back," Tom answered.

"Order more," Mr. Dearborn said firmly.

"This time the economy's different. Keep your eye on that Sears-and-Roebuck outfit. They're going for broke right now, I think it'll work for them. Pretty soon they're going to be bigger than Montgomery Ward."

Tom really hadn't planned on a conversation about business but Mr. Dearborn continued.

"You pay attention to your dad, watch him," Claire's father added. "Your family's been successful for years, he's a sharp fellow. I hope you plan to stay in the business when you get out of school."

"I guess so, that's all a bit far off for me yet," Tom said with a shrug.

"It'll be here before you know it. The hardware business will change, I think there will be chains of hardware places in a few years, sort of like department stores, the little mom-and-pop places will go away but your dad's wholesale business will do well with some planning," Mr. Dearborn answered.

Where did the guy get this stuff?

No wonder someone this smart, and this rich, has a sharp daughter, Tom thought to himself. It's like he knows the future. Tom glanced at Claire, who had her best "I'm bored" look as she ate her pizza.

Mr. Dearborn glanced at a mantel clock on the sideboard as it chimed eight o'clock and noted, "It's getting late, do you need a ride home?"

"Oh no," Tom replied, "I'll call my dad."

The thought of leaving the Dearborns made him sad, Claire's parents were really nice. Mr. Dearborn directed him to a phone in the huge kitchen, which had an island in the middle between the sink and stove. What an odd way to build a kitchen, Tom thought.

He picked up the phone, waited for the operator and gave her the familiar number. His mom answered and said one of them would be right over.

Mrs. Dearborn thanked Tom profusely again, he nodded, put on his hat and coat and walked outside as Claire followed, her arms crossed over her sweatshirt to keep warm. She led him down to the far end of the porch, away from the lights by the door. A glass-brick wall brightened the far end of the home's front.

"Thanks for coming," she said softly. "Oh, here's a little something." Claire reached into her hip pocket and pulled out an envelope and handed it to Tom. "Merry Christmas!"

He held up the envelope to look at it in the dim light, addressed to "Tom" in the same perfect cursive as the note in his locker.

"Should I open it now or later?" Tom asked.

"Hmmm, later," she answered with a wink, her hands in her hip pockets.

Now what was the girl up to? Going home suddenly seemed like a great idea. He stuck the envelope in his coat, he would not forget it.

Claire folded her arms across her sweatshirt again and let out a "Brrr!" accentuated by a frosty cloud from her mouth. "I thought your dad would be right here."

"Me too, but if you're cold, I guess we can get on the bus and get warmed up," Tom replied with a grin.

Claire snorted, grabbed her middle and bent over laughing.

"Oh, Tom! You are on a roll tonight!" she gasped between giggles, fanning her face.

It was the first time he heard her say his name.

"Maybe," he replied.

That did it.

Claire swooned against the glass bricks with a loud thump as she went into hysterical laughter, a hand across her forehead. Tom could hear her laughter echo from neighboring houses in the still night.

Suddenly, the Dearborns' front door opened and her dad stepped out on the porch and looked down at them, puzzled.

"It's okay, Daddy!" she said as she fanned herself, choking back more laughter.

The door closed, they were alone again.

She stood up, took a deep breath, and Tom put his arms around her waist. He pulled her toward him as she reached around his neck.

"Thank you, I had a good time, and I hope the Christmas tree is what your parents want," he whispered. The porch light caught a gleam in her blue eyes just as they kissed. Oh my, this girl could kiss.

This time there were no nerves.

They embraced, then Claire leaned back and smiled, her eyes still sparkling in the dim light.

"Oh, what a perfect evening, thanks for coming. I want you to know…"

"TOM! TOM! Speak to me!"

Tom's mind jerked across seven decades from Claire's cold, dark porch to Hickory Bough's warm, bright dayroom.

"You've been sitting there all morning!" He looked up and there were a worried Gaylene and Josefina. Gaylene shook his shoulder.

"Oh, uh, I guess, uh, I'm fine. I had one of my fainting spells, takes a while to recover," he mumbled.

"Well! It's time for lunch! Let's eat!" Gaylene said as she marched toward the dining room.

Tom took his cane and with a little effort boosted himself off the sofa and followed the chaplain into the dining room.

So if it was lunchtime, he had been sitting there four hours?

Just to make sure, he turned around and glanced back at the board:

- Greet our new resident: Claire Dearborn.

Chapter 6
Taking Notes

"Hey old man, you still among the livin'?" Tony asked as he rolled in Tom's door that afternoon. "Sorry, didn't notice you sittin' out there, been busy chasin' nurses."

"Oh, I'm fine, that was a bad one," Tom answered, rubbing his temples. He told his friend of the surprising name on the board, then described his flashback and the memories that followed of the Claire he knew long ago.

"So was she a rich brat?" Tony asked in fake seriousness.

"Oh no, the Dearborns were old money, didn't have to put on airs, they got along with everybody," Tom replied.

"Claire, well, she had her own personality, she wasn't outgoing like her father, you had to get to know her. She was something of a loner, didn't have many friends, and she had some unusual ways. But I don't think that was because her family had money. It was just her, and somehow I found it charming."

"Obviously this issue concerns the patient," Tony said with a fake scowl. "Tell me more! Lie back on the couch and tell Dr. Tony, shrinkology expert, all your problems."

"So first, what was in the envelope she gave you?" he asked.

Tom thought for a minute.

"Gee, I don't recall, I guess I'm having a senior moment," he said.

"I have some of those. The doctor wishes to know, what was the question?" Tony replied.

"Oh my, the notes, the letters, they blur together. She wrote me all the time.

"Our sophomore year, and on, we exchanged combinations to each other's lockers, I'd open up mine and here would be a sheet ripped out of a spiral notebook, folded up every which way, and stuck on the little shelf above the coat hook. I thought that funny, a ripped-up, carelessly folded piece of paper. But her hand writing? Flawless, absolutely perfect, she made straight-A's in penmanship.

"She would leave one liners, stuff like, '*This home ec class is so boring! I know how to bake cookies—and I'll bake you some anytime you want. You're my big cookie!*' They always brightened my day.

"The last summer the Dearborns went to the Broadmoor was 1946. She wrote me every day. I'd rush home from the warehouse to get the mail and there would be a letter with a Colorado Springs postmark. I loved 'em, she'd describe what they were doing: playing golf, riding horses, we took the tram up Pikes Peak, whatever."

"So why did her old man stop taking the fam on the big junket to the Rockies? Bucks or boy?" Tony asked.

"Well, yes, it was b-o-y," Tom answered. "She told me the next summer they were staying home and I asked why? 'I told daddy I'm not going without you!' she told me firmly, hands on her hips. So her dad said that wouldn't work and, if that's the way you feel, we'll stay home. That floored me."

102

"That evening over at the Dearborns turned into a big deal in my family. One of the low points came that Christmas Day."

"How so?" asked Tony, "Did the tree fall over?"

"My mom, I loved her dearly, but she could really be a *mom*," Tom said with a sigh as he thought back.

Tom described how mother Bentley had baked a ham and the family had a great holiday meal after opening presents. All of the conversation had been about his brothers, the hardships of war, their long trips home across the Atlantic packed aboard impossibly slow Liberty Ships, then crowded troop trains.

Tom's brother, Phil, finally interrupted, "Enough about us, so what's been happening in dear ol' Randall?"

"Well, your little brother has a girlfriend," mom replied in the flat tone she might use to tell everyone she mopped the kitchen Sunday night.

Tom felt his face go the color of the beets in front of him.

"So! Who's the lucky catch?" Phil asked.

"Claire Dearborn," Mom answered in her monotone.

"You mean Bruce Dearborn's little sister?" Chuck asked with surprise.

"Yeah," Tom muttered, staring down at an unfinished ham slice.

"I bet she's a real beauty by now, but I remember her as this kinda' plain, skinny kid," Chuck added. "A bunch of us guys would go over there and she'd be riding around on her bicycle in front of that funny house."

"Well, how did you pull that off, you sly dog?" Phil asked. "Did you tell her you're rich?"

The older brothers burst out laughing.

Tom thought he would die.

"Now boys," dad said, interrupting the merriment as he raised his hand. "They're in ninth grade, it's just a puppy love thing. I know it'll be over in a few weeks, we were all fourteen once. It's not like they're married."

The room grew silent as the older boys sat and looked admiringly at their little brother, his head in his plate.

"But if you play your cards right, you will be. Good goin', little buddy," Phil said solemnly.

"If she's as much a woman as her brothers are men, I know she'll make something of herself. They both came home with medals on their chests, they did more than we did to fight the Nazis, they're the talk of the town."

"Gus got the Flying Cross for saving his bomber, the Luftwaffe shot it up pretty bad," Chuck explained. "He was co-pilot, two engines out, the pilot wounded. They couldn't make it back to Deenethorpe so he put the plane down, almost a crash landing, at Lakenheath. The whole crew lived and most of them walked away, thanks to him. Anybody else in the right seat and they would've ditched in the North Sea. We won the war because of people like him."

Tony looked blankly at Tom.

"So what's wrong with that?" he asked. "Sounds like you impressed your bro's."

"I guess nothing," Tom answered. "But it embarrassed me."

104

"So, was your dad right? Was it a high school fling, an infatuation?" Tony asked, "Or, did she tease you for years and then run off in the night with the Gypsies?"

"Oh, Tony! You don't know how close you are," Tom replied.

"We dated, if you want to call it that, all through high school. Nowadays I guess people would say we were 'an item.' Looking back at it, I know there were other girls who liked me, I can think of this one cute redhead who hung around me, Pam something, can't think of her last name.

"I think I looked good back then, and pretty popular. But no, that's Claire's steady, leave him alone!

"I had Claire Dearborn, *the* Claire Dearborn, what gal in Randall could top her? She had looks, she had smarts, she had taste, and her family had as much money as the rest of the town put together. A little funny turned, but still....

"She felt the same about me, what guy at Randall High could beat Tom Bentley?

"She could be amazing. I won the election for class president my junior year. A bunch of the pep club guys were my campaign committee, if you'd call it that. Claire showed up at our planning meeting and sat in the back of the room, listening. The guys agreed to have me go 'round and do a stump speech in each home room, they would paint some big banners and hang 'em in the halls.

"As we left, I stopped and told her, 'Thanks for coming but you didn't have to be here.'

"She just smiled that pouty smile and said firmly, 'If you want it, I want you to have it.'

105

"Lo and behold, these small, white posters started appearing everywhere, dozens of them, in all the halls and above the lockers. They all said 'TOM BENTLEY PRESIDENT '49' in big, blue watercolor letters—perfectly printed block letters. I only knew one person who could write that well.

"I went in the boys' restroom off the main hall one afternoon and there they were, one above each urinal. Hoo boy! Then I went to track team practice that afternoon and guess what I saw plastered all around the boys' locker room?

"I was afraid to ask how, I won in a landslide."

"Maybe you should've run for governor or somethin'," Tony suggested. "Sounds like you had the best campaign manager since Hillary Clinton. And did you have rivals? Were there any guys scopin' her out?

"I don't think so, but I might have been naïve. She was a prize, alright, but so aloof, so quiet, so reserved. She could be off-putting. And given who her family was, I think she intimidated other boys," Tom said. "I never felt like I had competition.

"Right at the end of our junior year, the day everyone picked up their senior rings, we went to the office together during lunch to get ours. We walked out in the hall, I took mine off my ring finger, I might have had it on five minutes, and handed it to her. She put it on her index finger, then she took her ring off and handed it to me. I slid it on my pinky.

"We said nothing, almost mechanical. We smiled at each other, we just knew. 'I'll wear it proudly,' she told me seriously.

106

"We were just together—all the time. My grandson calls it 'hangin' out,' doing nothing in particular, just being with each other, and that's what we did mostly.

"Their house had air conditioning, the first place in town to have it. Needless to say I hung out over there all summer. We weren't overly romantic, no passionate making out like that night on the bus—well, not much anyway.

"I like such honesty in my patients," Tony interjected, "Or are you being completely honest, my friend? Tell the doctor!"

"Well, did I mention that gazebo way at the back of the Dearborns' big yard? It was fifty yards out there from their porch, right where their yard went off into the woods.

"Well, you know, there were some nights with a full moon, lightning bugs, chirping crickets, we'd cuddle out there. There were these big lights on the porch and there could be eyes watching from the house so we never got carried away, we were pretty innocent by today's standards.

"We'd talk about things."

Tom stopped and thought for a moment.

"Hey, I remember one of the first nights we ended up out there after wandering around the yard at dusk holding hands, she wrapped herself around me like she'd do, then she stared at me for a moment and asked very seriously, 'Do you think I'm pretty?'"

"Whoa, Nelly! The patient better know the answer to that one!" Tony laughed.

"True, I'm kinda' dense sometimes but I knew what she wanted to hear," Tom answered with a blank look.

"I started to say, 'Are you kidding me?'

107

"Here she was, this absolutely, stunningly beautiful girl—a tall blonde with gorgeous blue eyes. Yet she wonders if I find her attractive? So I started to say, 'Oh c'mon, Claire! Don't you see guys looking you over? There's just gotta' be a reason!'

"Well, if I'd said that it would not have come out right. So I sat for a moment and then told her, 'You are more than pretty, you are the most beautiful girl I have ever seen.' I hoped that would be enough.

"She furrowed her eyebrows, thought for a moment, and said, 'Okay.'"

"I was like, 'Where did that come from?' She could shoot stray bullets.

"As I said, we were just sort of, I don't know, there with each other—all the time. We ate together in the cafeteria when are schedules matched. She came to my track meets, she came to my Scout courts of honor, I went to her band concerts. We went to First Presbyterian Sunday mornings, then to BYPU Sunday nights."

"Be-you-pee-you what?" Tony asked with a puzzled look.

"Baptist Young People's Union, the youth group at the Baptist church."

"Remember, I'm Catholic," Tony said with a smirk. "I have trouble keeping up with presbytopians and baptisimists or whatever. You Protestants are hard to follow."

"Sorry about that.

"Over time, our families became close because of us. Our parents got to where they were always going to one home or the other to eat or visit; really special.

"She and I and our dads played golf a few times at the club. I'm not much of a golfer but she did well from the ladies' tees up front. She has long arms and, good golly, she could get some drives off. I did better on the greens.

"I trimmed their hedges when the gardener didn't do the job just so, the way Mrs. Dearborn wanted. Claire would make sandwiches for dad and me at my house when mom went off someplace. Hey, I remember driving home from the warehouse one afternoon and there was Claire in her pedal pushers, mowing our lawn when the guy we hired to do the yard skipped town. I doubt if she had ever pushed a mower in her life.

"One of the best times, when was it?, right before Christmas 1948, I think. My folks and one of my brothers were with me over at the Dearborns one night for dinner. We had a great meal, then we all went back and gathered around their big piano while Mrs. Dearborn played. We all sang, really belted 'em out, swinging our cups of eggnog; great time.

"I remember we were singing *Walking in a Winter Wonderland* and we got to the line about '*He'll say 'are you married?'' we'll say 'no man,' but you can do the job when you're in town.*' I glanced at her just as she looked at me.

We both blushed, I guess that was the first time I had the what-if thought go through my head. We were seniors in high school, maybe this could be a permanent deal.

"Our friends joked The Malt Shop should put a sign on the back booth that said 'Reserved for Claire and Tom' because we always sat back there and talked. At the far end of the room from the jukebox, you could hear the music but still talk comfortably. And we talked a lot."

"Talked about what?" Tony asked, shifting in his wheelchair.

"Oh, I dunno' what, hopes, dreams, ideas, goals. She was—is, maybe—thoughtful, intense and deep. What were we going to do with our lives? At that point we just assumed whatever we did we would do together, we were just always together.

"She would sit around quietly, thinking and listening while other people talked.

"Her folks invited me over Christmas morning, maybe my senior year. Her dad would always read the Christmas story out of the Bible before they opened gifts.

"Mr. Dearborn came to that verse in Luke, '*But Mary kept all these things, and pondered them in her heart.*' He sat there with this big, black Bible in his lap, he paused, then looked at Claire, chuckled and said, 'That sounds like you, sweetheart!' They all laughed, she just sat there.

"But then sometimes she'd go off on stuff, talking with those narrow blonde eyebrows furrowed, peeking out behind that wisp of hair that always hung over her face, slicing the air with her thin fingers. 'I think *this*, we should do *that*!'

"Like in 1948, the time we were sitting back there in our Malt Shop booth. The election was a month off. Would it be okay for us to support President Truman? Our families are Republicans and he's a Democrat. But he's from Missouri, does that make a difference? Yes, we should support President Truman!"

"And?" Tony asked.

"As though it made any difference, we were seventeen, we couldn't vote."

"I always liked 'give 'em hell, Harry,' great President, my man!" Tom's friend replied.

"I became her alarm clock. She had her own phone in her bedroom—a big deal in those days. I'd call and wake her when I got up. I never saw it but I had this mental image of Claire, no makeup, in her bathrobe and fuzzy slippers, her hair all mussed up, yawning as she shuffled into the kitchen for breakfast after I called.

"She would have absolutely died if I had seen her like that, she was so particular about the way she looked. But I would have thought it cute."

"Maybe she didn't do cute," Tony replied.

"No, she didn't.

"Whatever, we were in our own little world," Tom continued, "I'm not sure what people thought. One summer, it must have been between my junior and senior year, Mr. Ross, the chemistry teacher, worked part-time at the warehouse. That wasn't unusual, dad would bring in teachers to work over the summer, as much as anything because they didn't make much money. We were unloading a boxcar on the siding.

"Oh, talk about hot! We took a break, standing under a fan, and Mr. Ross struck up a conversation. 'What are you up to these days, Tommy?' he asked.

"I said, 'Not much.'"

"'You still chasin' that Dearborn girl?'

"I turned red, then hemmed and hawed and said something about 'we're seein' each other.'"

111

"'That girl is always doing something surprising but keep goin', she's a winner!' he told me. I thanked him for the advice, and we both went and got a cold drink. Even a guy as clueless as he was had picked up that we were always together.

"She helped my reputation. I won a Kiwanis Club scholarship, me and some other guys. We could bring a guest to the presentation, so of course I invited Claire. Afterwards, the club president came around to shake my hand just as she went to powder her nose. I remember he glanced at her walking off, then back at me, and said, 'That's Campbell's daughter!' then grunted an approving 'Mmm-hmm!'"

"If you can't look good, get a girl who does," Tony said firmly.

"Ain't that the truth.

"Then our senior year: We had graduation a few months off, and I remember I sat in first-hour accounting when the PA clicked on and the office lady announced: 'The following people report to the principal's office.' She droned on reading these names and I jumped when she said, 'Tom Bentley.' I had never been summoned to the principal's office for anything. I started worrying, then the last name she called was 'Claire Dearborn.'"

"So were you in trouble?"

"Oh no, not at all, turned out we were all the winners of our senior class most-likely this-or-that contest."

"So what did you win, most likely to hook a rich babe?" Tony asked.

"Of course not, remember she had been called in too. Claire and I were voted the 'Glamour Couple of 1949' and we had to go get a portrait at the photo studio downtown for the yearbook."

"So did you vote for yourself?" Tony asked.

"Heavens no, we were chosen by some kind of committee of students and teachers, I had no idea."

"So what about the photo?"

"Oh, mom went nuts, said that was just the greatest thing. They drove me over to Springfield to rent a tuxedo. Dad had to help me with the cuff links, bow tie and cummerbund, and I got these shiny, patent-leather shoes. I thought I looked pretty good."

"And Claire?"

"Okay, now this was Claire being Claire: When I mentioned I was getting a tux for the photo she said she and her mom *bought* a dress—past tense. She knew, but how?"

"Didn't you ask her?"

"Maybe it was a coincidence, I don't know. I did ask, and she mumbled something about 'make the most of what you have.' It was another one of her surprises.

"Wait: I never thought of this before, Tony, but maybe she did know. She was the class valedictorian, maybe somebody slipped and said something. If anyone could keep a secret, she could.

"Oh, but she was *very* upset about having to give the commencement speech. She called me that night after she found out, very nervous.

"'Well congratulations!' I replied.

"'But I can't do *that*!' she gasped. 'I can't get up in front of all those people! Could you give the speech for me?'

113

"I laughed at her, which I guess wasn't very nice, and said 'It doesn't work that way. You earned the honor, you give the speech.'

"'Well it's no honor for me, I'm terrified!' she said. 'Could you at least write a speech for me? You're so good at that sort of thing.'

"I was dumbfounded, this was her show, not mine. But we got together that weekend and worked up a nice little talk."

"*Ghost writers in the skyyyy*!," Tony sang.

"Anyway, enough of that, back to the glamor couple: The school set the appointment that Saturday, and we were milling around in the studio's lobby. Then Mr. Dearborn's big Packard pulls up, he parks in front of the door and goes around and helps Claire out, she's wearing this frumpy overcoat; cold outside. She comes in and takes off the coat and, Tony, so help me, she looked like she stepped out of the cover of *Vogue*, this slinky black evening gown. The dress showed off her figure, tall and thin, with that blonde hair falling over her cheek."

"Tall and thin? Sounds pretty good, I'm a leg man," Tony replied.

"You remember those Black Velvet Canadian ads back in the '70s with some slinky blonde in a black dress pitching whiskey? That's her!" Tom added.

"I'm a gin drinker," Tony replied.

"Whatever, the rest of the kids' mouths dropped— and so did mine. They were there in Sunday, go-to-meetin' suits and new Easter dresses, Easter came in a few weeks, and me in a tux with a fashion model. Talk about feeding your ego," Tom added.

114

"And here it came: The two of us huddled in a corner of the studio, I had my arm around her while the photographer took pictures of the others; flash, flash, flash. I whispered, 'You look *gorgeous* in black!'"

She looked at me with that half smile and replied, 'I look pretty good in white too.'"

"Bam! Wow, I knew what she meant! I said, 'Well, I hope I'm the first to see it.'

"She squinted at me, those blue eyes sparkled, she put on a big smile, and answered, 'Only if you're looking up the aisle when daddy and me walk in.'

"My heart stopped, let me tell you! I would have the winner's prize for the rest of my life!

"We went last, I bet the photographer took ten photos of us while the other kids milled around, watching.

"And there we are to this day in the yearbook, I still have one in a box in my closet, holding hands and looking at the camera. I have this thousand-yard stare on my face. Claire has her usual, odd, pouty smile. Elegant!

"I remember noticing when the studio sent us proofs that I was finally taller than her. At last, thank-you growth spurt! But if she wore heels she was still taller than me."

"That doesn't sound so bad," Tony interrupted.

"Oh, it was. I had no idea what to do, I was out of my element. Then our class sponsor, the fine arts teacher, told us the glamour couple always does the first dance at the prom. But I don't dance."

"Really? Why not?" a puzzled Tony asked. "You have a club foot?"

"I don't know, my Baptist parents said dancing promotes sin and corruption."

"Sin and corruption sound pretty good to me, so what did Claire think? Was she into sin and corruption?"

"Not much. She ordered me: 'You *will* learn to waltz or *else*!'"

"Or else what?" Tony asked.

"I don't know, I just went with it like I always did. Claire had me over and she put some waltzes on the phonograph: one-two-three, one-two-three, one-two-three. We did it enough I got serviceable and I quit stomping on her feet. She has these long, narrow feet—easy targets. She never said a word but she'd wince whenever I landed on a foot."

Tony laughed, "I can imagine how that looked."

"Her mother got into it: how romantic! Her lovely daughter and her best beau were going to be stars of the prom! Claire's parents were pretty good dancers and would spin around the room while I slowly clomped around with their daughter," Tom added.

"I asked Claire what about other dances? What if they play a fox trot or swing or something? I didn't know much about dancing but I knew there were other dance steps and I didn't have a clue."

"'I'll take care of it,' she insisted. The band, sure enough, played a waltz and we started off the first dance after the big dinner. The whole class circled around us, applauding, as we whirled around the floor in the spotlight. What a magic moment!"

"So did you pull it off, or did you look like Groucho Marx?" Tony asked.

"I may have, but we did okay; nobody laughed. I even faked a swing or two later that left Claire giggling.

116

"They had the prom on a Saturday night out at the country club. Mr. Dearborn let us borrow his Packard. I drove over in dad's Nash. It was big but Packards were huge, like driving a truck, never mind the leather seats.

"I went inside to pick her up and Claire came around the corner in that slinky black gown. What a beauty, she had rolled her hair so it was in these long golden waves over her back and shoulder—an absolute stunner. I could hardly think straight.

"Mrs. Dearborn dug out the family's Kodak Brownie and took our picture, then had the drug store print up five-by-sevens. I had that photo in the lid of my Army locker in Korea.

"Tony, that picture kept me alive. Don't get yourself shot, big boy, that's what you're going home to."

"That sounds really special," Tony interrupted.

"But you know what sticks out from that night? As we went out the door, my arm around her, I heard her dad say quietly in that deep voice to Claire's mom, 'We are so blessed to have him!' That—that—really meant a lot.

"I wasn't some dirty, lecherous boy taking advantage of their chaste daughter, some hood they were scared of. They loved me almost as much as they loved her. I had sort of become their third son, and I guess Claire had become my parents' first daughter, in some ways."

"Lechery has its rewards," Tony added.

"And after that morning at the photographer, the thought flashed through my mind: Pretty soon you're going to go one-on-one with Mr. Dearborn and Tom, my boy, you're going to ask, 'May I?' And he will nod and in that deep voice say, 'Of course you can, son.'

"Then I opened the door for her and she scooted right across the seat up next to me and I told her, 'I'm sorry, I can't wait, you are so beautiful,' and I leaned over and kissed her. All that beauty—and the cinnamon was there as always. I could see her smile in the dark as she whispered, 'I know.'"

"Sheesh, that sounds kinda' vain if you ask me," Tony said. "Are you sure you really wanted this chick?"

"Sure, this was Claire. What she said and did were, well, different," Tom replied. "We were in love, we knew it, we didn't have to say it."

"Well, Dr. Tony thinks the patient needs more therapy but right now the doc is hungry, so let's go eat," Tony said.

As usual, he rolled out into the hall—backwards— as Tom's cane thumped slowly on the floor as he paced the wheelchair.

Chapter 7
The Dream

The waitress brought their Italian night meals and Tony took his fork and leaned over sideways to twirl up a big wad of spaghetti.

"Pardon me, but you've rambled all over creation," he said between chews. "This is all sweetness and light, when did the Gypsies show up?"

Tom took a drink, put down his glass and thought for a moment.

"Oddly, our own parents, our ever-loving and ever-doting parents, threw everything off."

"Really? I thought the parents were crazy about Randall High's glamour couple," Tony replied.

"Oh, they were, but their plans were not the same as ours."

"That's not unusual. I can think of some parents back on The Hill that had a different plan than the Army for their dear son."

"*They* knew what was best for us," Tom said with irritation.

"Claire's mom graduated from Cottey College, it's this elite girls' school up in Nevada, toward Kansas City. And if you are part of the sisterhood—and she certainly was—your daughters went there too."

"So where did you end up?"

"The University of Missouri, up at Columbia, again because of parental pressure. Dad insisted all Bentleys go to Mizzou," Tom explained.

"But if we obeyed our parents, we would suddenly be a couple-hundred miles apart. They meant well but what they wanted would hurt our relationship, and we knew it."

"So the two of you circled the wagons to fight off the Gypsies?"

"Exactly," Tom continued. "We sat out at there in the gazebo reading college bulletins we picked up at the counselor's office. What would work for us? I wanted to go into accounting, finance or business. She wanted to do philosophy or English lit and have some type of career, probably teaching."

"Ah, the moonlight, the roses and a college bulletin," Tony replied, "you crazy, romantic kids!"

"We went over all options. We had Missouri Mines up at Rolla, but it's an engineering school. There's a Pentecostal college over in Springfield, Evangel, but we weren't Pentecostals, and the small but very good Drury College didn't work. Maybe I could go to some college around Nevada while she attended Cottey, but there weren't any.

"After all this reading and talk, we thought things through and agreed we wanted to go to Southwest Missouri State College over in Springfield.

We made that our dream: Move to Springfield—the big town—and start our own life together, our own home.

"We could both take the classes we wanted and, neither of us said it in so many words, we knew in a year or so we would be married and living in an apartment on our own.

"One Saturday afternoon, we'd been to The Malt Shop for lunch, we were just strolling around, window shopping, holding hands. We ended up at Draper Furniture, looking at sofas, bedroom suites and stuff. I don't think I had ever been in a furniture store before. We said nothing but we both knew why we were there, it was part of our dream."

"Sounds like a plan," Tony said, "And as newlyweds in your own cozy little apartment you could make up for all that wasted time out there in the gazebo reading up on colleges."

"Of course, if we had done that where would we have ended up? Newlywed college students just barely scraping by?" Tom added.

"We probably would have had some tiny little place at the end of a dead end street, behind a railroad track and creek. But when you're in love, you don't care."

Tony shoved his empty plate aside as he attacked a slice of apple pie. "Now the treachery: How to sell it to the folks?"

"As usual, you're ahead of me," Tom said, wiping his hands on a napkin. "We decided if we could get one set of parents to buy in then the other go along. We decided to huddle with mine first, they would be the easier sell. Claire came over to eat one Sunday night and we started our agreed-upon talk after dessert.

"It did not go well?" Tony said.

"Nope. Mom blurted out, 'but that's a teacher's college!' as dad nodded in approval.

"'Look, we've thought about this too, and we know Missouri is best for you,' dad added, staring at me. We went around and around but both of them were firm. I was going to Mizzou. Period. I could choose a fraternity or stay independent. And, they brought up mom came from Jeff City, your grandparents are nearby if anything happens."

"Then over to the Dearborns?" asked Tony.

"Yep, the next Sunday and guess what Mrs. Dearborn said?"

"Let's see, another slam on educators: 'But that's a teacher's college!'"

"Tony, it was the exact same thing: 'We've thought about this too and we know Cottey is best for you.' She was firm, her daughter was going to Cottey.

"Now, Mr. Dearborn was the one who understood. The man had a gift for seeing where things will lead. He sat there quietly through the whole conversation, more of an argument, with his chin on his hand.

"'Jewel, I think we can work this out,' he finally said, raising his hands like a baseball manager calling time.

But no, Mrs. Dearborn remained adamant. That otherwise sweet, easygoing mother dug in her heels: Her little girl would follow in mom's footsteps, nothing further to talk about. And like any man who's been part of a successful marriage, he knew when to hold 'em and he knew when to fold 'em.

"He folded."

"A wise man, indeed," Tony said with a nod. "My marriage would have been better if I had folded sometimes."

"So commencement still rings in my ears, as we came up on stage:

"'Thomas James Bentley, cum laude, to the University of Missouri.

"'Claire Elaine Dearborn, summa cum laude, to Cottey College.'"

"By the way, how about that speech, did she get her tang tongled?" Tony asked.

"Oh, she did fine, but I could hear her knees knocking, her hands shook.

"You know what? It made me so proud to sit out there with the other kids and see *my* senior ring on *her* finger as she turned the pages. I sat there and played with her ring on my pinky. That's my girl up there, I'm so proud.

"The big surprise that night sat out in the parking lot. The Dearborns bought Claire a brand-new, green, 1949 Studebaker, white sidewalls, with those backward-opening suicide doors to the rear seat, really pretty. We walked out of the high school gym, Mr. Dearborn steered everyone over to it, then handed her the keys."

"My brother had a '50 Studebaker, one of those bullet-nosed things; ran good but used oil," Tony said.

"Claire gave her old man a big bear hug with a loud, 'Oh, Daddy!' as she hopped up and down from excitement. He held her back, looked at her proudly, and said in that baritone, 'Why don't you and Tommy take it for a spin? Be back at the house in an hour, we're having everyone over.'"

"So cruisin' in Randall began that night?"

"Something like that," Tom added. "Out came a different side of her I had only begun to see. There we were, roaring around, still in our gowns and mortarboards, honking and waving at people, we must have been a sight.

"I had never seen Claire so loose and free, so happy, having the time of her life. I had the luck to ride shotgun.

123

Somehow in her mind, I think, I was the only one watching. I bet we orbited the courthouse ten times. Mind you, an hour before she was shaking like a leaf because she had to give a little speech.

"That night I figured out the love of my life had three personalities, I guess you would say. One was the intense, quiet, aloof, intellectual, career-oriented, girl who thought everything through—that's who she was in public.

"The second was an emotional, chatty, fun-loving, sometimes-teasing girl who dearly loved her close-knit family—affectionate. And, she liked to cuddle. She would wrap herself around me out there in the gazebo, put her head on my shoulder, and sit there for hours while we talked. She had to know you—really know you—before you saw the second person. I may have been the only one outside her family who made the cut.

"Then somehow, somewhere, hidden in between those two, was a secret third person who I don't think anyone knew. This was the girl who could quietly steal around and pull off surprising and unexpected things on the QT, the quiet planner."

Tony sat listening and nodding.

"Okay, pal, that's enough.

"Dr. Tony, shrinkologist extraordinaire, has completed his assessment: Sounds like a severe case of boyfriend-itis. Your gal was insecure, an introvert and complex," Tony said, staring at Tom in mock seriousness.

"Complex dames are trouble."

"She was that: complex," Tom answered.

"She proved that still waters run deep. But I was in love with her and part of her charm was wondering: What's she gonna' do *next*?"

"Commencement night, when we made it back to the Dearborns, they had a big crowd with her family and mine, we had to park up the street and walk. What's the line in the Broadway show? 'One big happy family!'

"They hauled out the champagne and Mr. Dearborn even had the maid come out from the kitchen and join everyone in a toast to the two of us. I still remember that nervous little colored lady in her maid's uniform, self-consciously wiping her hands on her apron, then hoisting a glass of champagne with all the white folks."

"Then he took everyone in the den and unveiled an oil painting of Claire, big thing, right there next to her brothers' portraits. Now what did that cost? Everyone applauded.

"It was the only time in my life I ever looked at a painting of someone standing next to me. But whoever the artist was, some woman in St. Louis, caught her perfectly: the dark blue eyes, the wisp of hair over her cheek and that brooding half smile. It was beautiful, I wanted to steal the thing and put it in my bedroom."

"That might have been kinda' spooky," Tony suggested.

Chapter 8
We Can Do This!

"Hey, speaking of spooky," Tom added, "That night, our parents cooked up an idea for both families to go down to Eureka Springs for a long weekend at the Crescent Hotel, that big, old place on the hill above the town. We went in late August before we left for college. Our folks rented a whole floor, the Bentleys on one end and the Dearborns on the other, to see us off and have joint family reunions."

"With a guard and a machine gun in the middle to keep you two apart?" Tony asked with a wink.

"Oh no, nothing like that, prudish aunts and grandmothers cruised all over. But what a place, creaky floors, lights that didn't work, strange puffs of cold air, odd groans and other noises in the night, everyone loved it.

"Everyone talked in the bar down in the hotel basement, the manager closed off part of it for our group; hospitality suite."

"So did the hotel have a gazebo?" asked Tony.

"Close. It had this nice, formal garden in the back with a great view of the town down below. A big thunderstorm came up that Saturday night and it left everything outside wet, cloudy and misty.

"The two of us snuck out there in the dark so we could be alone, we knew what was coming and how hard it would be. Claire fought back tears as we both said, 'We can do this! We will make this work!'

"Another magic moment: I wrapped her in my arms and we kissed passionately, then I looked up and noticed

127

someone watching from the second-floor porch. Uh-oh! But it was my brother, Phil. He gave me a big grin and thumbs-up. He understood, he and his fiancée married that fall.

"We got silly the next day. We'd go in shops, holding hands, and amble back in the back between the shelves, alone, and sneak a kiss or a hug; goofy, silly kids! It got to be a game to avoid the spinster aunts and our parents wandering around.

"Phil caught us again. We were back behind some bookshelves, wardrobes, or something in this antique furniture place across from Basin Park. I looked at her—the fun-loving Claire was in full force—and she squinted at me with this mischievous 'I *know* you wanna' kiss me!' look she had.

"Boy, did I. I cupped those pale cheeks in my palms and I smacked a good one on those pouty lips. Just then I heard a cough, we jumped. Phil quietly said, 'Your mom's coming, Claire.'

"We broke it off and I nodded. 'You owe me one,' he said, smiling. Claire ran off with a bad case of giggles just as her parents walked up.

"'How do you do that?" her father asked me, watching his usually stoic daughter run away, laughing.

"Never mind," I answered. He winked at me.

"Our parents took all these photos of the two of us, walking up and down the crooked streets. Frankly, I wasn't impressed with the town, really run down and seedy back then.

"But as usual, Claire's dad could see something the rest of us couldn't. 'You watch, some developer will get a hold of this place and the tourists will be so thick you can't stir 'em with a stick,' he told me as we ate the last afternoon we were there.

"And you know what? He was right. They built that big statue of Jesus up on the hill across from the Crescent, and they started that Passion Play thing in the '60s. And now, I don't think you can get a room on summer nights," Tom added.

"Truth be told, I bet ol' Campbell made a few shekels off it."

The Hickory Bough dining room had emptied.

"Tom, my friend, things remain too wonderful. Where's the pain? When do the Gypsies steal her off?" Tony asked.

The old man sat quietly, rubbed his face and tears started.

"Maybe some other time, it still hurts, sixty years and it still hurts," Tom replied.

Tony's usual snarky smile went blank.

"Sure, pal, maybe some other time."

The two buddies slowly made their way back to their rooms. Tom took a shower, swallowed his before-bed pills, read his Bible for a few minutes, slipped in bed and turned out the light.

He dozed right off in a fitful, uneasy sleep.

Troubling memories returned in troubling dreams.

There they stood in Claire's violet bedroom with her mom and the maid—he had never been in her bedroom, although he had been in the Dearborns' home dozens of times—helping her pack for Cottey.

It was a teen-age girl's bedroom.

He looked around, Claire had up a dozen photos of him or the two of them. The one her mom had taken right out in the den on prom night sat on her nightstand next to the phone they had talked on for hours.

His girl had an immense closet, a big walk-in thing, filled with racks of clothes, most on hangers from A La Mode, and shelves of shoe boxes from Kinnard's.

Imagine, Tom thought, a closet so big you could walk into it? No surprise, it smelled of cinnamon. And she had her own bathroom, no trips down the hall.

The Bentley's huge Victorian gem had little bitty closets only as wide their doors, plus one toilet downstairs and a second upstairs.

Dozens of dresses and multiple pairs of shoes, along with hose and girly underwear, went in four big freight boxes for shipment to Nevada, all carefully labeled Railway Express Agency, to be hauled over to the station.

The little pillow she slept on every night went in the last box closed.

Then Claire came over to help Tom and his mom pack.

It was a teen-age boy's bedroom.

They stuffed two suitcases and a duffel.

Done.

Labor Day came and went. Tom offered to take her to Springfield for dinner at a nice place the night before she left. But Claire thought about it, as always, and candlelight and silver weren't her plan.

"Let's just go to The Malt Shop for old times' sake, back in our booth."

Name it, girl, whatever you want.

She got silly again and made Tom drink her usual strawberry shake with his burger and she had his usual cherry Coke. Some of the old gang happened by to wish them well.

Claire quietly munched her fries, then stopped and looked at Tom as her blue eyes twinkled. With a mischievous grin, she asked, "Do you have a nickel?"

"I think so," Tom replied, digging in his pocket. "How about a dime?"

"That'll work," she replied, and took the coin. She got up and walked up front, stopping at the jukebox. Her fingers went down the list of records, she dropped in the coin and the big Wurlitzer started its soft clunks as it put another record on the turntable.

Vaughn Monroe leaned into *There! I've Said It Again.*

Claire smugly strolled back to their booth, staring at Tom with her half smile.

Tom looked blank.

"How? I didn't know they still had that record! It's been four years, it should be long gone," Tom said, surprised.

"I have ways, I thought I'd save it for a special moment—like now," she cooed, reaching out and taking his hand. "Just a little something to help you remember our good times, my darling. You listen to *Your Hit Parade*, just think of it as this week's 'Lucky Strike Extra.'"

The Malt Shop's dance floor may have been bigger than a phone booth, but not much. For the first and only time, Tom and Claire were on it. It wasn't as much a dance as holding each other, cheek to cheek, and swaying as they sang their duet again:

"I try to drum up,
A phrase that will sum up,
All that I feel for you.
But what good are phrases?
The thought that amazes,
Is you love me,
And it's heavenly."

A couple of booths erupted in cheers as Tom moved his face up and under the ever-present wisp of yellow hair and intentionally, this time, kissed her earlobe.

The Wurlitzer gave three plays for a dime and Claire had punched in a couple other slow songs. Tom, awkwardly, danced on. Other couples put down their burgers and joined their moment.

As usual, Tom drove Claire's Studebaker when they were together and they cruised around town talking for a while in the dark. Then there was some serious cuddling in the front seat after he parked at the Bentley mailbox.

"I guess I better let you get home," he said finally, opening the driver's door.

Claire slid under the steering wheel and started the engine. "Tomorrow's the day, it will be hard but we can do this!" she said, looking up at Tom.

"I know, I know. Good night, darling," he replied as he kissed her forehead. She smiled and drove off.

Mr. Dearborn called the next afternoon, insisting he come by and pick up Tom to go see Claire off at the station. It seemed odd, he could have driven himself, but Tom went along with it. Claire and her mom met the men at the

132

station parking lot, standing beside her Studebaker. Tom hugged her and she gave him an affectionate squeeze back.

"Here," she said, handing him the keys. "Daddy says I can't take the car so you can have it for now."

Tom looked blankly at her and her smiling parents.

"Go ahead, son," Mr. Dearborn said. "You can't take the train to Mizzou so you'll be doing a lot of driving. I know you'll take good care of it."

He knew they meant well but Tom took it as a slight: You can't have our daughter so we'll give you her car.

He mumbled, "Thanks, I'll be careful."

They walked out on the brick platform just as the big Missouri Pacific locomotive rumbled in, pulling a line of blue-and-cream cars that stopped with a slow groan. The conductor busily helped passengers off and on as Tom and Claire shared a good-bye kiss. Claire got on and that was that. The girl he saw daily disappeared as the engine honked, then pulled out in a cloud of diesel smoke.

Gone, for a whole month.

Tom's parents weren't excited about him driving "someone else's car," as his mother put it coldly, but it was a deal. It beat having dad make the round-trip, plus Tom could come home on weekends.

Two days later he loaded up the Studebaker with his stuff and headed north to Columbia—alone. It felt odd, driving Claire's car without Claire. He caught a whiff of cinnamon sometimes over the lingering new-car smell.

He checked into his dorm and immediately sat down, ripped out some notebook paper and jotted off a

133

quick letter, said he missed her, stamped it and dropped it in the big box marked MAIL in the lobby.

The next day, on his way back from the campus bookstore, he went by the lobby's mailbox wall and looked to find his. He peeked in the little window, he had mail! He did the combination, opened the door and to his surprise he found the usual, perfectly written "Tom Bentley" above the address.

It had a Randall postmark, not Nevada.

He split the envelope open with his pocket knife and caught the usual whiff of cinnamon as he unfolded a page written in the familiar, elegant cursive:

Oh, Tom, my dearest love,

I'm writing this as the men take my college things out and I hope it finds you as soon as you arrive in Columbia. I dread the weeks ahead without you here to hold me. You mean more to me than you will ever know, and have for longer than you know.

I already miss you, even though we will see each other in less than an hour at the station, isn't that silly? I hope you enjoy my parents' little gift!

Please write often and let's meet back here in Randall in a month. You are in my prayers every morning and my thoughts every minute.

We can do this!

Your dearest friend and devoted lover,

Claire

His eyes watered.

College turned into a blur, buying books, meeting a roommate from St. Joe, the cafeteria, figuring out the location of everything on the sprawling campus. He got fitted for his ROTC uniform, Mizzou made "rotsy" mandatory for freshmen and he decided to go Army rather than Navy, although that brand-new Air Force ROTC program dangled an attractive third option.

Bentley men always went Army.

Classes began, the season's first home game at Memorial Stadium proved noisy fun, with everyone dressed in black and gold as the Tigers marched to victory over Oklahoma A&M. He rushed but decided to stay independent.

He made it a point to learn the Mizzou fight song: *Every True Son*.

Quicker than either of them expected, the time came for the first weekend back in Randall. So the semester went—two or three letters a week and monthly trips home. Christmas break came and they were together again— hangin' out every day—for a couple weeks.

The routine repeated that spring.

Claire made it home from Cottey after spring finals a day before him. It was a sticky, late-spring afternoon when he drove the Studebaker onto the Dearborns' circle drive and parked at the front door.

He had hugs at the front door from Claire and her mom.

They sat in the air-conditioned den and laughed about college life, stories and details left out of the dozens of letters that had wound back and forth between Nevada and Columbia.

Best of all, they just sat and looked at each other: together again!

Summer break, life returned to normal. They grabbed some sandwiches for a bite to eat and, as the sun set, they wound their way, hand in hand, back to their gazebo.

They sat down on its little bench again.

They were happy, they had done it! They were half-way through this parent-induced trial. And maybe with a little coaxing, the folks would let them transfer to Southwest Missouri in the fall?

It might be worth a try. They rehearsed what they would say:

We're good kids, you know that, we have obeyed you and done as you wished, now can you make an exception?

Please?

They talked well after dark.

A few nights later, back in the gazebo, they cuddled once more, listening to an owl hoot somewhere out in the woods. Tom had his arms around her, Claire had her head on his shoulder as he nuzzled her hair, highlighted by the porch light at the other end of the yard.

Cinnamon, life doesn't get better than this.

They whispered to each other:

Darling, it's worth a try, maybe this time the folks will say okay.

Maybe Springfield—our dream, our own home—can really happen.

I know sweetheart, why can't our lives be like this all the time?

You're so special, I want you with me every day.

I do too, you make me complete.

136

But what if they say no again?

Well, we've proved we can do this.

I can do it because you're the most important thing in my life.

And mine too.

Just one more school year and Cottey's history.

Then we'll both be at Mizzou, right?

Mizzou has married student housing, we can make our dream home in Columbia just as well, right?

Of course we can.

Darling, wherever, my home is in your arms.

That's the way I feel.

Whatever happens, I want you here, next to me, forever and ever.

Promise, you're mine?

Promise.

Me too.

You're so special.

And you are too.

Now, kiss me.

Chapter 9
The Telegram

Between hanging out with Claire and fulltime work at the warehouse, Tom didn't pay much attention to the news. His dad in a concerned voice over dinner one night asked, "What do you think about this war in Korea?"

War? What war?

Tom knew he couldn't find Korea on a map.

"You're in ROTC, son, do you think you'll get called up?" his father asked seriously.

Tom hadn't thought about that.

ROTC? Just another class—Introduction to Military Science—plus drill on Thursday afternoons and periodic inspections. They did weapons training, target practice with the M1s could be fun, he made sharpshooter. He proved pretty handy with the Brasso and inspections had been no problem.

Tom, after all, was an orderly guy. He followed directions well and people liked his perky, upbeat, can-do personality. He rose to the top of the detachment, unusual for a freshman.

But hey, wasn't that a good thing?

Claire came over to the Bentleys one night and voiced her views as only she could.

"Look at this mess!" she said, waving the latest issue of *Look* with a cover story on the fighting. "I've thought about this. President Truman should do something, we can't just let these Communists run over a country!"

But they were in Missouri, far away. It was all theory.

The telegram came the afternoon before the Fourth of July, a Monday. His dad had Tom, as usual, at the warehouse when he heard a phone ring, then someone yelled "Telephone, Tom, it's your mom!"

Now that's odd.

Anything special and mom would have called his dad. Tom picked the receiver off the desk and managed "Hello?"

"Tom, you better come home, you have a telegram from the Department of the Army," his mom said. Her voice sounded worried.

Wait: It sounded like her when he was a little guy, eight years earlier, when he heard her talk about his brothers enlisting.

He checked in with his dad and told him what had happened, who quickly announced "Let's go!" as he jumped up from his desk. Both headed out to the parking lot at a near run.

"What do you think's going on?" Tom asked as they got in the Nash.

"I know exactly what's going on, you're getting drafted," his father said, frowning. "The only good thing is you'll get an officer's commission out of this, maybe that'll keep you out of the trenches. You'll be a ninety-day wonder, a second lieutenant, by this fall. You better brush up on your Korean."

Tom sat stunned.

Dad and been in World War I and through the ordeal when his brothers went to war, so he knew the drill. But Tom Bentley? He was still a teenager, what did he know about war?

They parked in the driveway and Tom dashed up the sidewalk to the porch as his mother came out and handed him the yellow envelope. Tom tore it open and carefully read the message, then slumped against a pillar.

"Well?" his mother asked.

"I have to report for officer's training at Fort Leonard Wood one week from today," Tom said quietly.

His mother started crying.

"Oh no! We went through this with your brothers and I thought we had war over with," she said between sobs, wiping her eyes on her apron.

"The good news is you'll be up the road, close," his dad said with a sigh. "Leonard Wood's closer than anywhere else they could've sent you."

His parents hugged and he stood there, trying to think what to do next.

Claire.

He trotted in the house and picked up the phone in the hall, waiting for the operator.

"Number, please."

"8935"

"Thank you."

She answered on the second ring, "Hello?"

"Hi, it's me," Tom answered grimly.

"You don't sound happy, what's wrong?"

"The Army called me up."

"They what? I don't understand."

"Because I'm in the Reserve Officer Training Corps, see, I have been called up for officer training, I have to report to active duty," Tom explained. "It's this war in Korea."

Claire gasped. "No! Will I see you again?"

"The good part is I'll be at Fort Leonard Wood, just up Highway 66, I should be able to get home a few weekends."

"I'll be right over!" she answered, slamming down the phone, and in a matter of minutes the Studebaker pulled up and jayparked by the Bentley mailbox. Claire jumped out and jogged up the sidewalk in snappy white Capri pants and an aqua top. Tom met her on the porch steps and they hugged.

There wasn't much to say, their lives were about to change more than they could possibly imagine. And once again, they could do little. They sat on the big porch swing, holding hands, as they talked to Tom's parents; numb.

"I went through this thirty-three years ago," his dad finally said, "May of 1917. I still remember the dread when I got that draft board letter. They put me on a troop train and off I went to Fort Sill down in Oklahoma, then to France.

"Belleau Wood, oh my, I still have nightmares.

"At this point all we can do is take care of details. We need to call a lot of people and send some letters and telegrams; get everything ready," he added.

"Let me know if I can help," Claire said stoically as she got up, reaching out to brush Tom's cheek. She smiled weakly at him, then shuffled down the steps, her shoulders hunched over. Tom had never seen Claire walk that way; defeated.

"Keep me posted!" she called sadly as she walked through the gate. He stood and watched as she got in her car, did a U-turn, then waved as she drove off.

"Poor girl, she's not taking this well," Tom's mother said, watching Claire drive away.

"I don't think any of us are," his dad replied.

Phil came over for dinner to offer encouragement and they sat and talked into the night. Tom went to bed early and slept surprisingly well.

The Bentleys and Dearborns had a big picnic at Dearborn Park for the Fourth but it wasn't fun. The weather turned Fourth of July-hot and no one wanted to talk about the one thing everyone had on their minds.

Tom's brothers chatted with him a little but were more interested in their new wives. He envied them.

As usual the Bentleys, except for Tom, skipped the actual show as dark came on. Fireworks made his dad think of Belleau Wood again, not a good thing.

"I saw enough of 'em in France," he explained as they left. Tom and Claire held hands on a blanket next to her parents, watching the noisy pyrotechnics overhead.

Tom got up the next morning as he heard dad going out the back door for work. He went downstairs to get something to eat and as he passed the phone it rang.

Tom answered.

"Calling for Tom Bentley," a woman said in a firm voice.

"This is he," Tom replied, wondering if it were the Army.

"This is the office of Campbell Dearborn. Mr. Dearborn would like to have you come in for a meeting this morning, can you be here at 10:30?"

Now what?

Surprised, Tom answered "Sure."

"Please come to the Merchants & Planters Bank Building, take the elevator to the eighth floor, and identify yourself to the receptionist. Good day," and the line clicked dead.

He could not imagine.

He made some toast, told mom about the call, then went back upstairs to shower and shave and put on one of his nicer shirts and a new pair of slacks.

Tom decided to walk downtown even though mom offered her Oldsmobile. He went down the front steps, crossed Ninth and set off down the hill.

He quickly decided he'd made a mistake. It was only 10 o'clock but already hot. He turned into the bank building, then found the men's room and went in to get a couple of paper towels to wipe his sweaty face.

He went down a narrow hallway to the side of the bank lobby to the elevator. He hit the call button and was surprised to find no one in the car when the doors opened. It was one of those new automatic elevators with no attendant. He pushed the "8" button, the doors closed by themselves and up he went.

Amazing.

The doors opened to a business office lobby, a receptionist chewing gum and reading the paper sat across from the elevator behind a desk. She laid down the paper and looked up with listless indifference as he came toward her.

"Yes?"

"I'm here to see Mr. Dearborn."

"And your name?"

"Tom Bentley."

144

"Just a minute," she said, smacking her gum, as she called Mr. Dearborn's secretary. "There's a Tom Bentley here to see Campbell."

The receptionist's bored look suddenly turned to rigid attention, she bugged her eyes out and glanced up at Tom nervously.

"Yes, yes, I'll send him in right now!" She hung up the phone, stood up and motioned down a hallway. "Please go right on in, Mr. Bentley!" the receptionist added brightly.

Tom couldn't recall ever being called "mister" before.

He thanked her and noted she watched him as he walked toward a door marked PRIVATE. He started to knock but decided to just turn the knob and walk in.

Mr. Dearborn's secretary jumped up as he came in and offered her hand. They shook and she motioned toward the office of the boss.

"Please go right in, Mr. Bentley!"

Tom stood at the open office door and nervously peeked inside. Randall's wealthiest man worked from a big room with mahogany paneling, photos and certificates hung on the walls. He couldn't help but notice a photo of Claire's dad shaking hands with President Roosevelt.

An oscillating fan on top of a corner filing cabinet slowly waved back and forth to take the edge off the already hot day. Mr. Dearborn sat behind an enormous desk covered in papers held down by paperweights to keep the fan from scattering them. He was in shirt sleeves with his suit coat hung over the back of a big leather chair.

He talked on the phone as he waved a "come here" to Tom.

"We'll take ten percent, yes, I think it'll work. I'd like a bigger share but that would exceed my authorization and I'd have to go to the board, that would slow you down. I'll have the money wired to you this afternoon," he continued.

"Listen, I've had an emergency come up; personal stuff. Let me call you back later. Yes, yes, good-bye," and hung up.

Tom had been staring out the open windows at a splendid view of the little town spread out below and the rolling, green Ozarks off in the distance. Up here, he looked down at the Limestone County Courthouse weather vane for the first time.

He found the view beautiful and forgot for a moment about why he might be there.

"Tom! Thanks for coming, have a seat," Mr. Dearborn said as he stood up and motioned to a couple of overstuffed chairs in front of his big desk. He walked around his desk, then across to the office door and quietly closed it.

Tom didn't know what to do, was he in trouble? No, he and Claire hadn't done anything untoward out there in the gazebo. Well, no, they hadn't, no, but this was her father.

"Please have a seat, young man," Campbell said in his resonant baritone. Tom sat down with his back straight in one of the big chairs as Claire's father sat down in an identical seat across from him.

146

"Thank you," Tom managed, in awe of the impressive surroundings. He always thought his dad had a nice office at the warehouse but this topped it.

Mr. Dearborn sat quietly for a moment, looking down at the carpet. He wiped his forehead with his shirt sleeve, bit his lip and stuck his thumbs under his suspenders.

"I am the only man in the world who loves Claire more than you," Mr. Dearborn slowly began.

Uh oh, here it comes.

"I went home Monday night and as I walked in the door Jewel met me with this scared look on her face. I asked what was wrong?

"'The Army has called up Tom,' she told me. 'You better go see your daughter, she needs her father very badly.'"

Oh, so this was about the Army. Tom relaxed a little.

"I went down the hall and knocked on her door and she asked me to come in between sniffs. There she was, sprawled across her bed crying her eyes out. She had thrown a pile of used tissues on the floor. My little sweetheart grabbed another one out of the box and blew her nose as I walked in, her eyes all red and puffy.

"'Your mom told me the news,' I told her.

"'Daddy, you have to *do* something! You know a lot of people, you can change this!'" she cried. "I don't want to lose Tom!"

"I sat down on the edge of the bed, she sat up, I put my arm around her and I cuddled her as she started boo-hooing again. I told her I know a lot of people, true, but I don't know anyone who could help Tom. When the Army calls, you go.

"That didn't help, she started bawling again.

"I thought about it all evening and all day yesterday. We went to bed last night after we got back from the fireworks, and I was lying there in the dark, staring at the ceiling, listening to Jewel snore, thinking.

"Daddies don't like to see their little girls cry, what could I do?"

The scene struck Tom dumb.

Stoic, always-in-control Claire, crying her eyes out over *him*? No, that could not be.

"I finally came up with a name: Frank Pace. He's President Truman's secretary of the army now," Mr. Dearborn continued. "He's from Arkansas. I know him, we've done a little business together, fine fellow."

"And?" Tom asked weakly.

"And, if you want, I could make a phone call to the Pentagon. Things could change for you very quickly. It's possible you would suddenly get a deferment, or you might be stationed here in the States, or maybe you would go to Europe. That Berlin airlift mess seems to be settled. Maybe you'd wind up aide-de-camp to some general; cushy job."

A fix.

Such a thing had never crossed Tom's mind.

Stuff like this only happens in movies or in radio dramas, then the bum-bum-bum-bum music plays. One man doesn't just call another and something this big mysteriously changes, even when one of the men is Campbell Dearborn.

This might be illegal, is Mr. Dearborn some kind of crook?

No, it could not be.

"I know my girl—your girl—would be very happy. But it's your choice, I'll do what you want," Mr. Dearborn added.

Tom sat, stunned, feeling the fan blow back and forth across the back of his neck. A phone rang down the hall, a regulator clock ticked on the wall.

"Mr. Dearborn, gee, I don't know what to say. I hadn't even thought of such a thing," Tom said quietly.

"Nor had I, I would not have thought about this if she hadn't pushed me."

Claire strikes again.

Tom clenched his fists and bent over, nervously looking at his feet. He felt his face go red.

"I... I... I with all my heart want to make Claire a part of my future," Tom said slowly, wiping the beading sweat off his face. "God blessed me when she came into my life."

"I figured that out, son, that night you came over to help with the Christmas tree. You bounced around like you just hit the daily double at Hot Springs. She was your prize. And I had never heard our quiet Claire laugh like that.

"She glows around you, you bring out the best in her.

"And hey, I'm a guy, I understand these things. I remember how I felt when Jewel and me were dating, I thought she could walk on water. She was just the most wonderful thing ever—and I guess I still feel that way after thirty-one years.

149

"So I know how a guy feels when he's smitten by a girl. Smitten you were, and are. You're as crazy about my daughter as she is about you."

He paused.

"And when the time comes to pop the question, Tom, you have my permission, just let me know first," Mr. Dearborn added.

Oh, wow! First we're calling the Pentagon, now we're proposing marriage. And how many boys get pre-approved?

Tom sighed loudly, leaned back and then looked up at the ceiling. The clock ticked on.

"It's very tempting, one phone call and this could be over and done, at least officially. But my brothers, my father, my grandfather and my great-grandfather all served honorably in the Army, wherever they went. Why should I be the exception?" Tom asked.

"As much as I'd like to say yes, I have to say no, don't call. Maybe it's honor, maybe it's duty, I don't know. But if I go, then I go."

Mr. Dearborn tilted his head and stared at his daughter's beau intently.

"You really are a keeper, son, I'm impressed," he replied.

"You know her brothers' service records, and I did my part in the Great War. I survived combat but nearly died of the Spanish flu on the way home. Jewel waited here for me. I knew that, and I think that's the only thing that kept me alive.

"I know Claire can bring you home the same way her mother brought me home. Stay focused on her.

"But what do we, you and me, tell my daughter?" Mr. Dearborn asked.

"Tell her you did all you could do," Tom said with a shrug.

"You're right, I did. And my wife and I will be praying for you every day. Let's hope this whole mess gets over with soon and you can come home, then the two of you can settle down," the father answered. "You're sort of family already and you can make it official."

Mr. Dearborn stood up and offered his hand. The two shook and he led his visitor out with his hand on Tom's back.

"I don't know how to thank you," Tom said as he walked slowly to the door.

"I do," Mr. Dearborn said firmly.

He stopped as Tom turned back to him.

"Always take good care of my little girl," he said firmly. "She is more special to me than you can possibly know. She's a handful sometimes, but God blessed us, too, and showed us great favor when she came into our lives. I pray she does become a part of your life, for keeps.

"Always do your part to make her happy."

Tom nodded and walked out. The secretary, then the receptionist both quickly stood and smiled as he walked by. Tom smiled back.

He stopped by The Malt Shop for a cold cherry Coke-to-go to ease the hot uphill walk home. He decided it best not to say anything about Mr. Dearborn's offer. Pretty soon the big yellow-and-green house came in view up the hill as we walked in the shade of the big oak trees along the street. He crossed Poplar, went through the gate and up the

151

sidewalk and the steps. His mother came out the front door as he came on the porch.

"What was that all about?" she asked.

"Mr. Dearborn is a really nice guy, he just wanted to give me some pointers on the Army," he replied.

"That's nice of him, come on in and let's get busy," she replied.

The rest of the week flew by. On the day, Tom and his dad got in the Nash, drove up Highway 66 to Waynesville, then turned south into the Army post. The two hugged, shook hands and Tom's Army career began.

The next three months proved the hardest time of his life.

Tom fell out before dawn for exercises, drill, classes, inspections, gunnery practice—all in a hot Missouri summer. He lost weight even as he gorged at mess.

But an orderly person like Tom fit into Army routine, he scored well.

The letters to and from Claire began again, and he managed a few leaves with short but enjoyable visits. Just to get inside the Dearborns' air-conditioned home with Claire was a treat after days in the hot sun. All he did was lie on the floor and sleep, his head at her feet, as she sat on the sofa reading.

He made it.

It all wrapped up with a commissioning ceremony on an October Friday. His parents drove up and his mom beamed as she pinned lieutenant's bars on his uniform.

Thomas J. Bentley had been made a second lieutenant in the United States Army, an officer and a gentleman.

But a big question hung in his mind as the ceremony ended: Classmates went to combat units—field artillery, infantry, armor. Lt. Bentley went to the Quartermaster Corps. Had Mr. Dearborn made a call anyway? He had no way to know, and he did not dare ask.

Or then again, maybe the Army picked up on his Bentley Hardware experience.

He had a few days' leave before he left for duty and they rushed down U.S. 66 to meet Claire's train. She came back from Nevada to see him one last time before he shipped out.

Close, but they made it.

The Bentleys walked onto the platform as her train pulled in. And there she was, dressed to the nines as always, in a navy blue and white suit with a matching white hat as she stepped down out of the vestibule. The conductor held her hand and its little white glove as she gracefully went down the stairs and into the crowd.

"Stunningly beautiful as ever," Tom thought to himself as he pushed forward to meet her.

Tom, still in uniform with the brand-new bars in place, finally stepped in front of her. Claire stopped, put down her suitcase, and the blue eyes got big. She stared at his uniform and uttered a loud and emphatic "Nice!"

Sometimes he could impress her.

Tom managed to pull her aside and kiss her, and as only Claire could, she threw her arms around his neck and kissed him back passionately. Everyone drove over to the

Dearborns to eat and the talk went on a long time until the Bentleys finally decided to head home. Tom nodded off in the floor again and they had to poke him when they finally left.

"Let's go get a photo of the two of us tomorrow," Claire suggested as they walked out on the porch.

"Sure," Tom said with a yawn. "Pick me up in the morning." He went to sleep in the back seat before they got home.

But he was up and ready Saturday morning. Claire came by in her blue and white suit but without the hat and got him, making sure his uniform was just so, and they drove downtown to the studio. They were back where the Class of 1949's Glamour Couple had caused such a stir less than two years before.

The rest of the weekend turned into a whirlwind of friends and family before church Sunday morning at First Presbyterian. Tom sat numb beside Claire and her parents through the service, too much to think about.

Maybe the next time he was in a church he would be in a flag-covered box.

Maybe he and Claire needed to do something.

Now.

They drove to the Dearborns after church for fried chicken and iced tea. They finished dessert and the two of them slowly walked down the hall, past the grand piano, holding hands, onto the wide, covered porch and sat down in two big wicker chairs.

Their gazebo stood out there at the edge of the yard. A golden autumn afternoon spread out in front of them with just the slightest breeze, just a whiff of a chill, to rustle the red, orange, yellow and brown palette before them.

Change had started.

Another hour and they would drive to the station for Claire's train. They sat in silence for a few minutes, both in dread that this golden autumn day would end too soon.

"That was delicious, good lunch," Tom finally said, trying to get the conversation started. Claire continued to stare at the trees. He squeezed her hand lightly and she squeezed back.

She turned to him with her usual half smile but it slowly turned to a grimace, hidden partly behind the ever-present wisp of yellow hair.

"This is hard," she said.

"I know," he replied. "We need to get married before I leave."

What did he just say?

It were as if there had been some deafening explosion, a bomb had gone off, some huge boom or bang, like one of the howitzers he fired in training.

But now they sat in an equally quiet silence.

What had he done? It had not come out right.

The silence hung on until Claire sighed loudly as she let go of his hand, crossed her arms and looked down at her skirt, thinking.

She did not act surprised.

"If you ask me, you know I will say yes," she said deliberately, slowly measuring each word. "I guess we could drive down to Miami, Oklahoma, and see a justice of the peace tonight. But you know it's not what we want."

The silence got louder.

Claire sniffed and started again.

"Next spring I'll graduate from Cottey, and we know this mess in Korea will be over with," she continued slowly. "They say this big battle they just had, where is it? Incheon? Is a success and the Communists are on the run. General MacArthur told the newspapers it'll be over by Christmas, and I guess he knows what he's talking about.

"By next June you'll be back, and I know you'll be some kind of war hero or something, like my brothers," she added, looking at him and forcing a smile.

"We can have a big church wedding with all of our friends and family. The organ will play, the choir will sing, it will be wonderful! You can walk me down the aisle in that handsome uniform of yours after the pastor makes us husband and wife. My bridesmaids will take my train off and we'll dance together at a big reception out at the club. Everyone will be there!

"Oh, that uniform, you look wonderful in it!" she continued, reaching out to feel the lieutenant's bars and running her fingers lightly down his sleeves. She gazed at him with a broad smile.

"I'll start classes at Mizzou next fall. We can start our own home, we'll be together all the time, just like we want."

So did she say yes, or no?

Were they engaged, or not?

It was just so typical of her, Tom could never quite be sure what Claire thought. But he knew after five years, after holding that hand so often and looking into those blue eyes, not to ask.

How far they had come since that afternoon in chemistry class, yet sometimes he still felt he didn't really know her.

Was she in love with him? No doubt, yes.

Was he going to be a part of her life? Probably, but when?

Somehow, it always worked out, Claire would pull off one of her big surprises.

Maybe she would again.

He leaned over, brushed the wisp of hair back and nuzzled her cheek. He caught a whiff of the pleasant cinnamon, as always, reminding him of her and all that she meant to him.

He gently kissed her cheek. His lips tasted salt, which startled him. He opened his eyes and looked at her, close up. The lovely blue eyes looked back at him through welling tears.

Tom had never seen her cry.

Stoic, ever-confident Claire, crying.

This had gone all wrong.

He didn't know what to say or do to make it right. He wanted her more than anything in the world and obviously, in her own way, Claire wanted him. But because of some madmen half-a-world away, a pair of innocent not-quite-twentysomething kids in Missouri would have to wait.

"Okay," Tom mumbled. He swallowed hard, his face burning and red.

They sat silently for maybe a half hour, staring at the autumn before them, holding hands. Claire sniffed a few times and wiped her eyes with her fingers. A couple of squirrels came out, hunting here and there for acorns, scampering across the leaf-covered yard. They seemed to give up after a while and went to wherever squirrels go.

She finally shook his arm, stood up and said, "We better go."

The maid had placed her suitcase by the front door and her dad brought the Packard around.

Tom and Claire rode in the back seat with her parents up front, making small talk. They had a short wait at the station until her train pulled in, Claire gave each parent a peck on the cheek, then turned and wrapped her arms around Tom's neck, hugged him, and gave him a passionate kiss.

The hug lingered, then she pulled away, looked at him longingly and she said a simple "Good-bye."

Claire turned to the conductor, he helped her up the step stool and stairs, and she disappeared. She reappeared at a window above them, sat down and waved at her threesome below. The conductor yelled "'Board!" The locomotive honked and the train pulled away.

Claire was gone again.

Now his eyes watered.

Her parents dropped him off at the Bentleys and got out of the car to wish him well. Campbell gave him a firm handshake and Jewel hugged him lovingly, adding "We'll be praying for you!"

Two empty days went by until his dad drove him back to Fort Leonard Wood.

Despite the happy talk by General MacArthur, things were not going well and the Army was in a hurry. Lt. Bentley would receive his advanced quartermaster training

158

from called-up reservists aboard ship on the long voyage across the Pacific.

A troop train took him and hundreds of other men west. There he was, getting off the train in Oakland, then buses to the barracks, waiting a day or two for something to happen. He was an officer and had to order around men older than him. That felt funny.

He finally boarded a ship with dread. Tom stood on the deck, looking up, as they steamed under the Golden Gate Bridge and out into the Pacific.

Tom woke up in a cold sweat. He had to get up in the night as men his age do. He looked at the clock on his nightstand: 1:33. He got back in bed. He knew what would come next in his dreams but managed to go back to sleep anyway.

Chapter 10
Reputation

Tom crossed the Pacific as the chipper, it's-almost-over confidence of MacArthur and other generals evaporated.

China entered the war, the Soviets sent "advisers" and fighter jets.

The game changed.

Korea endures brutally cold winters and the young lieutenant had the misfortune of arriving at Incheon as the first bad storm of the season hit, coming down the gangplank in driving sleet. The cold made constant relocations all the more difficult as the Army and its allies shifted back and forth to avoid the enemy.

UN troops fought into Seoul—what was left of it—then retreated out. Back in, then back out.

How could the Quartermaster Corps do its job in this chaos? Supply lines decayed into a mess, needed supplies ended up missing, misplaced or stolen.

The stressful officer's school back in Missouri last summer began to seem like a rather pleasant holiday, compared to what he now faced.

But Lt. Bentley quickly realized he didn't have the worst of it.

Shell-shocked combat soldiers with hollow eyes told horror stories of human waves the Chinese threw across the border. UN machine guns and artillery mowed down a row, then another wave of pitiful men, most didn't even have weapons, would just step over the bodies and keep coming.

Return fire and air support weren't enough. UN troops that had roared toward the far border of North Korea as 1950 ended now were thrown headlong backwards, to the south.

How many men did China have? Would they ever stop coming?

But dependable Tom did the best he could. Somehow, some way, he managed to get the job done. Successful armies have lots of stuff—ammunition, food, clothing, supplies—and it's the quartermaster's duty to get it there.

Lt. Bentley developed a knack for improvisation that sometimes bent Army rules. He never broke, but he bent. He earned a reputation: If you need it, Bentley gets it. He gained a couple of experienced sergeants who stayed in after World War II, helping him immensely.

Combat officers loved him and so did his men. Guys in his platoon told with pride who they reported to.

You'd see their lieutenant out there in the snow and mud unloading trucks right along with the lowly black privates. Most shavetails didn't do that sort of thing. He pushed himself, he set an example his men followed. Push, push, push—they got it done because their officer did his part.

A promotion to first lieutenant came in record time with new, company-level duties. Someone up the chain of command had noticed.

Winter turned to spring, which helped, plus thousands more American, British, Canadian, Turkish and Australian re-enforcements marched onto the peninsula below the UN flag.

More troops?

More stuff.

There came the afternoon they unloaded a big convoy, finally getting matériel squared away. The trucks drove off and the young lieutenant sat down on the ground with his men for a break.

"Sir, you been goin' at it pretty hard, you need some R&R," a chipper buck sergeant, new to the unit, volunteered between swigs from a dirty canteen. "You know, there's a village back there a mile or so, we can set you up with an 'American princess' who could, uh, help relieve your stress."

It shook Tom.

Him?

A prostitute?

Tom bit his tongue and thought for a moment.

"Sergeant, back in Missouri I have the most beautiful young woman you ever would want to see waiting for me. I'll wait for her."

The noncom nodded, then quietly got up and shuffled off between the crates.

That offer, that disgusting offer, rolled around in Tom's head. No doubt the man meant well and wanted to help, in his own way. And, the sergeant probably thought he could score points with his lieutenant.

Tom avoided the seamy parts of Korea, just as he did in Missouri. He had principles. But sometimes, he learned, a principled QM takes on unofficial duties.

One afternoon following mess he spotted a chaplain and a sergeant in kitchen whites struggling to carry a big cookpot between the tents. Now, that's something you don't see every day.

He would have ordered them to halt, except the chaplain wore captain's bars. Lieutenants don't order around captains, even if they are chaplains.

"What's happening, gentlemen?" he asked as he walked up.

"Budae jjigae," the cook replied.

"Do what?" Tom asked.

"Our table scraps, leftovers from lunch," added the chaplain. "The Koreans use 'em to make budae jjigae. I think it translates as 'army stew.'"

"And?"

"There are some Canadian missionaries near here, run a little church and orphanage, lots of hungry kids to feed—and more every day. We set the pot out, the MPs let 'em come in and empty it," the sergeant explained. "I'll pick up the pot tonight."

"So they're eating our scraps, our trash?"

"Yes sir," the sergeant replied, wiping his hands on his apron.

It stunned him, just how miserable are these poor people?

"Here, let me help you," Tom said, grabbing a side of the heavy pot.

Helping deliver table scraps became part of Lt. Bentley's off-the-books routine.

Fresh out of a rare shower, Tom sat on his bunk in his skivvies, his dog tags dangling from his neck, to write Claire once again. As usual, he opened the lid of his trunk, looking at their prom night photo as he wrote.

164

He wrote his usual I'm-working-hard-but-thoughts-of-you-keep-me-going letter and went to bed.

He heard no artillery that night.

Claire mailed him lots of other photos: her commencement at Cottey, standing between her parents in cap and gown; and that fall a rare color photo came of her dressed in black and gold, standing between The Columns with Jesse Hall in the background on the Mizzou campus with "*Every Daughter!*" written in the corner. And just after New Year's 1952, a letter arrived with a photo of the Dearborns' latest Christmas tree and "Remember?" written under it.

Most still smelled of cinnamon even after a slow-boat trip across the Pacific. Tom liked to sniff the pages; so pleasant.

The shell exploded with a deafening blast outside his tent one bitterly cold night in early 1952. Shrapnel ripped through the canvas.

The concussion threw Tom from his bunk as he jerked awake in blinding pain from a chunk of hot metal that tore into his thigh. Blood gushed. He picked himself up and stumbled around in the dark to his trunk at the foot of his bed, flipping open the lid. He felt around for his dress uniform tie to make a tourniquet, all while holding the blown-open leg.

Someone turned on a light in the partially collapsed tent and there below, in the middle of the screams and chaos, he saw their prom photo. He groped frantically for the tie, splattering blood across Claire's face.

He found the tie and managed to wrap it around his leg and stanch the flow. Medics rushed to help. One gave him morphine and helped him down onto a stretcher. Somewhere, repeat fire started and the enemy shelling stopped.

Tom's behind-the-front unit supposedly had set up out of artillery range, several miles behind the lines, he couldn't remember where exactly. But such is war, nothing could be certain.

They loaded Tom and other wounded men in the back of a deuce-and-a-half that bounced off down a snowy road in the dark to a clearing.

Not everyone made it.

Medics put his stretcher on the ground inside a tent and covered him with a blanket. At first light he heard an odd thump-thump-thump-thump and looked out a tent flap to see one of those new helicopter things. It landed with a blast of air, then medics picked him and other wounded men up and placed them aboard. Up they went.

Tom had never been off the ground, but the novelty of a helicopter ride did nothing to ease the throbbing leg.

They flew a half-hour to a field hospital, then medics unloaded him and took him into a big tent with the standard red cross on top. Soldiers joked the cross provided an easy bullseye for the enemy.

They put him out and a surgeon picked chunks of metal out of his thigh, then sewed a row of stitches. Nurses patched him up before the anesthetic wore off.

The next day an Army convoy moved him to the coast, then Navy medics loaded him on a ship headed for a

Tokyo Army hospital. He would stay there several weeks to allow the leg to heal.

Tokyo stunned him. The big war had been over more than six years but much of the city remained rubble, with dead weeds and tree sprouts poking up through dusty remains. It left Tom in awe as a bus taking him to the hospital from the dock wound through empty streets.

"My gosh, what do Hiroshima and Nagasaki look like?" he mumbled to himself. If nothing else, the Army Air Force had been thorough.

No wonder Japan declared itself a "peace state" after the war.

But Tokyo beat Korea, at least people weren't shooting at each other. The wound slowly healed but physical therapy proved tricky. An infection set in, penicillin shots began, and more days of bedrest. The medical staff cautioned he would be able to walk but anything strenuous was history.

A limp would be permanent.

It came as tough news for a former track team member and avid Scout hiker.

A bird colonel came by one afternoon to pin a Purple Heart on Lt. Bentley as he sat up in bed. How crazy is that, a supposedly behind-the-lines QM officer wounded in action?

Tom gained a little every day. A physical therapist gave him a crutch and he learned to navigate around the hospital at a slow, clunky pace.

At least he still had two legs, not everyone around him did.

What would it be like to clump around on three legs all the time, he wondered? The crutch made his armpit ache.

He hobbled to a Protestant chapel service one windy Sunday morning, a clear day as a stiff breeze whipped in off Tokyo Bay, cool and damp. Snowcapped Mount Fuji loomed off to the southwest against a clear blue sky, providing a scenic counterpoint to the rebuilding city's ugliness.

Lent had begun, Easter would be here soon and the chaplain gave his ragtag, torn-up congregation of halt and lame encouragement that, through Jesus, God offers hope for all of us.

Tom needed to hear that. He had spent more than a year stretched to his limit—and then to nearly have his leg blown off.

But it could have been different, he reminded himself. If those chunks of metal had flown at him a few inches differently than they did, or if the shell landed over a few more yards, then it would have been over.

Tom wanted to go home, but not that way. He wanted to see Claire standing beside him, not crying behind him.

"Will this war ever end? Lord, help me!" he mumbled in prayer during the benediction as the service ended. He took time to stop and thank the chaplain for his encouragement as the others clumped, limped and rolled out.

The chaplain invited Tom to have a seat and share his story.

"I've done my part, now I want to go home," he said, ending with a sigh.

"Don't we all," came the reply.

"Chaplain, I know that, but I have a beautiful young lady back in Missouri and I miss her more than words can tell, and I miss my parents too."

"If you're in here you can get leave when your wounds heal enough," the chaplain suggested. "If you can get the money you could probably go home, at least you'd get to see her for a few days."

Oh?

"And how am I going to do that?" Tom asked, puzzled.

"They started a commercial airline flight out of Tokyo back to the States, Northwest Orient flies out of Haneda Airport over on the bay. It's pricey but it certainly would beat wandering around Tokyo with nothing to do," the chaplain suggested. "Also, the Air Force has VIP flights out but I don't think an Army lieutenant has much chance of getting on, so check out the commercial option.

"Talk to the USO, they can help you; blessings!"

They stood up, shook hands and Tom gimped down the hospital corridor as fast as his crutch could thump to the USO office.

Was it true? Could he fly home?

Yes it is.

We can make arrangements for you, the flight lands in Minneapolis. Maybe you could meet your girl and family there? The flight's always packed, hard to get a seat, but we'll try.

Swell, please do!

Chapter 11
Just Like V-J Day

Approval came for a two-week leave in April, either side of Easter. Perfect! He wired his dad asking for airfare, suggesting they meet in Minneapolis over the holiday. Getting down to Randall from Minnesota might be too much to ask.

He received a telegram the next day: DONE STOP RESERVATION MADE SEE YOU MINNEAPOLIS BERGEN HOTEL APRIL 8 STOP DAD.

What about Claire?

She gushed her side of the happy story as they cuddled once again on a big leather sofa in the hotel lobby:

April Fool's Day, cold, gray and snowy in Columbia; dreary. She was depressed as she trudged across the Mizzou campus, not only from lingering worry about Tom's wound but because of an unexpected midterm B- in her English lit class on Chaucer.

"Claire Dearborn did not go to college to earn B's!" she told Tom emphatically, poking his chest with her finger and scowling. She had to do better, this was not good enough.

She ambled up the steps to her dorm, stomped the snow off her boots and went in the entryway to take off her coat and muffler. She saw a handwritten "Claire See Me" note on the big clip by the door to the house mother's office.

Now what?

She poked her head in the door as she pulled off her hat and gloves and found the house mom at her desk.

171

"You wanted me?" Claire asked, peeking around her wisp of hair.

"Yes, you have a telegram," the house mother replied, handing over the yellow envelope.

Oh, no.

Now what? Telegrams mean bad news, she thought. Had Tom been hurt again? Were her mom or dad sick?

"Do you mind if I sit down before I open this?" she asked.

"Certainly, have a seat."

She sat down in a straight-back chair by the door, her hands shaking so hard as she ripped open the envelope she tore the telegram. She nervously unfolded the yellow sheet:

ON LEAVE MEET ME 8 APRIL BERGEN HOTEL MINNEAPOLIS STOP LOVE TOM.

She shrieked and jumped straight up as she waved the telegram.

"Yes! Hallelujah!"

"What's up?" the surprised house mother asked.

"My boyfriend's coming home on leave from Korea!

The house mom came around from her desk and they hugged. Happy news!

"That's wonderful, I know you're excited!"

"You don't know! You don't know!"

Claire ran upstairs to her room, dropped her books on her bed and ran back down to the dorm phone booth in the lobby. She shut the door, picked up the receiver, dropped a dime in the slot, dialed zero, and waited.

"Operator."

"Yes, I'd like to make a collect call to Randall, Missouri, my name is Claire" and gave the operator her folks' number.

There were the usual clunks and thunks as the operator finished the connection and the phone in the Dearborn kitchen rang.

"Hello?" the maid answered

"I have a collect call from a Claire, will you accept the charges?"

"Yes!

"Claire, honey! Have you heard the news?"

"Yes, that's why I'm calling! Oh my, what do we do?"

"Just a minute, let me get your mom."

Claire's mom quickly came on the extension and they exchanged "Can you believe it?" several times.

The Bentleys had called Jewel and they firmed up travel details. His parents and Mrs. Dearborn would fly with her to meet Tom. Campbell had committed earlier to an extended East Coast investor tour.

Mr. Bentley booked Claire on a flight from Columbia to St. Louis, she would meet the parents there at Lambert Field. They would fly on together to Minneapolis.

Claire cried.

Finally! This was just too good to be true! Her Tom, coming home to her, however briefly.

But flying? Wait a minute, could she get on an airplane?

"I'll have to think about that," she told her mom nervously.

"But if I have to walk I'll be there!" she added firmly.

Claire gave her mom love, said "'bye," then headed upstairs to her room. She had plenty to do and few days to do it.

Forget Chaucer, for now.

She waited outside on a chilly, bright morning with a handful of other passengers at the fence behind the Columbia airport's terminal, nervously eyeing the little airliner with Ozark Air Lines in green and white painted above seven little windows. The stewardess came out, opened the gate, and off the group went across the tarmac.

Claire found airports and airplanes intimidating. Flying was not at all comfortable and too cramped, but faster than a train. And on this trip, time was of the essence.

Claire dug in the seatback pocket for "the bag" the pleasant stewardess had pointed out to her jittery passenger. The DC-3 lifted its tail wheel off the runway and banked east, with a few light bumps, toward St. Louis. Out her window, she could see the Missouri River's green ribbon rolling away in the distance and the dome of Missouri's capitol over in Jeff City on the horizon.

She never used the bag. You know, it really is kind of pretty up there.

They met easily in St. Louis, the parents in from Springfield, then everyone boarded another flight north.

The four of them crammed into a cab at the Twin Cities' Wold-Chamberlain Field and they watched the unfamiliar city roll by in silent excitement.

The taxi dropped them off, Jewel picked up the fare, and they shuffled inside to the desk after a bellhop put their bags on a cart. Mr. Bentley signed at the front desk and got the room keys as a tired Claire surveyed the hustle and bustle of a big-city hotel lobby in late afternoon, right when guests arrive.

What a beautiful place, she thought, looking around. Lots of marble with dark wood paneling lit by big brass chandeliers hung from a soaring ceiling. A wide staircase past the elevators led up to a mezzanine of meeting rooms.

And what an odd assortment of people milling around: A priest holding some woman's purse, a middle-aged woman carrying a clipboard and pen, some swarthy businessman wearing a heavy coat and hat as he smoked, hustling bell hops in their dapper uniforms pushing luggage carts, a pale little girl in a wheelchair, some crippled soldier hobbling around on a crutch.

Wait!

Yes! He's *here*!

"TOM!" she cried.

Claire shrieked, dropped her coat and purse, and ran to him, calling his name again, as a yellow cloud streamed behind her head.

Tom had just stepped in the door, waiting for a moment as his eyes adjusted from the sunshine outside, when he heard his name—and here she came at a dead run.

"Hold it! Don't knock me over!" he called as he put his free hand up.

She caught herself in time and stopped as Tom dropped his crutch and hugged her, knocking his Army cap off. They kissed passionately as a sudden wave of applause and cheers erupted in the lobby.

"Isn't that sweet?" someone said loudly. "They look just like that nurse and that sailor on V-J Day!"

The parents were close behind her and hugged Tom when Claire, finally, let go of him. His crutch got lost in the crush until his dad stumbled over it.

"Hey everyone, let's go eat!" Mrs. Dearborn called out as the happy greetings wound down, and the five of them headed to the hotel restaurant.

Everyone asked him the same question: How was your flight?

Tom shook his head.

"The only thing that takes longer than flying the Pacific is sailing the Pacific," he said with a shrug as they sat down. "We flew for an entire day and we were only to Anchorage—half-way here. Edmonton got hit by a snowstorm last night, we barely were able to land. We had to wait for hours after we refueled before the weather cleared, then they had to plow the runway and de-ice the plane.

"We were supposed to get here early this morning. As it turned out, I guess we landed right behind you this afternoon."

The four of them looked him over and Tom sensed it, how had he changed in one-and-a-half years?

And he did the same.

The adults were the same ol'-same ol', his dad had put on a little weight and lost a little more hair. Chunky Mrs. Dearborn, well, turned out to be a little more chunky.

But Claire, oh my, Claire!

Any girlishness in her had vaporized. She was a woman.

He could not take his eyes off her. Anything that lingered from that just-blossomed fourteen-year-old he first knew had vanished. Sitting in front of him was a poised, beautiful, adult—even if she did go screaming through hotels.

She looked different and, could it be?, even more beautiful.

He stared at her. Claire brushed the usual wisp of hair back from her face and rested her cheek on her palm and stared back. The blue eyes twinkled as brightly as he had ever seen.

He winked at her.

She winked back.

"Are you really here?" she asked as the waitress brought their salads, staring at him.

"No, I'm not," Tom added. "I have been caught up into the third heaven. All I see is some glorious, angelic being."

Everyone laughed.

"Silly boy!" Claire replied with a go-away wave.

The fivesome talked long after the pie and coffee had disappeared. His dad signed for the check and they adjourned to some big sofas in the middle of the lobby and talked on.

Tell us about the night you were wounded. What has the war been like? Will it end soon? What's Korea like? What about the people? How is your leg? What about Tokyo?

177

A big grandfather clock across from the front desk chimed ten o'clock and the adults finally decided to go up to their rooms.

"You kids come along soon, I know you're both tired and we can talk tomorrow!" Mrs. Dearborn urged as she headed to the elevators.

Tom and Claire said sure, be there in a minute.

Claire turned and studied Tom as he sat, self consciously.

"You've changed," Claire said softly with her half smile.

"I've been thinking the same thing about you," he replied.

"How so?"

"You're a woman now, a very beautiful woman. You're not a girl anymore."

"Thank you."

"And how have I changed?"

The eyebrows furrowed as she looked intensely at his uniform.

"You're more mature too, you have an edge," Claire answered.

"How so?"

"What's the word, 'confidence?' I don't know if that's it, maybe 'swagger' says it better. You're still the Tom I know but you're more in charge, or something."

"I hope that's a good thing, I want to be what you want in a guy," Tom said, still enjoying her blue eyes. "Sometimes I've had to be very demanding to get the job done. I guess it shows."

"I'm not complaining. Hey, we're both tired, let's pick this up in the morning," she replied.

"Good idea, and I need to change the dressing on my leg."

Tom took his crutch and boosted himself off the sofa with an appreciated, if not helpful, lift from Claire. They slowly walked to the elevators through the nearly empty lobby and went up to their floor.

Claire shared a room with her mom and Tom and his folks had a bigger room down the hall.

"Good night, darling," he said as he held her cheek and kissed her at her door. Cinnamon.

"Thank you for coming, you really don't know what this means to me," she replied, holding him for a moment.

"Oh yes I do!," Tom said, smiling. "But don't thank me, thank my dad. I bet my ticket cost as much as I'll make this year."

Everyone slept in the next morning. After a few phone calls back and forth, they met downstairs in the restaurant for brunch. Then the mothers trotted off with happy waves to Dayton's for shopping. Tom's dad decided to "go for a walk, nice day outside."

"Wish I could go too," Tom said as he hobbled back to the lobby's big sofa and sat down next to Claire.

"No you don't, you'd rather be with me," Claire said, teasing.

"Well, if I have to!" he replied with a grin.

They sat closely—but not exactly cuddling. A constant stream of guests, visitors and bellhops walked by, many glancing down at the handsome young lieutenant and the tall blonde girl.

"This is almost like being back in the gazebo," Tom said, looking around.

"The word here is *almost*," Claire replied with a grimace. "The only audience we had out there was a couple of raccoons."

"Oh, I always suspected we had an eye-from-on-high watching us from the house," Tom replied with a chuckle.

"That's true, my parents' bedroom windows look out on the backyard," Claire answered matter of factly. "I'm sure there were glances out our way. But I can hear it all in my mind: 'Hey, that's Tom out there with her, we don't need to worry. Come to bed, Campbell!'"

They laughed.

"Well, if it's too busy here we could go upstairs," Tom said with a sly smile.

"No."

"So you don't trust me?" he asked.

"Rather, I don't trust *me*, darling," Claire answered as she laid her hands on his and grinned. "I can only imagine what that crazy girl on the bus would do with you in a hotel room! I may be a woman but she's still deep in here, you know!" she added as she tapped her chest.

They both laughed.

"Well, tell her there will be a day!" Tom said.

"I will, and I'm sure she'll make it worth your wait," Claire said with a sly smile.

"We've done this right and we shouldn't change things now," Tom said, squeezing her hand. "You are my

180

prize, my gift, and, how shall I say? I'll unwrap it when the time is right!"

Claire covered her mouth and laughed.

"Silly boy!"

His smile disappeared as Tom turned serious.

"What's wrong?" Claire asked.

"I can't believe the horrible things I've seen done to women, or the horrible things women have done to themselves. The term's 'American princess.' I've been offered one."

"And?" Claire asked, nervously turning her head.

"I didn't think twice. I told them I have a girl back home, I'll wait for her."

"Thank you."

"I know it's to survive, so I don't judge them. When you're desperate...."

"But how awful is that, selling yourself to strangers, strangers who don't even speak your language?" Tom asked. "Guns and bombs don't do all the damage in a war.

"And, I guess, after seeing such awful things, it's why I treasure you all the more."

They sat silently smiling at each other.

Then Claire coughed nervously.

"I, well, to change the subject, if you don't mind me asking, could I see your wound?"

Tom sat back on the sofa, surprised.

"Uh, I don't think you want to."

"Is it that bad?"

He sighed.

"Yes.

"The stitches, thank the Lord, are out, itched like crazy. There's a big scar from just below my hip to my knee, pretty gruesome. I'll be okay, the Army will give me some sort of disability, but I won't ever run again," he explained.

"Can you love a cripple?"

The thought horrified Claire.

"I didn't know, I'm sorry, of course I can," she replied softly. "I'm just glad to still have you!"

"Or, what's left of me," Tom replied with a weak smile.

They sat quietly, holding hands, as Tom stared absentmindedly at the hotel door. A bellhop came through with a luggage cart and a tall businessman followed him.

Claire's dad.

"Look!" Tom said, nudging Claire and pointing.

"Oh my!" Claire gasped as she jumped up and trotted toward her father, nearly as fast as when she ran to Tom. "What are you doing here?" she called out.

Tom grabbed his crutch and hobbled over.

"New York can wait, this is more important, little girl!" Mr. Dearborn said as he kissed her forehead and hugged his daughter.

"And am I so glad to see you, young man!" he said, turning to Tom and offering his hand and a slap on the back. "How's the leg?"

"Better."

"Mom's off with Mrs. Bentley shopping, is she ever going to be surprised!" Claire gushed.

His arrival made the happy reunion even better. They stopped at the desk, Claire asked for an extra key, and the three of them headed upstairs. The bellhop dropped Mr. Dearborn's luggage off and Tom picked up the tip.

"Well, this is cozy," Mr. Dearborn said, looking around as they walked in the smallish room. "I guess I'll have to have housekeeping bring a rollaway, but I don't know where they'll put it. I may have to sleep in the bathtub."

Tom noticed an odd piece of furniture as father and daughter chatted: a television, the first he had seen.

"You have a TV?" he asked.

"Yes, mom and I watched it this morning, I bet your room has one," Claire answered. "Who knows when we'll have television in Randall?"

"Hey, I was so tired last night there could've been an elephant in our room and I wouldn't have noticed," Tom replied.

He turned a knob and with a loud click the set began humming as it warmed up. Shortly, a black-and-white image of some quiz show slowly appeared on the little screen.

It enthralled him.

"Wow, I guess radio will be gone in a few years," he said to no one.

"Not necessarily," Campbell said, hanging his clothes in the closet. "Radio will change but it'll be around a while with music, news, whatever. You won't find them putting those things in cars," he said motioning at the set.

Just then the lock on the door clicked and the mothers came in with their arms full of packages. Mrs. Dearborn spotted her husband, gasped "Oh, honey!" and dropped her load on the bed as they embraced.

The six of them spent the afternoon talking and Tom shared his stories—and frustrations—about the war. Claire, her hands in her lap, hung on every word.

Thursday, everyone decided to go see a movie. Tom managed to hobble a few blocks down the street for a matinee of *The African Queen*. Loaded up with popcorn, sodas and Jujyfruits, his thoughts turned from Korea to Africa, and a different war, for a couple hours.

Except, the Pathé newsreel with fresh Korean battle scenes didn't help. Tom fidgeted, drawing worried glances from Claire.

"Humphrey Bogart has nothing on me in the frustration department," Tom said as they stood to leave as the credits rolled.

"But all the boats you were on worked, didn't they?" his dad replied. The chatter continued as they headed back to the hotel.

Time flew the rest of the day but they did nothing in particular. The talk went into the evening in the Bentley's big room. In a pose like those brief weekends during Officer Candidate School, Tom went to sleep on the floor with his head next to Claire's feet as she read that evening's *Minneapolis Star*.

The parents chuckled at the sight: Their kids in a familiar pose, just like old times!

Good Friday, Tom's last day in Minneapolis, and everyone became melancholy. The flight to Tokyo left after midnight, early Saturday morning, and the last hours they had together meant all the more.

A church down the street from the hotel had a Good Friday service and all six took Communion quietly as the somber worship ended. Tom packed his freshly done laundry, put on a clean uniform, and the six of them ate a final dinner.

The parents saw him down to the front door at eleven o'clock and there were hugs, kisses and handshakes. Claire decided to ride out to the airport to give Tom a final sendoff.

The cabbie held the door open for her as she scooted half-way across the back seat, arranged her feet around the hump in the floor, and Tom sat down next to her, laying his crutch across their feet.

Then they were off through dark streets.

"How long will this take?" Claire asked Tom.

"Oh, I don't know, ask the driver. I think it took us a half-hour to get here when I came in," he replied.

"No, I mean, how long will it be until you're home to stay?" she said, looking at Tom intently.

"Oh."

He thought for a moment.

"Well, there's scuttlebutt that the UN and the North Koreans talk, but who knows?" he replied, shaking his head.

"Tom, please, I need to know something, this just drags on and on."

He hung his head.

"I know, darling. Believe me, there's no one more frustrated about things than me," Tom answered. "But it's out of our hands, just keep praying."

"Look, I started at Mizzou last fall because you would be there—but you're not," Claire said firmly with irritation. "The girls in the dorm tried to match me up with some boy and I told them no thanks, I have a guy in the Army.

"But do I? I don't know if I can go on like this. Can't you do something?"

"I've done all I can, the answer's not up to me."

"What can you do that you haven't tried?" she snapped.

The tone surprised Tom.

"Are we having an argument?" he asked innocently.

"No, I just need answers!"

"Claire, remember when I said we should get married before I left, then you said you wanted to wait. So here we are, we're waiting."

"But that was one-and-a-half years ago. I thought we'd be planning our first anniversary about now."

"Well, the Communists didn't cooperate," Tom said, trying to make a joke.

Claire didn't laugh.

"I'm working on it," he said. "I want to transfer back to the States because of the wound," he said, rubbing his leg. "I know it could happen. Best of all, maybe they'll let me go Army Reserve and I could finish my commitment down in Missouri. That's a definite possibility. Or, maybe they'll post me at Fort Lee in Virginia, quartermaster command, or maybe Oakland."

Claire sniffed and wiped her nose.

"More than anything, I guess I just need to know: Do you still want me?"

The question made Tom's jaw drop.

"Why, yes, of course, more than you can possibly know!"

"You've seen so much of the world, you're an Army officer, some girl from a little Missouri town may not interest you anymore. That's my perception.

"If not, let's end it now."

Tom gasped.

"No! Are you kidding me? No! Absolutely not! Sweetheart, your perception is not reality! Claire, I want you, you are my dearest possession! Do you feel that way about me?"

Claire gulped and quietly nodded.

"Yes, but I need to know you care. I think of so many things, I come up with plans. I'm beginning to have doubts," she whispered weakly.

Tom had been caught off guard. He took her shoulders, turned her and looked straight into her damp blue eyes as streetlights flashed by.

"Listen to me! Listen to me! You do not know how badly I want you! You are my greatest possession.

"Claire, please darling, you are everything I want in a woman—in a wife. You do not know how badly I want to come home, to be with you every day. Believe me, no one wants this over with more than I do," Tom said firmly, almost begging. "And if anything, the last three days have convinced me even more how very special you are.

"I want you more than ever."

He leaned over and kissed her oddly uncooperative lips. The girl who put herself into every kiss just sat there.

"Okay, but it's just so hard," she said as she cried.

Tom wrapped his arms around her and she laid her head on his shoulder. The golden hair enveloped him once again.

Cinnamon.

"Oh please, darling, stay with me on this. You're the most precious thing I have," he whispered. "You're what keeps me going. I've seen guys around me go crazy, some shot themselves. Me? I go on, I have Claire. She's waiting for me, that means everything, I can make it through another day."

She nodded silently and wiped her eyes again.

"Are you still my girl?"

"Yes," she answered with a weak sob. He dug a handkerchief out of his pocket and handed it to her.

The cab drove on through the night.

They pulled up at the terminal, the driver shut off the motor, came around and opened the door to help them out. The couple stood at the curb looking at each other as the cabbie took Tom's duffel out of the trunk.

They embraced.

"Trust me, I'll be home as soon as I possibly can and we'll get to live our dream yet—the two of us—in Springfield, Columbia, Randall, someplace. Please be patient, I still have the dream, and it's you. My home is with you," Tom said, looking into her damp eyes.

"Okay."

They kissed passionately as the cabbie admired the big airplanes on the other side of the fence.

"Good-bye—again," she said with a sigh, wiping away tears.

Tom helped her back in the cab, closed the door and handed the driver a twenty.

"Take good care of my girl," he said.

"Yes sir!" the cabbie replied with a brisk salute.

Claire turned and waved through the back window as the taxi drove into the night.

"I'm getting tired of this, Lord," he prayed as the cab disappeared. "Thank you for making her for me, but when can I have her for keeps?"

A skycap came for his duffel. Tom went through the usual check-in formalities at the ticket counter and walked out to the gate through the deserted terminal. Boarding wouldn't be for another hour. A clutch of passengers and well wishers sat around chatting at the gate as he found an empty seat in a dark corner.

He stared absent-mindedly at a big travel poster proclaiming JAPAN, NORTHWEST ORIENT AIRLINES around a lovely pagoda. The picture didn't match the Japan he knew.

Claire's questions left him deeply troubled.

"Where did that come from?" he mumbled, shaking his head, reflecting on their awkward cab ride. What caused all that after the sensual, very promising "she'll make it worth your wait?"

Had Claire changed more than he knew?

That's all he needed with the other stresses: girl trouble. Claire had been a constant since that afternoon in chemistry so long ago.

Could he lose her?

No, he did not even want to think about that.

Okay, granted, maybe this outburst came from the second, emotional Claire, but it worried him—a lot.

It had been the closest thing to a fight they'd ever had. If always confident, we-should-do-this Claire had doubts, maybe this relationship wouldn't work after all.

189

Maybe she saw no way to pull one of her surprises—and she knew it.

Would two sweet Missouri kids and their dream be another war casualty?

Chapter 12
Randall! Next Stop!

The long flight back proved even more tedious since he had no eagerness to arrive.

As soon as he returned to duty, Tom followed up on his promise, formally requesting a transfer.

Denied.

The command needs you, Bentley, your skills cannot be lost, you're too good.

Thank you, I guess.

His can-do reputation had grown, Lt. Bentley continued to make an impression someplace up the chain of command, but at least they put him in an office job at Incheon as the hospital discharged him. He wouldn't have to lie in his bunk and listen to artillery anymore.

The war had fallen into a stalemate with a definite front. Stay away from the line and life could be something approaching normal.

Tom tried to put a positive spin on things in a letter but it didn't sound very convincing, he thought. The good news: a promotion to captain.

He checked for mail as he left the hospital, finally, to head back to Korea. Tom found an envelope with the always perfect "Lt. Thomas J. Bentley" and his APO address, the first since he left Minneapolis.

He always tore into Claire's letters but not this one.

Was it a Dear John? Was it "forgive me?" What would it be?

He took a deep breath, then stopped in the hallway to read it, setting his crutch aside and leaning against the wall. He noticed the envelope had a Minneapolis postmark and the single sheet of stationery inside had a Bergen Hotel address at the top.

He held his breath:

My dearest Tom,

I cried all the way back to the hotel from the airport because I realized I upset you. I don't know what the poor cab driver thought.

Things did not end right for us and it's all my fault, I let my emotions get in the way. I want you NOW!

But when I stop and think about things, then I know I am still committed to you—and to us. I feel sorry for myself because you're not here with me, and I guess I don't think about how hard it is for you over there, all alone.

You do not know what seeing you meant to me, maybe I can go on for however long this takes. Thanks more than you know for making all of this happen.

I count the days until we're together at last in our own home, sweetheart. I count you my dearest friend and greatest treasure.

All my love,

Claire

So it was "forgive me."

"Whew!" he exhaled

Perhaps they were okay after all. But that near-argument still troubled him, and what did she mean by "*maybe* I can go on?" Maybe *not*?

The gears inside that blonde head were grinding away faster than usual, and that might not be a good thing.

The months rolled by, another summer, fall, bitterly cold winter and spring, but Capt. Bentley basically had a desk job. What he did closely matched the paper shuffling and stock checking back at the warehouse.

A year had come and gone since Minneapolis and the letters continued back and forth. Claire neared her Mizzou graduation and he wanted to be there, badly, to see it.

The rumors got louder—some sort of armistice, or ceasefire, or something—was in the works. But what to believe, after months of whispers and gossip?

Finally, 27 July 1953, it ended. The hearsay this time proved true: No victory, but the shooting stopped.

Capt. Bentley could go home.

He jerked awake, the nightstand clock showed 7:56, nearly 8 o'clock, breakfast waited. Tom had been in bed a long time, but after a night like this, who could feel rested?

He dressed, took his morning pills, grabbed the cane and tapped his way down the hall to the dining room. Tony stopped finishing up the morning's special, breakfast tacos, and greeted him with an enthusiastic, "Hey!

"What are these things?" he asked, pointing at his plate as Tom sat down. "Tex-Mex for breakfast? Lemme' tell 'ya, those people are takin' over!"

"Considering their food that's not a bad thing," Tom replied as the waitress poured his coffee. "I don't hear you complaining about Italian food."

"Well, that's different," Tony replied. "But, you ever have a frozen margarita? Now those things are great."

Tom stopped chewing and put down his fork.

"No, don't drink much," he mumbled.

Tony put down his fork and stared at his friend.

"You don't look so good, pal, another rough night thinkin' about her?" Tony asked.

"Yeah, what else is on my mind these days? At this stage of my life breakfast tacos are as good as it gets."

Tom briefly went over the troubling things from being too good.

"I never had that problem," Tony replied, using a bit of tortilla to sop up salsa in his plate.

"I had to wrap up once the shooting stopped so all of us could ship out. I tried everything: The commercial flights? Booked solid for months. How about an Air Force VIP flight? Of course, Army captains are not VIPs. A cargo flight? I thought about stuffing myself in a box and addressing it to my folks. But seriously, nothing," Tom said.

"Finally at the end of October, three long years, they put me on a ship for Oakland. You don't know how wide the Pacific Ocean is, that trip just went on and on. It was the slow-boat-to-China in reverse. If I had found an oar, I would've opened a porthole and rowed to get to California faster.

"We docked in California at Thanksgiving and I was push-push-push, let me go-let me go! My desire compelled me, I have to get home to Claire!

"But the Army? 'Oh, you're in a hurry? Tough luck, sir, so are ten-thousand other guys. Take a number.'

"Finally, I got the word, I would get processed out and be home before Christmas.

194

"I firmed things up, I had a ticket to leave 20 December that would get me into Randall on the evening train, 23 December, Christmas Eve-eve, whatever."

"So you were happy, I guess?' Tony asked.

"I used some of the last cash I had on me to send telegrams to my folks, to Claire to meet me at the station, and one to Sol Wiesen, the jeweler. I still remember it: NEED ONE CARAT YELLOW GOLD ENGAGEMENT RING SMALL FINGER BUY CHRISTMAS EVE STOP TOM BENTLEY.

"I had it all worked out: It would happen in front of the tree in the Dearborns' den on Christmas Eve after we came back from church. I'd get down on one knee, show her the ring, and she'd scream 'Yes!' Mr. Dearborn had asked me to let him know first so I figured I'd call him that morning. Everything, at last, was set!

"Must've been a long train ride," his friend said.

"Oh, you can't imagine! But officers went in sleeping cars so I had a roomette at the back of the train, quiet back there, by myself. A moon came out and I spent a lot of time staring out the window crossing Arizona that night, thinking just how it would be, rehearsing our meeting at the station, then giving her the ring in front of the tree.

"The bad times were over! I knew life would be beautiful now.

"The train would pull into the Randall station, I'd jump down the stairs and there she would be with her little smile, waiting for me in the dark. I would sweep her off her feet, kiss her, and hug her so hard I might squeeze her to death.

195

"We did it! I'm home! Let's get married!

"The train got to Kansas City right on time. Then the train south finally left and I remember the stop in Nevada, thinking this is where she had come and gone so many times. It was getting dark and started spitting snow.

"When we got to Randall, the train started slowing down so I reached up in the overhead rack, got my duffel down and headed for the vestibule just as we passed the big Bentley Hardware sign up on the warehouse roof. What a thrill to see that again, started snowing hard.

"The conductor came through announcing 'Randall! Next stop!' That's when things veered off.

"The Gypsies finally showed up?" Tony asked.

"Yes, the conductor had to squeeze through a mob getting off to open the Dutch door and lower the stairs. So much for bouncing down into her arms."

Tom's voice cracked as he wiped his eyes with his napkin.

"Here I was, having to wait some more for all these people, but I finally got down to the platform, stepping into this swirling crowd pushing and shoving in the snow. I knew she was in there somewhere, I just had to find her.

"But in a few minutes everyone was off, a handful got on and the crowd thinned quickly, people wanted to get out of the snow. Still no Claire.

"She must be in the waiting room trying to stay warm, that was it! I was so discombobulated that when I finally made it over to the station I started to push through the door marked COLORED. Well, she wouldn't be in there."

"Probably not."

"I finally made it into the waiting room; empty. Maybe she waited in her car? I walked out the front, not a Studebaker to be seen. About then the locomotive honked and the train left.

"The clerk at the window yelled, 'You gonna' be here long? I need to lock up.'

"So I thought I'd call, the agent gave me ten dimes for a dollar, then I went to the pay phone and got thrown for a surprise.

"Claire hid in the phone booth?" Tony asked.

"Well no, Randall had dial phones, no more 'number please.' It took me a minute to figure it out, but I dialed her number, 8935. It rang and rang and I was about to hang up when Mr. Dearborn answered."

"And?"

"I told him it was me, he sighed and said, 'I'm afraid there has been a change in plans, Claire will not be able to come to the station.'

"That shocked me, I asked if she was okay? He replied, 'Oh, as far as I know she's fine.'"

"Now that's odd," Tony said.

"Exactly, '*as far as I know she's fine*.' I thought what a funny thing to say. So I started to ask and he interrupted me: 'I think we need to explain some things, Tom. Why don't you come by for breakfast in the morning, say about eight o'clock?'"

"Geez louise, she stood you up!" Tony said, sitting upright. "After three years, she stood you up!"

"You got it," Tom replied, wiping his eyes again. "It was over."

He sighed and shook his head.

197

"Her biggest surprise ever. I got my dad on the phone and he drove over to get me. 'I thought you had Claire pick you up?' I said that's what I thought. I asked him what he had heard and he didn't know a thing.

"It was a long night after I greeted the folks, but at least I was in my own bed."

"And breakfast?"

"It was tough getting there, snowed all night, streets were bad. I didn't even have to knock, Mr. Dearborn opened the door as I crunched up to the door.

"He looked awful. My first thought was ohmigosh, Claire died."

"Apparently not," Tony said, scowling.

"He invited me in and took my coat. Her brother, Bruce, was there with this toddler in the floor. Bruce got up, shook my hand and said, 'Welcome home, soldier, I'm sorry.'

"Sorry for what? Before I could say anything he picked up the kid and introduced him, 'This is our son, Robert.' Cute little thing, wavy brown hair.

"Mrs. Dearborn came up the hall about then wringing her hands and she looked like death warmed over, I had never seen her so pale and sad. We sat down at the table.

"Mr. Dearborn said grace, kind of an unusual prayer about 'help us to trust you in all things,' then looked at me after he took a drink of coffee.

"'I expected Claire to tell you about all this,' he started, with irritation.

"Tell me what?" I asked.

"He continued, 'As you know, she graduated from Mizzou in August, we went up there for commencement. She told us while we were there she had been offered a scholarship for women to Columbia University's law school in New York; very exclusive. She passed the law school admissions test, she left for New York early this month to get an apartment. She will start classes in January.'"

"So she and the Gypsies had been gone for weeks, and she didn't say anything?"

"No."

"Man, I thought I dated some cold babes," Tony said, shaking his head.

"Truly, I was speechless," Tom said, his voice shaking.

"Her parents were falling all over themselves, apologizing, they were upset too. 'I'm sure she will write you or call you in a few days, she's very busy right now,' her mom said with that worried look on her face."

"And did she?" Tony asked.

"No."

Tom sat quietly, staring at the table as he threw his napkin in his plate.

"I never heard a word, sixty years have gone by.

"I thought about contacting her, maybe going to New York to look her up. But I talked myself out of it. I was beyond bitter. I figured if she still cared she would do something."

The two friends set in silence.

"That is brutal," Tony said with a sigh.

"Her last couple letters were oddly worded. She rambled on about needing a plan for life, that we each had to think about what we wanted to do, they sounded different. I didn't think about it at the time, she could go off on tangents, and I just figured she was thinking out loud after graduation.

"Mr. Dearborn hemmed and hawed about 'of course we're proud of her accomplishments' but obviously they were hurt by what happened, the way it happened."

"What about the ring?" Tony asked.

"When things settled down, I mentioned I had planned to propose to Claire that night."

"'We know,' Mrs. Dearborn said, shaking her head, she'd started crying. That shocked me. Then Mr. Dearborn explained Solomon Wiesen, the jeweler, had come by the bank to ask about a loan. He told Mr. Dearborn about my telegram.

"Mr. Dearborn explained, 'I told him I figured as much. Tom is a fine young man. I told him a long time ago he had my permission for Claire's hand when he was ready.' I replied I had intended to call him that morning, as promised.

"I had to slide over to Mr. Wiesen's shop in the snow to tell him things were off.

"He brought out the ring, beautiful."

The friends sat in silence for a few minutes.

"In some ways my life ended about then," Tom said with a sigh.

"That's the most cruel thing I ever heard," Hickory Bough's manager of snarky remarks said with a rare solemn look.

"So are you gonna' look her up—or are 'ya gonna' shoot her?"

"Don't tempt me," Tom answered firmly.

"I wonder if she's avoiding me? I don't see her in the dining room."

"Don't know, she may be in such bad shape she can't get in here. I doubt if she even knows you're here."

"I guess you're right," Tom said as he got up from the table. He took his cane and the friends started their usual slow march back to their rooms.

"Let me know what you decide, you poor guy," Tony said as he wheeled his way down the hall.

What to do?

Tom sat down on the foot of his bed and looked out at the dumpster. "I know how you feel," he said to the big metal box.

He prayed, he thought, he worried. Maybe it wasn't her, maybe there were two Claire Dearborns in the world. But not likely. And if he saw her, what would keep him from blacking out again? Just seeing her name sent his head spinning in his worst attack since he moved to Hickory Bough.

And what would she look like? He didn't look like he did in 1952 and he doubted if she did. Maybe she was bedfast with tubes running out of her, maybe she was ugly, like those poor people sitting around the dayroom.

No, he had to see her, if for nothing else to ask "why?"

201

Chapter 13
Are You Friends?

He let another day pass as he tried to think of something, anything, besides Claire. Tony and some other guys came by and they talked baseball. Spring training loomed around the corner, would the Cardinals have a great year?

Tom got out the iPad and tried to read some books, he surfed the 'net, he got out some old photos and put them up in his room. Something, anything, to do.

But it was no use.

Tom slept on it another night and mulled over things again. He finally decided to go after breakfast but he didn't know which was Claire's room. The nurses' station will know.

He took a deep breath, picked up his cane and ambled toward the big horseshoe out in the dayroom. He tried to look nonchalant as he came up to a young lady busily typing on a computer.

"Yes?" she asked, looking up.

"Excuse me, but what roo-, uh, suite is that new lady in, Miss Dearborn?"

The nurse ran her finger down a list on the counter.

"You mean Judge Dearborn? She's in C 4, are you friends?"

"I don't know," Tom replied as he shuffled off.

He had never been down C Hall on the other side of the dining room. He tapped by the doors marked "Linens" and "Oxygen NO SMOKING," then past C 2, where some elderly man watched television, then he spotted the little sign: C 4 Claire Dearborn. The door stood open and he stopped short, he froze.

Could he do it?

All the years, all the good times, all the hurt. He shook, everything, all of it, back on him—now. He gripped the handrail to make sure he didn't black out and fall again. He carefully peeked around the door and looked inside.

And there she was.

Claire wore a light blue bathrobe and sat in a wheelchair. The slender build was long gone, she had put on a lot of weight. The still-beautiful hair had turned fifty/fifty gold and silver, wrapped up in a bun, so the ever-alluring blonde wisp over her cheek had disappeared. The flawless complexion had turned wrinkled and weathered.

But this was Claire, no doubt about it.

Two nurses busily took her blood pressure and temperature, tapping the numbers in a laptop.

No, he could not do it.

It still hurt too badly, it made him angry.

He turned and shuffled back to the dayroom, found a big chair, and sat down heavily with a sigh.

"Good morning, Tom! May you be blessed with a good day today!"

The familiar sing-song of Gaylene interrupted his funk. She stopped and looked at him with her usual big smile, which quickly turned to a frown.

"Oh my! Tom looks like he has a big problem he's worried about!" she said.

"Yes, yes, I do," he answered.

"Well! I'm here to help! Tell me what's bothering you!"

204

"Gaylene, you don't have the time."

"It's something big, I know!"

"Yes, yes it is."

"I'm not worried! Tom Bentley always does the right thing even if it's hard, I know it! God will give you strength!" she gushed.

"Thank you, I try," Tom said, adjusting his glasses as he looked blankly across the room.

"You go ahead and do what you know needs to be done! 'Bye for now!" And with that the bowling ball rolled toward the kitchen.

"... *Always does the right thing even if it's hard,*" spun around in his head.

Gaylene was right, he had to go see Claire. If he didn't do it now they would meet some other time around Hickory Bough and it would be even more awkward. Why did God do this to him?

"Awkward, awkward," he mumbled to himself. "Lord, help me."

He leaned forward, stood up and shuffled back down C Hall. Tom stopped short of Claire's door again, then peeked inside.

She now sat alone in the wheelchair, dozing.

He pitied her.

Oh my, that statuesque young woman, tall and thin, with long, beautiful golden hair, the one he had known and was so proud to have on his arm. She had become sick, wrinkled and obese.

It shocked him, he stood for a moment in the door, staring at her.

205

"Here goes," Tom whispered. He took a deep breath, took a step forward and tapped twice on her door with his cane. Claire jerked awake and looked up at him with dull, watery blue eyes.

"Yes?" she said.

One word of that voice, that low, very feminine voice, and more memories flooded back. The voice sounded older, with a quiver, and he could make out a strong lisp to the S.

But it was Claire.

He stood for a moment longer, then spoke.

"Claire, it's me, Tom," he said slowly.

The old gentleman braced himself. Yes, he half-way expected her answer but it hurt terribly when he heard it:

"Tom who?"

That Tom, Claire, once the love of your life. The man you teased by saying "I look pretty good in white too." The man you wrapped yourself around for hours out in the gazebo. The man you daydreamed about marrying and moving to Springfield with. The man you wore out pens writing letters to.

That Tom, the man you kept alive through a horrible war because he thought about you every waking moment and in most of his dreams. You gave him hope, and as it turned out a vain hope.

That Tom.

What happened?

Why did you do what you did?

Why did you hurt him?

Did you ever really care?

Tell me!

206

He sighed and stood quietly for a moment longer, then cleared his throat.

"Tom Bentley."

Claire raised her hand. The dull eyes focused on him intently, then she frowned.

"No! No! This is... so... Why did you come back?" she asked angrily, her eyebrows furrowed.

The lisp was noticeable.

It took him aback.

"Claire, I didn't come back, *you* did!"

"I don't want to hear it! Go away, leave me alone! Get out! NOW!" she shouted, getting red in the face, shaking her fist.

Tom steadied himself, he had never, ever seen Claire angry.

He didn't expect this. He hoped for something between Claire throwing her arms around him and begging "forgive me!" to that familiar half smile and a quiet "hello."

He had not been ready to be yelled at.

Tom shook his head and quietly turned back into the hall. He grabbed the handrail, so upset he could scarcely stand. Tears ran down his cheeks, he breathed in gasps.

But he would not black out. No, not now.

That would let her win.

Tom Bentley would get through this.

He stomped angrily across the dayroom and veered into B Hall. He could see Tony looking in B 9's door. Seeing the empty room, his friend wheeled around to back toward his own room when he saw Tom steaming down the hall.

"Ah! There you are! Did you look her up? How did it go?"

"It didn't!" Tom shouted as he turned into his room, sat down on the sofa and angrily threw his cane on the floor.

Tony backed in behind him.

"So what do you do now?"

"I'll call Tom Junior and tell him I want to move, I can't stay here!"

Tony looked shocked.

"Oh buddy, I'm afraid I can't let you do that. You belong here, you have to stay!

"Everyone thinks you're a swell guy, Gaylene, Josefina, Clémence—everybody—even Mrs. Stevens.

"And Noisy Nancy, stay for Noisy! You make this dump a better place, don't let what happened sixty years ago mess up your life now! Think about the future!"

Tom sat with his arms crossed and grumbled to himself.

"Thanks, I needed that. Tell you what, let's get the dominoes out," Tom suggested to change the subject.

They played until noon, then went to the dining room. Corned beef and cabbage made Tom mutter "this completes the worst day I've had since my wife died."

He went back to his room and laid down for a nap but couldn't sleep—and didn't want to risk it after the awful night before.

It's bad when a person is scared to go to sleep, and Tom was.

208

But he did.

He woke up an hour later and shuffled outside to Hickory Bough's little garden by the dining room. The sun would cheer him up. Not a breath of air stirred, so for a late-winter day, if one sat in the sunlight, things would seem pleasant. Tom figured he'd enjoy the outside for a while, then maybe go ride a bike in the exercise room.

He sat on a bench and rolled things over in his mind: "No! Claire's history, time to move on, pal," he muttered, angrily pounding his cane on the pavement. "She hurt you once, don't let her hurt you again! Forget her!"

But then what?

He did not want to rot away at Hickory Bough, ducking down halls to avoid someone. Maybe he would move to Bella Vista after all and Tom Junior could just drive, hang it! But Tony had a point. He had friends here and he felt safe in a way he didn't back in that big, empty house, living alone.

Hickory Bough may not be home but it felt better, safer, at least until now.

He slammed his cane down again in frustration.

Little did Tom know he was being watched.

That night after dinner, Tom went back to his room and got ready for bed early. The doctor had given him sleeping pills but cautioned him to "take them sparingly, only when you need to." If there ever were a time he needed to, it was now, so he took one.

He slept like a baby.

He woke the next morning feeling better than he had since he saw that name on the white board. He finished

209

dressing and took his morning pills when he heard a tap on the door.

"Come in!"

"Mr. Bentley? This is for you," Clémence said as she stepped in and handed him an envelope.

He thanked her, took the envelope and shuddered as he saw it. A letter-perfect "Tom Bentley" in beautiful cursive jumped out at him. He knew exactly who wrote it.

Tom held it to his nose and sniffed: cinnamon.

He was afraid of it.

He put the note down on the end table and scratched his chin, what to do? He sat down on the edge of the bed, thinking. She probably wrote to tell him to buzz off. "Well, what could be worse than what happened yesterday?" he muttered.

He picked up the envelope, ran his finger under the flap and pulled out the sheet of stationery.

Tom,

Please forgive me for what happened but you startled me. I didn't know what to do, I thought maybe I had a bad dream.

Is it really you? Are we meeting again? I saw you outside just now and I could tell you were very upset. I'm so sorry, it's all my fault.

Please come back whenever you want. Let's talk.

Claire

No "devoted lover," not even a "dearest Tom," but no "go jump in a lake, chump!"

He'd think about it but he would not get in a hurry.

After six decades, what were a few more days? Claire could just wait if she was going to act like that.

210

He might never go back.

But he had to find something to do to get his mind off her. After breakfast, he pulled out a box of books from the closet Judy hadn't opened; read something. He saw *Crime and Punishment*, no, too depressing. Then *The Great Gatsby*, a terrific book about a guy losing his girl. No, certainly didn't want to read that.

Then below he found some big, blue flat book. He dug it out: *Rampart, Our Bright Future, 1948-49, Randall Public Schools*.

Oh no, but he had to look.

He thumbed through the yellowing annual to the last page of the senior class, labeled "Our Best." And right below it, in the largest photo on the page, stood the "Glamour Couple of 1949." There they were, holding hands. He wore the rented tux, Claire had on that slinky black dress with flowing hair falling over her cheek.

Gosh, those two kids looked good.

Did he ever look that young?

And Claire, could this possibly be the same crippled old woman down the hall?

It did not seem possible.

He threw the yearbook back in the box and decided to go to the exercise room.

Chapter 14
Ask Not, Want Not

A week-and-a-half went by. There were movies, books, spring-training baseball on TV, and dominoes with Tony. Then Tom Junior, Judy and the grandchildren surprised him one Saturday morning.

"Hi, Pop!" Tom Junior called out and Hannah added a perky "Hi, Grandpa Tom!" as "my kids" strolled in B 9.

"Well, what a pleasant surprise! You always come on Sundays," the old man replied with a smile as his daughter-in-law bent over to hug him. "What's up?"

"Judy wants to go to this art fair down in Springdale, Arkansas, today so we thought we'd stop since it's on the way. We managed to lasso the kids, Hannah's home on spring break," Tom Junior explained.

Just then who should come through the door, head first as always, but Tony. He had met Tom's family and the little crowd quickly made lively chatter. They talked for a while, then Tom Junior mentioned "we better be going" as he inched toward the door.

Things started to wind down as another wheelchair came through the door: Claire, pushed by Clémence. Obviously nervous, Claire sat up and mumbled, "Oh, you have company," and motioned for the nurse to back her out into the hall.

A shocked Tom waved off Clémence, who darted out the door.

"No, no, I want you to meet my family," Tom said in a friendly tone. This was different, he was on his turf, in his room, in a good mood.

"Claire, this is my son, Tom Junior; my daughter-in-law, Judy; my grandson, Chad, he's a senior at Randall High; and his sister, Hannah, a sophomore accounting major up at Mizzou.

"And, I don't know if you've met Tony, Tony Di Burlone. He lives down B Hall from me. We're buds.

"Everybody, this is Judge Claire Dearborn. We, umm, uh, we knew each other in high school."

There were nods and how-do-you-do's all around as Claire and Hannah shook hands. Then Tom Junior and his family excused themselves so they could get on the road. Tony quickly rolled out right behind them, knowing he'd be out of place.

They were alone.

Claire looked at Tom. Tom looked at Claire.

"So, you were married?" Claire asked cheerfully.

"Yes."

"And your wife?"

"Widowed, 1980, cancer."

"I'm sorry, and her name?

"Nobody you knew, not from around here."

"Oh? Well then, how did you meet?" she asked, still smiling.

"Okay, well I guess, whatever then, Linda, Linda Brown," Tom said with a forced smile. "She died at 39."

"It must've been hard," Claire replied.

"Very."

Tom sighed.

"We met at the warehouse, married in June 1961. She moved to Randall from Clarksville, Arkansas, after she graduated from high school, 1959. She came up here to take care of a sick great aunt. Randall didn't have a nursing home worth talking about back then."

Claire listened, smiled and nodded.

"And you, did you marry?" Tom asked, cheerfully.

Claire sat silently.

"No."

They sat in awkward silence for a minute or two with forced smiles. The silence echoed louder than the multiple TVs down the hall.

"Tell me about her," Claire finally said pleasantly.

Tom shook his head.

"My granddaughter, Hannah, you just met, is her spitting image. She was petite, Linda had shoulder-length brown hair and big brown eyes, cute and perky, always a big smile. She just showed up one day behind the front desk in the lobby, the new receptionist, personnel hired her. Tough job, it seemed whoever had it didn't last long so I paid no attention at first, just another face, another come-and-go temp.

But she turned out different, always pleasant and smiling, outgoing, greeted everyone with a 'good morning' or a 'good afternoon.'

"She handled the phone and the mail like a pro, always organized, everybody liked her; chatty. She became very good at taking messages for dad, my brothers and me, reminding us of meetings and appointments. 'Remember to come back from lunch early, Tom, you have that store manager meeting!' that sort of thing.

215

"We got to talking one morning when I passed her while she sorted stuff into the mail room pigeonholes. Like I said, she was short and she had to stand on her toes and hop to reach the boxes on the top row. It looked funny.

"I stood there with my coffee, watching her jump and laughed at her. She stopped, looked at me and laughed too. 'Can you buy me some stilts?' she said with this big, perky smile.

"We became friends after that, we'd chat in the break room, 'How's your day goin'?'; that sort of thing. My, my, she always was just so pleasant to be around," Tom said, lost in thought.

Claire nodded, still smiling.

"I took her to The Malt Shop one day for lunch, I guess our first date and, well, one thing led to another. I proposed at a little New Year's Eve party some church friends put on as 1960 ended. I clued them in.

"I put my arm around her, pulled her close, and popped the question as we all stood around waiting, just before the clock chimed midnight. She answered, 'Of course!'

"So I whipped out this engagement ring, bought it from Wiesen's with my savings, right at the stroke of midnight and her eyeballs nearly popped out, three carats, big one. I thought she would pass out from shock. I slipped it on her finger, she waved her hand around and gasped, 'It's so heavy!'

"That night turned into a real New Year's celebration for everyone," he added, smiling at the memory.

"She wanted a simple little wedding back at her home church in Clarksville, all basic and quick. Her folks didn't have much money. I offered to help but no, they wouldn't hear to it. 'They have their pride,' is the way she put it.

"Okay, fine. So instead, I offered her a dream honeymoon: Where would you like to go? Name it, anywhere in the world! Mexico? Hawaii? Europe? South Pacific?

"I think the longest trip she'd had in her life to that point was the move up here from Clarksville, two-hundred miles. She sat there with her chin in her hand, tapping her finger on her lips for a moment and breezily replied, 'No, just a night up in the Ozarks, that'll be fine.'

"I repeated: 'Your choice, I'm here to make you happy.'

"'No, that's all I want.'

"So we had a two-night stay in a little lodge up in the mountains on Highway Seven, very pretty, very basic."

He paused for a moment.

"I think with Linda, well, she proved you only know what you've seen. Her family didn't have a lot, long trips never happened. Their idea of a vacation was to hop in their old Chevy station wagon and drive over to see Linda's grandmother in Fort Smith Sunday afternoon. So she couldn't fathom, say, a month in Tuscany."

Tom paused.

"She never asked for much. Eating out, even The Malt Shop, burgers with the kids, always became a big deal."

Tom paused again, then chuckled.

217

"Ha! I guess we made all the little old ladies chatter, small-town busybodies! Did you hear? The boss's son married the receptionist! She's ten years younger than him! He robbed the cradle, imagine that! You *know* they have something to hide!

"I'm sure some watched the calendar very closely. Of course, nothing happened. Tom Junior's sister, Brenda, arrived a couple months past our first anniversary. Tom Junior joined our family two years later. We lost a baby three years after that."

He paused, took off his glasses, and wiped his eyes.

"She loved our big, old house on Poplar, so different than the little shotgun house where she grew up. Linda asked if we could live there after we were married, her old aunt had passed away by then.

"I still lived with my parents and they thought having her move in a swell idea. So we shifted things around and they both lived with us until they passed away. It became our home.

"She and mom hit it off, very close, Linda became the daughter mom never had," Tom added pleasantly.

Claire coughed.

"Your mom gave me a hug at that birthday party you threw for me our junior year and said I was the daughter she never had," she interrupted.

"Well?" Tom said flatly.

"Uh, okay."

"Anyway, three generations in one home!" Tom said with a dreamy smile.

"Old habits die hard, Linda proved that true. She could be thrifty to a fault, saving aluminum foil and jelly glasses in the kitchen, that sort of thing. She grew up with nothing and I had to push her sometimes: You're a Bentley now, we have the money, get what you want!

"I'd take her down to A La Mode for her birthday and make her buy clothes. We'd walk out, I'd be holding a bunch of dresses on hangers and she'd have an armload of boxes. Linda would shake her head in disbelief. We stuck it all in the trunk, then I'd walk her down the street to Kinnard's to buy shoes.

"I bought her a brand-new Buick for our tenth anniversary, really pretty. 'But I can't drive *that*!' she gasped when I took her out to the stable and gave her the keys.

"So I asked, 'why not?'

"'Well, it's, it's just too *shiny*!' Linda answered with her hands over her face in shock. Of course, she loved it, hauled our kids all over town. And sure as anything, you'd see Linda Bentley's Buick parked at Gibson's, that cheapo discount store we had back then.

"And we finally did some travel. We took the kids to Disneyland on the train one summer, another year we drove to the Grand Canyon—in her Buick—that sort of thing.

"I loved to bless her, to make her happy beyond what she could imagine. She always would just be so grateful for anything."

Tom thought for a moment.

"Well, she did start dressing better and she started thinking up trips we could do. She got interested in antiques, bought some nice collectibles with mom's advice.

"But always, one of her great lines was, 'Ask not, want not.'"

Chapter 15
Either/Or

Claire sat with a forced smile, listening, thinking.

Tom Bentley—*her* guy—married to someone else? Having children with another woman? It seemed so hard to imagine.

Yes, to be frank, it did bother her. Even after all these years it made her uneasy, even if she had been the one who passed on him.

Was she jealous?

Well, yes, yes she was.

"She sounds very different than me," Claire said, awkwardly smiling as she shifted in her wheelchair.

"Yes, you could depend on Linda. If she said she was going to be somewhere, she was there," Tom said curtly.

That did it.

The pleasantries ended, the forced smiles turned to frowns.

Tom felt his face go red, Claire blushed.

She grabbed her chair's armrests and sat up.

"Tom, look, I never said I'd meet you at the station."

"So you know what happened that night?"

"Yes."

"No, as a matter of fact you didn't tell me anything, you told me nothing at all! Can you see the problem?

"Could you have at least said something— anything?" he asked with anger. "It hurt badly—very badly!

"I counted on you! I counted on you through that whole bloody war, and when at last I came home to the beautiful woman I loved and adored, you abandoned me.

"You hurt me, you hurt my family, you hurt your family!"

"Now wait, that's not true!" Claire replied defensively. "My family was very proud of me."

"So tell me," Tom snapped, "what looked better than what I offered you?"

"Tom, please, don't say it that way!" Claire pleaded, shaking her head and raising her hand.

"Okay, to be frank I gave up."

Claire wiped her eyes.

"I let my emotions take over without thinking things through."

"But why? I made you a part of my life for eight years. I knew you were the one," Tom replied sharply. "I thought you felt the same way."

"Only eight years, eight years? Try fourteen years!" Claire snapped back. "And what good did it do me? Nothing! You wasted my time!"

He grimaced at the insult.

"Fourteen? I don't understand. We met that afternoon in chemistry class when..."

"Try third grade!" Claire shot back, pointing at Tom. "Remember Miss Humphries?"

Tom rolled his eyes.

"Oh, that witch! She was awful, one of the worst teachers I ever had. Who could forget her? But what does she have to do with me?"

"Everything," Claire replied with condescension.

"Huh?" Tom said as he sat up, puzzled.

"That's when I first saw you," Claire added, shaking her head.

"Miss Humphries had given us some kind of assignment to write a sentence with words—nouns, verbs, adjectives—she put on the blackboard, or something like that. We were supposed to pick out several words and write a complete sentence. She gave us a few minutes and then she called on each of us to read our sentences aloud.

"I remember she called out 'Thomas!' and you went first. You stood up, read your little sentence and started to sit back down. 'That was awful!' she yelled at you. 'I work so hard to teach you children and that's the best you can come up with, young man? You just stand there for a while! You are an embarrassment!'"

The painful memory came back to Tom as he put his hand on his forehead.

"Oh, I remember that. I had done the best I could, little kid that I was, then she started off about how I made her look bad."

"Exactly!" Claire replied.

"I sat in the row across from you and up a couple seats. I turned back to look at you. We were all scared to death she would call one of us next. There you stood, alone, in the middle of the class, ready to cry.

"I felt sorry for you," Claire continued. "You seemed like a nice boy, you handled your part of it well. I got a crush on you that day, an innocent little girl's third-grade crush.

"I decided I wanted you to be my boyfriend, in the way an eight-year-old thinks about such things."

Tom sat with a blank stare.

"I had no idea."

"No, no you didn't!" Claire added, frowning and shaking her finger at him.

"I watched you for years, everyone liked you, good ol' Tom Bentley, everybody's pal! And I tried to make you notice me. You like *them*, why don't you like *me*?

"What's wrong with me? Why won't you talk to me?

"You would be sitting at a cafeteria table eating lunch, talking with a crowd around you about sports, cars, movies, what's on radio, everybody laughing. And me? I sat down at the end of the table quietly eating my sandwich, hoping you'd say something to me.

"I was introverted, shy, I thought everything through. What does he mean? What if I do this? What if I do that? Should I say something?

"I wasn't outgoing. But you seemed so nice, so sweet, I kept trying.

"It wasn't until that afternoon in chemistry, ninth grade, after I finagled my way into your lab group, that you noticed me, six long years later.

"All of a sudden, miracle of miracles, you spoke to me in the hall! I almost fell over, it shocked me! You'd walked past me a thousand times.

"Then you bumped into me in the library, you looked at me and smiled before you walked off. He actually touched me, oh my! I was so spacey I had to grab the shelf to keep from falling over!

"Then that day in the cafeteria, you sat down and ate with me! Then you called me one night! Wow! No boy

224

had ever called me and then to get a call from you—from *you*!, my dream guy!—oh, I could hardly breathe!

"*Finally*, he noticed me!" Claire nearly shouted. "It really could happen! My dream could really come true! Tom Bentley, the big man on campus, the most popular guy in school, the cute guy all the girls giggle over, might be *my* guy!

"I told myself, 'Claire, sweetheart, you're this close—*this close*—don't mess this up! Do whatever it takes: Just get him!'"

Tom sat speechless.

"Was I that dense?"

"Yes."

He sat quietly, shaking his head.

"If I missed you it certainly wasn't intentional," Tom answered. "I remember looking at you and you looked back after that test tube blew up, or whatever. I didn't know much about girls, you know, pretty girls. I had gal pals but, hey, that's different. I didn't know what to do.

"You captivated me but I thought you were mad at me, laughing at me, or something."

"Not at all!" Claire said, the eyebrows furrowing. "You were my knight in shining armor, my first love, and I hoped, I prayed, that Tom Bentley—someday, please Lord!—would like me too. You were everything I wanted in a boy.

"You were smart, you were polite, you were cute, you were clever, you were popular—everyone liked you!"

"Well, you didn't give me much, uh, feedback until that trip on the bus, I felt very awkward."

"And I had feedback from *you*?" Claire snapped.

"We were both an innocent fourteen, I'd never had a boyfriend. Like you, I didn't know what you thought of me, although you suddenly had noticed me," she replied.

"Talk about awkward, I just threw myself at you on that bus—and hoped. My worst fear was you'd yell 'Get off me!' and make a scene. I would have died."

They stared at each other in silence.

"That night certainly changed things for me, and you?" Tom finally asked.

Claire leaned back in her wheelchair, clapped her hands and laughed, lightening the mood.

"Oh! I must've been a sight when we got back to the school," she said.

"How so?"

"Remember? It was late, cold, everyone wet and tired, slogging around, miserable. And here I came across the parking lot to my father's car—skipping! Happy, happy, happy! I was as dizzy as a termite in a yo-yo.

"It worked! It worked! Hallelujah! Now Tom Bentley's *my* boyfriend! I caught him! Life is wonderful! Dreams come true!

"I got in, leaned over and gave my father the usual peck on the cheek and he said, 'My, you look happy.'

"I caught myself. 'Oh, it was a really good game,' I told him.

"My wise and perceptive father leaned on the steering wheel, looked at me out of the corner of his eye and said, 'You don't give a Fig Newton about football, what's his name?'

"I felt my cheeks go red, I stared at the floorboard, then mumbled, 'Tom Bentley.'

226

"He sat back and raised his eyebrows. 'That's right,' he nodded, 'I think the Bentleys have a son about your age.'

"Oh, I wanted to crawl under the seat, so I started apologizing: 'Really, Daddy, he's very nice, all the kids like him. I know you'd like him, he's really intelligent,' on and on I went.

"'I can understand that, the Bentleys seem like good folks,' he replied, nodding.

"I yakked about you all the way home.

"Our maid got off Saturdays so mom would get up early and make pancakes and bacon. Saturday morning breakfast always was something special my family did.

"You know me, I'm not a morning person, I'd shuffle in the dining room in my bathrobe, yawning, with a bed head, and mom would be all chipper as she brought a big plate of pancakes and a bottle of maple syrup from the kitchen, 'Good morning, sweetheart!'

"That day, we were sitting there quietly eating and my father looked at mom, coughed, and said very formally, 'Jewel, our daughter has a gentleman of interest.'

"'And who might that be?' mom asked. I blushed and told her. 'Why yes, I know his mother from Junior League, she's very nice; nice family.'

"Then I turned into a blabbermouth again, their quiet daughter went off like an auctioneer. I jabbered on and on about you and how wonderful you were—until I noticed my parents looking at each other, winking.

"I shut up.

"That Sunday afternoon after church I wrote you that note. I started it ten times before I finally decided that it said what I wanted. I dropped it in your locker Monday morning, I couldn't bring myself to hand it to you."

"So how did you know where my locker was?" Tom asked.

"My locker was directly across the hall from yours our freshman year," Claire replied curtly.

"Oh."

"I guess I kept on talking about you and it was a month later when we were getting ready to put up the Christmas tree that mom suggested, 'Why don't you ask Master Bentley to come over and help us?'

"It took me a half hour before I got the nerve to call you. You know, back then girls *never* called boys. I just could not do it!

"And well, there you were. I was just beside myself—my dream, truly, had come true! To have you in my house, spending an afternoon with me, one on one, I had no words!

"I guess I made a good impression on your folks," Tom replied.

"You certainly did," Claire said. "I was an independent kid but my parents' approval meant something. I asked them after you left, 'Well, what do you think?'

"'I like him, he seems to be a fine young man,' my father said when I came back in from seeing you off. Mom nodded in agreement, 'He's sweet, he's a really nice boy, very polite.' That meant a lot."

"You know, I remember that first time we went to The Malt Shop together, you seemed very concerned about

228

people seeing us," Tom asked. "Were you worried it would get back to your folks?"

Claire slapped her forehead, leaned back, and laughed again.

"Oh no! Truth be told, I wanted people to see me with you!" she answered. "Look over there! Mousey Claire's sitting with the most popular guy in school! How did she pull *that* off? What does the big-man-on-campus see in *her*? He could hang out with any girl he wants!"

"It meant that much to you?"

"Yes."

She thought for a moment.

"Yes, yes it did. I idolized you, I wanted to show you off."

"Why didn't you tell me all this while we dated?"

"Why should I? I had you at last so it made no difference—or I thought I had you.

"But after fourteen years, I gave up. I waited and waited, I finally decided you would never be mine.

"Dadgummit, Claire, think! This has been silly, third grade!

"Here I was, graduating from college and still chasing some boy I saw in elementary school.

"That's crazy! By then, I had seen you three days in three years, and our parents had forced us apart for a year before that.

"It would never happen, I quit!"

"But the war wasn't my fault," Tom pleaded, "I was madly in love with you, I loved you as much as I thought you loved me."

"I knew that, or I thought I knew that," Claire replied, "but this whole thing became unrealistic, maybe I was wrong. Maybe Tom Bentley wasn't the guy for me. Maybe I should strike out on my own. Maybe I should live a different kind of life.

"And another thing: What future did I have back here in Randall? I knew you would take over Bentley Hardware someday and I would have to live the rest of my life stuck here in the Missouri boondocks.

"I was about to receive a bachelor's degree with a dual major, with highest honors, and what could I do in Randall? Get a job flipping burgers at The Malt Shop? What career?"

"You could do all kinds of things!" Tom replied brightly, spreading his arms. "Didn't you see that? When you got that law degree you could hang a shingle for your own practice, or maybe you could run for Limestone County's prosecuting attorney. Or, maybe you could run for the General Assembly, go up to Jeff City every year.

"And what about working for your dad? He had a whole gaggle of attorneys putting together his big deals."

Claire stared out the window, lost in thought.

"I guess so, but I didn't know what my father did," Claire replied. "He just got up every morning, he left, then came home that evening. I wasn't like you, he didn't involve me in his business. My father kept all that to himself."

"That's true," Tom agreed. "My dad had me unloading boxcars and taking inventory as soon as I could push a two-wheeler. But my point is, you could have had a career and you could have had me too."

"Don't be silly, women didn't do things like that in the '50s and '60s," Claire scoffed.

"Oh? But you are not just any woman," Tom said firmly. "You *are* a Dearborn, and you *would* have been a Bentley.

"Remember who we are: This town shoots fireworks on the Fourth in Dearborn Park. The softball and baseball teams play on the Bentley Fields behind the warehouse. Your brothers were war heroes and mine did their part.

"Every charity in town receives big donations every Christmas from our families. Bentley Hardware paid for the vo-tech wing at the high school.

"Everyone in Randall and Limestone County knows our names. They know we are fair, honest, hard-working, church-going people, we aren't out for personal gain.

"Don't discount yourself!" Tom added emphatically.

"And politics? I doubt if there has been a Republican candidate for a statewide office in Missouri in the last hundred years who didn't get a donation from the Dearborns, the Bentleys, or both. If you ran for office the whole party mechanism would have been behind you. You would have been a leader, an example to other women. They would have had printing presses cranking out Claire-Bentley-for-this-or-that yard signs and handbills for weeks.

Claire sat, listening. Now she was speechless. Why hadn't she thought of all this?

And what of that name?

Claire Bentley.

It rolled around in her head. It hadn't occurred to her in years.

"Go bigger," Tom told her. "You could have been Missouri's first woman governor or U.S. senator. You might have beat Jean Carnahan and Claire McCaskill to Washington by a decade."

Claire sat, staring blankly.

"I guess I didn't think things through after all," she agreed. "That's not like me.

"When I graduated from Columbia, all the talk concerned East Coast jobs: clerk for a Supreme Court justice, a junior position with some high-powered New York or Philadelphia firm. The class losers took corporate jobs out west, Pittsburgh or Buffalo.

"Nobody talked about other stuff, like going back to Missouri.

"I guess I was like what you said about Linda: You only know what you have seen. I never saw that. I saw attorneys—what I was about to be—as something to do with the East Coast and Washington."

"So let's back up," Tom replied with sarcasm. "Just how did you end up in New York in the first place?"

"It dropped in my lap," she replied.

"Here came spring 1953, I would graduate that summer. I had been plugging along in college and that was almost over. What next? I didn't know, and marriage was out with you gone.

"I went to Mizzou's counseling department and they made an appointment for me with some minister there in town. He came highly recommended, had worked with a lot of students, especially coeds.

"We had a good meeting in his study, very jovial, friendly, outgoing. He asked what I was good at, what do you like to do? He said I should write out a plan for my life—big picture stuff.

"Honestly, Tom, I didn't say anything about my boyfriend in the war. Somehow at that point I just figured you would fit in with, well, whatever.

"He suggested I apply for this women's scholarship to Columbia University's law school. He said I'd be great at law because I was so thoughtful and logical, plus I had a bachelor's coming in philosophy, a great background going into law.

"Now, that sounded different! That could be better than anything else I had.

"I applied, took the law school admissions test, passed easily and they made me an offer: A full ride— tuition, books, housing, everything paid—and I would be living in New York City for a couple years. What a deal!"

"That does sound pretty good," Tom agreed.

Claire wiped her brow.

"Exciting, I wanted it! This is where the decision came, my emotions took over, and I didn't think it through: What about Tom?" she said with a groan. "I had no idea when—if ever—you would be home. And if you did, you may not want some girl from backwater Missouri.

"Darn it, I had waited long enough! So I went over to Western Union and sent the foundation a telegram on a Friday afternoon. I took the offer.

"Three days day later, Monday, July 27, I heard a radio bulletin: a ceasefire had been signed. That meant you were coming home, finally, at last! But I had made a commitment.

"Oh God, please, what had I done?" she whispered, "Suddenly, everything went wrong. I wanted you *and* I wanted New York. But it had been so long and I still didn't have you. How much longer would it be—if ever?

"So I tried to rationalize things. Maybe you were a will-o'-the-wisp, just some crazy, silly dream. What did I have to show for the past three years but three days in Minneapolis? Nothing!

"I knew I had to try something else, I had to give myself a new dream."

"Why didn't you tell me?" Tom interrupted. "I would have backed you all the way. Dad had to go to New York several times a year on business, a trip he did not like. He would gladly have let me stay there instead and work for the company while you were in class. We could have lived our dream in New York. Imagine that!"

"I didn't think of that. In my mind it was either/or, law school or you. And, I didn't want it to sound like a Dear-John if I wrote and told you what I decided. I still thought the world of you. I knew you were sweet, you were kind, but maybe you weren't the guy for me.

"At that point I felt like I would never have you. Ah, but I *could* have law school!

"So, maybe I wasn't supposed to marry. I'm something of a loner, maybe I should live some different kind of life.

Tom twirled his cane and tapped it on the floor. Claire paused and wiped her eyes.

"Look, I'm sorry, I truly am, I know I handled it poorly," she added. "And my parents let me know it—boy, did they let me know it."

"Oh? What happened?" Tom asked, looking up.

Claire sighed and her eyes began to water again.

"My father and I were very close. He made me his special princess, he loved you because you loved me."

"That's not unusual, most daddies think of a daughter as a little princess. I thought of my daughter that way once," Tom said.

"Oh, our relationship turned into more than just a father-daughter thing, as nice as that is," Claire added as she sniffed and wiped her nose. "He literally saved my life."

Tom scowled.

"The fire?"

"Yes."

"You never told me what happened."

"I know, even now it's hard to talk about," she said, her voice shaking.

Claire sat for a moment, breathing deeply.

"I would have died had it not been for him. I was four years old, we lived in a big old house that looked a lot like your family's place. I had a bedroom upstairs, I woke up hot in the night.

"That seemed odd, it was late fall and cold outside. I smelled a funny odor and looked around and I could see smoke curling around on the ceiling. I called for mom but heard nothing.

"I kicked my covers off, sat up on the edge of my bed, stepped down and burned my foot on the floor. I screamed, still nothing.

"Little kid that I was, it terrified me. I could see smoke or vapor coming up off the floor, I guess the fire down below heated the varnish and it was cooking off."

"My, that's awful," Tom replied.

"I started screaming, 'Mommy! Daddy! God, help me!' and just then my father burst through the door, picked me up and went running out in the hall.

"Out there, the smoke was so thick I could hardly see. The flames were starting to burn through the stairs as he held onto the railing with one hand and me with the other. It was so hot I felt like we were in an oven. He tripped at the bottom of the stairs and nearly fell.

"He got us out of the house more by feel than anything. I coughed my little head off.

"We stumbled down the porch into the front yard and there stood mom, my brothers and the maid in the dark, on the sidewalk. I saw them lit in yellow by the flames as my father ran toward them.

"I turned around to look back at the house and I could see flames through my bedroom window, right where I had been a couple minutes before.

"That close to death, the worst night of my life."

Claire sobbed and dabbed her eyes.

"I don't need to tell you about the worst night in my life," Tom said bluntly.

Claire started crying.

"I guess not. Oh Tom, again, I'm sorry."

She wiped her eyes with a tissue and took a deep breath.

"It was all a mix-up. When my parents woke up and smelled smoke they panicked, mom thought dad would get me and dad thought mom would. Everyone else got out in the yard and of course they asked each other, 'Where's Claire?' My father, my wonderful father, ran into a burning house to save me.

"He held me, kissed me and hugged me out there in the dark as the firemen pulled up, there wasn't much they could do. We stood out there in the cold night in our pajamas watching that beautiful old house burn down. We lost everything, all that was left of our old home was that gazebo in the backyard.

"That was our gazebo, Tom."

"I can't imagine," Tom said. "I remember waking up that night when the fire trucks came roaring up Poplar."

"That's why my father and I became especially close," Claire said softly.

"Mom and I went up to St. Louis for nearly a year to live with my aunt. Dad and my brothers got a little apartment here in town so the boys could stay in school. After the trauma that night, I went something like six months before I saw my sweet father again. We came back that summer to visit him and my brothers. We drove over to see the crew building our new house, the one you knew.

"Dad made sure we had a new fireproof home: concrete block, one story, you could step out on the ground through a window from any room.

"I remember dad standing there watching the masons put up the walls, shaking his head saying, 'never again, never again.' Then he hugged me."

"So I take it your relationship became, well, strained, when you went to law school?" Tom asked.

"The worst—the worst—argument we ever had came the night he drove me to catch the train to New York. We had to go over to Springfield, the train stopped there at something like two in the morning.

"He kept after me: 'What about Tom? I'm happy for you, I'm proud of you, this is wonderful, but you have to tell him something. You need him, sweetheart, you two can work something out.'

"He knew I hadn't said anything to you because, like I said, I didn't know what to say.

"I finally snapped and yelled at him, 'I'll do this my way!'

"I don't think any of we three kids had ever yelled at him. It shocked him, he was terribly hurt. Here was his princess, the little girl he snatched from death, talking back!

"He pulled over on the shoulder of the highway and we sat there for a few minutes with the engine idling in the middle of the night. He finally put the car in gear and we drove on in silence.

"Why did I do that? I don't know," Claire continued. "Why didn't I listen to him?

"My father, the most intelligent and insightful person I have ever known, he was a blessing. He had that peculiar gift for seeing the future, how things will work out—in business and in life.

238

"He knew I should have you, whatever I did with my life, you should be a part of it. 'You two complement each other,' he told me more than once.

"When we got to the Springfield station I got out, I got my luggage out of the trunk and I slammed the car door and stomped off. I didn't even tell him good-bye."

"Claire, I…" Tom said, shaking his head.

"We didn't patch things up for weeks. I was fed up waiting for you, mad at my parents and bitter. I had this big chance—my big opportunity—and no one cared.

"I had all these stupid daydreams for all those years and what did I have to show for them? Zilch! Nothing! Nada!

"I thought: 'Watch me, people, I'll prove myself! I'll do this *without* you!'" Claire shouted, waving her hand. Then she sighed. "And I did, but I did it alone. I didn't have anyone to share it with.

"It wasn't until that February that my parents called, person to person. I hadn't bothered to write them, much less you. We started to work things out on a pay phone out in the hall across from my apartment. My father told me you called from the station that night and how you came over for breakfast the next morning. Well, that pricked my conscience. It finally hit me what I'd done, how foolish I was. I treated you very badly.

"Then mom came on the line and told me that you had planned to propose on Christmas Eve, right there, in front of the tree. You were home, you had the ring, you and my father had talked, everything was ready—except for me."

Claire stopped and started crying. She pulled a handkerchief out of her pocket and wiped her eyes.

"What had I done?

"I went into hysterics right there, crying my eyes out. People opened their doors and stared, what's going on out there? Fourteen years, I came so near and yet ended up so far. Everything I had dreamed of was there—right there—and I messed it up.

"Me! The thinker, the planner, and yes, the sometime-schemer, and I lost it all!

"I lived with three other girls near campus in Morningside Heights. They made a fuss, trying to comfort me. I finally got ahold of myself and I started a letter to you that night but I never could find the right words, it sat on my desk for months. I never mailed it. I knew I should have and the longer I waited, the worse things were. So, I did nothing."

Claire sobbed more and blew her nose. Tom felt his anger turn to pity.

"I don't want to talk anymore," Claire said through sniffs. "Can you take me back to my suite?"

"Uh, you can't push yourself?

"No, I had a stroke three years ago, my left arm is nearly useless. I can't walk, I can barely stand, just enough to go to the bathroom.

"I lost my voice too and couldn't speak. I had a voice coach come in and work with me for weeks. I finally got to where I can talk again, except for this lisp. I hope it doesn't bother you."

"Not at all."

Tom sat for a moment then got up.

"Well, I guess I can push you back. Here, hold my cane."

He laid his cane across Claire's lap and off they slowly went down the hall and across the dayroom.

How odd, he thought as he pushed her along, his beautiful girl had become a crippled old woman yet here they were, together again. Was it by chance, by God's intervention or Claire's scheming?

He didn't know.

Neither said anything as Suite C 4 rolled into sight. He turned and wheeled Claire slowly through her door and stopped in front of her sofa.

"Thank you, I'll be fine now," she said looking back at him as she handed him his cane. "Can you come by tomorrow? Maybe we can talk some more?"

"Sure, maybe after Gaylene's worship service?" he replied.

"Oh! Have you met her?" Claire said, brightening. "Ha! What a character, she bounces all the time."

"I guess so, let's try to meet then."

Chapter 16
Who Am I?

The usual crowd assembled in the dayroom Sunday after Hickory Bough's biggest meal of the week for the chaplain's service. Josefina pushed Claire in and set her brake.

A women's trio from Gaylene's Hartville congregation sang a couple hymns, accompanied by a guitar. Gaylene gave a devotion on "How do you know when you are blessed?" There were prayers at the end, another hymn and the little crowd broke up.

"Coming over?" Claire asked pleasantly, looking up at Tom as he walked by.

"Sure," he said, handing her his cane.

"An interesting topic," Tom added as he slowly pushed her along through the dispersing crowd. One nice thing about pushing Claire, he thought: He could enjoy looking down at that still-beautiful hair. She kept it in a bun but it made him think of the young Claire, back when. Even at eighty, she had beautiful hair.

"She had a good point that even when you're having problems and things don't go well, you can be in God's will. Have the two of us been blessed and we didn't know it?" Tom asked.

"That's hard to remember sometimes," Claire agreed. "I certainly didn't feel very blessed those first months in New York."

"What can I say?" Tom answered.

"You can't say anything, my problem.

"Here I had this fabulous blessing, a great opportunity, a free ride to an Ivy League law school, and I ended up depressed, unhappy and bitter."

They turned into C 4, Tom parked the wheelchair and sat down on the sofa across from her, then looked around. He noticed someone had helped Claire decorate her "suite." Identical to his, the room had the same gray paint and blue curtains.

But Claire had made it her own.

There were lots of photos, some faded, on the walls of vacation trips. A youngish Claire stood at the Queen Victoria monument in front of Buckingham Palace, a middle-aged Claire and two lady friends posed before the Grand Canyon, a thirtysomething Claire laughed as she threw a coin over her shoulder into Rome's Trevi Fountain.

A dozen or so photos of nieces and nephews had been nicely arranged above the bed.

Tom admired the stopper, hung across from the sofa: A large, professionally framed, black-and-white of a fortyish Claire in her judicial robe with a Supreme Court justice, he couldn't remember the name, beside President Nixon in the Oval Office. Her smiling parents, older than Tom remembered them, stood on the other side of the President. Jewel held a Bible.

"Wow," he muttered in awe.

Another photo had a smiling group of judges in their robes gathered around President Carter. Tom had to look to pick out Claire in the back row. A gavel mounted on a wooden base with a brass plaque sat on her dresser.

But there were none of him. Tom bit his lip as he thought back to that day in Claire's bedroom, helping her pack for college, when every photo in the room had him in it.

A splendid view out her window also caught his eye. Claire's room looked out on Hickory Bough's little garden and beyond to woods in the distance. He saw no loading dock, no air conditioner, nor dumpster.

"Anyway, as you were saying the other day?" Tom asked.

"Oh my, so many years, what to tell? I clerked for Justice Whittaker on the Supreme Court in Washington. He came from Missouri, a Republican. I'm sure my name helped—back to what you said about being a Dearborn.

"From there I went to the Department of Justice, Eisenhower was in office, another Republican, that's how I got the appointment. I managed to lie low and keep my position while Kennedy and Johnson were in office, then I moved up to a deputy's office when Nixon gave me a higher appointment."

Tom nodded. "Washington is a long ways from Randall."

"Yes, it is. It's a unique place, very much a small town, though. In some ways it's more of a small town than Randall. But it's big-city with just the best of everything. It's all about who you know and what parties and receptions you get invited to, lots of gossip.

"After you have lived there you figure out that most of what we call 'news' just amounts to Washington gossip. People who live there think Washington is the center of everything—it's all about them."

"And there weren't any eligible young men in our nation's capital interested in a beautiful, well-educated attorney?" Tom asked.

"Oh, I guess over time I thought about it, you know I always think about everything. I decided I would stay single, I was not looking anymore. Washington had lots of single, professional women as role models and that's what I decided I wanted to be."

"Nobody interested you?"

Claire sat silently, looking out the window at the sunny afternoon. She sighed and answered, "Only one."

"I told you about Linda, tell me about him."

She shook her head and looked at her lap.

"It was the other great mistake of my life; Bert Trottel. It's hard to talk about all that."

Claire dabbed at her eyes with a Kleenex and took a deep sigh.

"Why?" Tom asked quietly.

"If your Linda was everything I'm not, then Bert was everything you're not. He was a liar, a cheat and a crook."

"Uh, can you explain that?"

"Oh! He was so tall, so handsome, so smooth, so debonair, so suave. Any woman would want to be seen with him," Claire paused and bit her lip. "Clark Gable didn't have anything on Bert.

"You know, it's one thing when a sweet, sincere boy you have known and admired for years, who you go to church with, and who your parents adore, says 'You look gorgeous!' It's quite another when some total stranger in a custom-tailored, Italian suit with a silk pocket hanky, too much Brylcreem in his wavy hair and a crooked smile swaggers up to you at happy hour, holding a martini, and says, 'You look gorgeous!'

"But he did, and I fell for him, I just went over the cliff. The ever-thoughtful Claire let her emotions take over."

"When did this happen?" Tom asked.

"We met at a congressional cocktail reception just before Christmas 1970. He was a bigshot lawyer from Cleveland. If you wanted a charter for a new bank, or you had business with the Federal Reserve, especially in the Midwest, call him.

"Other guys that smooth, that fake, that smarmy, made passes at me but they turned me off. But not this time, not smooth Bert. I just went crazy.

"There I stood in my little black dress, holding a plate of hors d'oeuvres and my usual Moscato. They had the reception in this swanky hotel ballroom. He walked up to me and just spread it on thick: 'Happy holidays! My, what a beautiful dress, you look gorgeous, you really do look great tonight. So, what do you do? Oh, that's fascinating! Tell me more!'

"He went on and on. Any other time a guy started talking that way I stomped off. They were pickup lines and, well, he picked me up. I gave him my business card.

"I guess I'd had a couple drinks and, frankly, even though I had decided to stay single, in the back of my head I had this scary thought floating around: 'You're coming up on forty, sweetie, and there's no man in your life: Spinster!'"

Tom sat quietly listening, stroking his moustache.

"I knew people started making assumptions about me. You think she likes girls? Do you ever see her with a man? She must be into women's lib, a bra burner, probably has a dyke girlfriend we don't know about.

"Remember, in the early '70s things were changing."

"So then?" Tom asked.

"He would not let go, Bert wooed me bigtime. He sent huge bouquets of flowers to my office for no reason. I got a singing telegram by a barbershop quartet on Valentine's Day. The four of them stood there wearing straw boaters and old-timey, plaid suits with spats on their shoes, harmonizing: '*A pretty girl, is like a melody, that haunts you night and daaaay...*' Don't you know that livened up the office?

"He asked me out, then made it a point to pick me up on Tenth Street at the Justice Department where I worked, just after five o'clock, in this unreal beautiful De Tomaso Pantera, just as everyone walked out of the building.

"I'd climb in his hot car, he'd idle up to Pennsylvania Avenue and wait for a hole in the traffic. Then he'd turn right, screech the tires, and VROOM!, up the street toward the Capitol.

"I could tell the gossip turned: 'Did you see that guy who picked up Claire? Wow!'

"We would go to dinner at some expensive restaurant, the maître 'd would greet Bert by name and seat us. The waiter and the wine steward, same thing: 'Good evening, Bert.' He would order in French.

"Then I'd be sipping some nice Moscato, waiting for my soup, and he'd lean over and whisper things like, 'I saw Pat Nixon sitting in your chair last week.'

"He had season tickets to the Washington Senators, right behind home plate, and the opera. He just fawned over me. Looking back, it felt slimy, but I ate it up. I could not, or would not, see through it.

"The summer of 1971, he invited me on short notice to go with him to his chateau in France for a week. I had to quickly shuffle things around to get off, but who could pass up that?"

"Sounds nice," Tom replied.

"I thought my family had money, but Bert had serious money. We flew first class on Pan Am to Paris aboard one of those brand-new 747s. That was just the best there was.

"He kept this Simca sports car at a hotel's garage out near Orly Airport and off we drove, south through the French countryside. We stopped and bought baguettes, cheese and a bottle of Burgundy, then had a picnic under the trees.

"Oh, so romantic! I'm surprised he didn't pay some guy with a beret and an accordion to show up.

"Then we drove on to this castle he owned, surrounded by manicured gardens and big fountains. It was all dreamlike: Me, the skinny, quiet, wallflower from Podunk, staying in a chateau surrounded by vineyards and beautiful woods owned by a filthy rich, big-time attorney? Oh my, I'd won the prize!"

"Claire, you were no wallflower," Tom interrupted.

"Whatever, but it excited me, maybe I really had made a catch! I wanted to live like that.

"My father, who had that knack for seeing where things will go, waved the first red flag. He and mom flew to Washington for my birthday right after we got back from France. The four of us went to dinner and Bert, naturally, buttered up my parents. He had done his research on dad and went on about how great his banks and businesses were.

"Mom sat there with stars in her eyes, absolutely smitten.

"We got back to my apartment and I sat down with my parents after we took off our coats and shoes. I sprawled across the couch and asked, 'Well, what do you think?'

"My father scowled. 'Be careful, my dear, be careful. There may be more here than you can see. Don't rush into anything,' he said, shaking his finger at me.

"At least he didn't mention you. Even after all those years I was scared he would start up: 'He may be nice but he's no Tom Bentley. You could've had Tom Bentley!'

"He put the first doubt in my mind, was Bert for real?"

"So did you rush into anything?" Tom asked. "Was there quid pro quo?"

Claire hung her head shamefully.

"Oh, Tom, please! Don't put it that way," Claire said, sniffing loudly. "Of course there was, I'm embarrassed by the whole thing."

"No judgements, we all make mistakes. Judge not lest ye be judged," Tom said softly.

"Thank you."

Claire started sobbing.

"Why? Why? I'm the smart one, I think things through, I'm logical, so why? Obviously, Bert was too good to be true."

She wiped her eyes and took a deep breath.

"Anyway, another big change came because of him. We were having yet another fancy dinner that fall, sitting there sipping some expensive champagne, when Bert leaned over and whispered, 'Have you ever wanted to be a judge?' I said something like 'Sure, of course!' I was a pretty good government attorney, I could handle myself in court, that would be a step up.

"I gained self confidence in law school. I learned how to stand up in front of people and state my case. You have to know how to do that when you're talking to a judge or jury.

"I'm glad of that," Tom answered. "Sometimes it amazed me how little self-confidence you had, like when you gave that shaky valedictorian's speech.

"There you were, a beautiful girl, you were poised, you had impeccable taste, you set the curve for the whole class, and you had a prosperous and successful family."

Claire nodded.

"Frankly, that might have been my problem all along," she said, shaking her head. "Who am I?

"Everyone in my family did well, could I measure up? My father: successful businessman. My mother: social leader. My brothers: tops in school, war heroes and business leaders too.

"And me? What could I do? I saw myself as a nobody. They did great, but what about me? Maybe that's why I wanted you, maybe that's why I wanted Bert."

"Nobody? Not at all, I think your life proved you a leader, not an also-ran," Tom said firmly.

"I guess you're right," she added, "and what happened next certainly gave me an ego boost.

"A few months later, early 1972, I got the call from a White House staffer. The President planned to nominate me to fill a federal judgeship in Dayton, Ohio. I nearly fell out of my chair. Bert knew who to call—and when."

"Sounds wonderful," Tom said, shaking his head.

Claire sighed. "No, that's when things started to fall apart.

"Bert planned a quid pro quo that, thank the Lord, I did not have to meet. The Judiciary Committee had approved me, I waited for a full Senate vote. It was expected to be automatic but then, Bang!, Watergate happened and Washington went nuts. That slowed everything down, which proved good for me.

"The Democrats controlled the Senate and I was afraid my nomination would get tabled since I'm a Republican. It did get delayed but the Senate approved my nomination anyway a few weeks later.

"Congratulations," Tom sad quietly. "I recall the Randall paper had a big story and your photo."

Claire sighed. "Thank you, but Watergate delayed things and helped me avoid a tragedy that summer."

"How's that?" he asked.

"It was one of those strange things, God's intervention, I guess," she answered with a far-off look out the window.

"I had been in meetings all morning to wrap up things with my staff before the move. I needed some coffee so I walked down the hall to the breakroom and sat down at the table. We always had a pile of magazines and newspapers there, we were all big readers. I was thumbing through the pile absentmindedly and I found a copy of the Canton, Ohio, newspaper from a few days earlier.

"Now, how did that get here? No one in the office came from eastern Ohio and I didn't know of any recent visitors we had from there. Puzzled, I picked it up and thumbed through it. And there, on page six, I saw the headline: 'Famed Cleveland Lawyer In Divorce Battle.'"

"Uh, divorce?" asked Tom, mystified.

"Yes, my Bert was married."

"And you didn't know?"

"Of course not! I got physically ill, I threw up there in the breakroom floor, vomit everywhere, spilled my coffee.

"Some of my staff rushed in and helped clean up the mess, the secretaries and paralegals all giggled about nerves over my new job. Thankfully, I grabbed the paper and snuck it back to my office before anyone saw it. They all knew about us, the flowers and the fancy car.

"I closed my office door and called his private number in Cleveland and got him on the first ring. I could scarcely breathe but I hissed, 'So you have a wife?'"

Tom squirmed on the sofa.

"Oh, smooth as ever! 'My dear Claire! Now, now, don't you believe everything you read in the papers! I'll be in Washington in a few days and I'll explain all this, don't worry about a thing. You just decide where and we'll have a lovely dinner.' And he hung up."

Claire paused and took a deep breath.

"I never heard from him again."

"Good riddance," agreed Tom.

"Yes, and as the trial went along it all came out, this was back when divorces weren't automatic.

"Talk about a bitter and spiteful wife—a woman scorned—this was the divorce from hell. She had saved it all up and spilled everything: Bert worked for the mob. That got the attention of the FBI and district attorney.

"He did legit bank lawyering as a cover. Among other things, his wife testified he had multiple mistresses in New York, Chicago and, yes, Washington. And well, that's alienation of affection in a divorce case.

"There were indictments, a big criminal trial, and the jury convicted him on multiple counts—wire fraud, conspiracy, accessory to murder, money laundering, tax evasion, sex trafficking—after one afternoon of deliberations. They threw the book at him, I forget how many years he got.

"They found Bert dead in that prison for white-collar criminals in Seagoville, outside Dallas, all very mysterious. Seagoville's low security, a country-club prison for wealthy, first-timers. That made it easy for someone, somehow, to snuff him; easy in and out. That's my opinion, anyway.

"I figure someone thought he'd sung to the FBI—knowing him he probably had—to cut his sentence or to get a better place to do time. Typical Bert, me first.

"And I have to point out, the Washington mistress was *not* me, Tom," Claire said emphatically.

"I, uh, wasn't going to ask," Tom mumbled as he blushed.

"Turned out silly Claire was one of multiple women he used. He had a big prize, some French gal, Oui! Oui!, set up in a penthouse apartment at, where else?, the Watergate to, how shall I say?, entertain clients—and himself. She had a new Mercedes convertible and open accounts at the best boutiques in Georgetown.

"And me? Dinner and baseball! I didn't know how to play the game because I didn't know there was a game.

"I could have worked him for my own fancy apartment or a hot car to replace my banged-up Datsun—if I were that kind of woman.

"Innocently, I thought him sincere. He must love me, like I love him."

"You loved him?" Tom asked.

Claire thought for a moment.

"No, 'crush' might be a better word. The whole thing afterward left me sick, disgusted with myself. He targeted me: How can I use this hick chick? He wanted to put me in reserve for when he needed help with some deal gone bad.

"Thinking back, I suspect the trip to France came after he and a main squeeze had a fight and she told him to get lost. It was all too quick, 'Who else could I get? Hey, what about Claire? The dumb thing won't know the difference.'

Tom sat with a blank stare.

"C'mon, is this real? This sounds like some potboiler novel," he asked.

"I wish it were.

"And see the other something-for-something? I realized that here I was, a rookie federal judge. The Midwest was Bert's turf. Think about it, it would have been very handy for a mobster in trouble to have a young, inexperienced judge who owed you her job. Some legal problem comes up, you steer the case her way and, Presto!, not guilty.

"For the first year after all this I literally was scared for my life. Was one of his hit men going to take me out? Did the mob think I knew something? It left me petrified.

"And what if I were called to testify at his criminal trial? But I was such a small fish I never got a subpoena."

Tom leaned over and shook his head. "I don't know what to say, I never heard about any of this."

"Of course not! Remember, the press went insane over Watergate and they threw Bert in the can before Nixon resigned. There were lots of other stories that never made it on the evening news."

The two said quietly looking at each other for several minutes, the TVs hummed down the hall.

The afternoon had gone fast and the bright sunshine had turned to a beautiful sunset out Claire's window. Josefina worked the C Hall, pushing the meal cart, and stuck her head in the room and asked, "Are you ready for the dinner, Judge Dearborn?"

She stepped back when she saw Tom on her sofa. "Oh, excuse me!"

"That's alright, sure, now would be fine," Claire replied. "Come in, come in."

"Well, I guess I better be running along, I eat in the dining room," Tom said as he took his cane.

"Oh no, please stay, please," Claire said, waving for him to sit. "Do you have anything for Mr. Bentley, he lives on B Hall?" she asked.

"Of course, ma'am, no problem. Mr. Bentley and I, we are amigos! I'll bring a meal but it will take a few minutes," Josefina replied.

"That's fine, Josefina, I eat too much anyway," Tom said. "Thanks."

The nurse brought in Claire's meal on a tray that snapped onto the wheelchair's armrests. Claire thanked her and took the plastic cover off the plate.

"Oh boy, dining at Hickory Bough: high adventure," she said with her odd smile. "At least my right arm still works or I guess they'd feed me through a tube."

"So why are you back here instead of Ohio or Washington or someplace?" Tom asked.

Claire swallowed, then pointed at her plate with her fork.

"Because I did too much of this, I put on a lot of weight, a lot of weight. I guess I look like a stuffed sausage to you but I'm actually down.

"Why can't I be like I was in high school? We'd go to The Malt Shop once or twice a week and I'd knock off a burger, fries, and shake—no problem! I still had that glorious, slim figure."

257

"Oh my, it was," Tom said with a distant look.

"And now? A nurse walks by my room eating a donut and I put on two pounds."

Tom laughed.

"I know that's right, I have to fight my weight too."

"I didn't watch my diet and I sat around all the time," she continued. "You don't get much exercise reading legal briefs and it caught up with me. It didn't help that I was knocking off two packs a day of Virginia Slims as I read. I had a couple of little strokes, warning shots, at least I stopped smoking.

"Then the big one. As usual, I had to huff and puff up the stairs when I went to bed, when all of a sudden…."

Claire sat quietly.

"Thankfully, I had my phone in my pocket, I called 911, and mumbled for help. The ambulance crew had to break down the door.

"I loved Hyde Park in Cincinnati, where I retired, but I couldn't live alone anymore so I sold my condo and moved to St. Louis to be near my brothers' kids. Gus and Bruce passed away a few years ago.

"But it didn't work. A year ago my nephew suggested I come back to Randall to live with Gus's daughter and her husband. They own my folks' house now.

"She's very sweet but, hey, Marty's in her sixties and couldn't keep up with an invalid aunt so we decided I should do some kind of assisted living.

"Here I am."

Chapter 17
Maybe and Thank You

A pleasant Sunday afternoon had dissolved into a chilly, clear evening.

"Well, enough about me! Tell me about your life. Can you describe how you came back to Randall, ran a business, had a happy marriage, everything sweetness and light?" Claire asked as she ate.

"Did you live out our dream? Did you have what I could have had, what I could have done, if I had just mailed you that letter?"

Tom shook his head.

"I can't say that," he answered.

Now Tom teared up.

He lifted his glasses and wiped his eyes. Claire stopped chewing, put down her fork and looked intently at him.

"What's wrong?" she asked, concerned.

Tom laid down his cane, clasped his hands and bent over for a moment. He looked back at Claire with tears running down his cheeks.

"I am an alcoholic."

Claire gasped.

"You? A good Baptist like you? I never saw you take a drink!"

"Well, you haven't seen me in sixty years, and I don't know how good a Baptist I ever was," he replied. "I didn't drink until I went in the Army. We had some officer parties that got a little, well, out of hand sometimes, thanks

259

to ample libations. But I never did anything serious until I got home," he answered, wiping his eyes.

"Oh no, after I disappeared," Claire said, wiping her mouth with her napkin. "I guess I messed things up more than I know."

"No, no, it's all my fault. There is this thing called self-control—and I lost mine."

"Oh Tom, that's awful," she replied, eyebrows furrowing.

"Early 1954, I just moped around that spring, working for dad at the warehouse. The Army let me finish my commitment in the reserves. So, my military career came to an end. You were gone, most of my Randall friends were gone, or married with their own families. Everything, together, left me empty.

"My folks bought their first television that spring and I sat around and watched TV—*Romper Room, Milton Berle, Howdy Doody, I Love Lucy*—when I wasn't doing odd work at the warehouse. I stopped looking up people or going out, I stopped going to church, I just turned into a recluse.

"Nowadays, people would say I had PTSD, back then they said you were 'shell shocked.' Whatever, it's the same thing. Getting out of the Army caused a lot of stress. The military consumes you and when it ends, what do you have to fill it?

"And, well, you know now what I went through on the personal side."

"Yes," Claire whispered, staring at Tom.

"My dad finally gave me a talking-to one night. I had a typical pose: slumped on the sofa in the parlor, watching TV. He came in, turned it off, then pulled up a chair and sat down right in front of me. 'You need to get movin', snap out of it!' he said.

"We agreed I should go back to Mizzou and pick up where I left off after my freshman year. So I bought one of those little two-seat Nash Metropolitans to drive back and forth to school."

"I don't know what happened to my Studebaker, I guess my father sold it after I moved to New York," Claire replied.

"Well, I wasn't in the mood to ask," Tom said. "I avoided your parents, I know they avoided me. I had a lot of hurt and they were, frankly Claire, embarrassed."

"I understand. I worried you would show up at my father's funeral when he died, I know you and my father were pretty close. Oh, that would've been awkward!

"Mom moved to St. Louis to live with Gus after my father passed away, we had her service up there in 1990," Claire explained.

"Your father died while Linda was in ICU," Tom replied. "I sat in her hospital room reading the *Ledger's* big obituary. I missed lots of things about then, at home and around town," Tom added. "I pretty much lived at the hospital."

"Anyway, back to the subject at hand: There I was back on campus the summer of '54. I ran into some old pals from my freshman year who also had been in the war.

"We got together one night at one of the frat houses for a party and, for the first time in my life, I got totally polluted, just blotto, on-the-floor, passed-out drunk. I don't know how I got back to my dorm.

261

"Oh my, my head hurt the next morning, my mouth tasted like I'd licked a toilet but, you know, in a way it felt good! For a few hours I didn't think about my problems. So I did a lot more parties, I pulled some real benders. I'm a happy drunk, I laugh a lot."

Claire sat holding her fork, horrified. Just then Josefina came in with Tom's meal.

"Is this okay, Mr. Bentley?" she asked, placing the tray on the sofa next to him. She stood up, looked at the pained expressions on the old friends' faces, said a quick "Excuse me!" and hustled out.

Tom ignored the meal.

"It went down from there and my grades showed it. I had straight A's my freshman year, before the Army, but I barely managed a two-point that summer, pretty poor for a kid who came out of high school cum laude, and at the top of his officer class. I got put on dean's probation one semester, things were so bad."

Claire took another bite.

"So you had problems too?"

"What's the old saying? 'He started drinking to drown his problems, and his problems learned to swim?' That was me.

"I came home the summer I graduated, '57, and went to work fulltime for dad. He made me vice president of sales, about the worst thing he could do. I lived at home and I knew I couldn't get away with drinking there, so I thought about moving out, getting my own place.

"But hey, the company had me on the road half the time and every hotel has a bar. I just made sure I had a separate bar tab I paid out of my own pocket so the booze didn't show up on expense reports."

"So your parents didn't know?" Claire asked.

"Oh, they knew, at least dad knew," Tom said, shaking his head. "I'm confident some customers made comments, a smart guy like him could figure it out. I started sneaking out to my car to get a drink, I kept a bottle behind the seat.

"But the hangovers? Oh, it showed. I got to work late, I forgot to file reports and attend meetings, I got irritable, I chewed out employees for nothing, I turned into a mess. That made me depressed, so I drank more."

"How long did this go on?"

"Too long," Tom replied, shaking his head. "There came a time when, as alcoholics put it, 'the whiskey turned on me.' It stopped being fun but I had been hooked, I had to drink.

"It came to a head one night in early 1959. I forgot something at the office and decided to drive over and pick it up so I could do some work. And of course, I could get a shot out in the car. I got in, reached around and took a swig, one for the road! I hid the bottle and backed out. But I knocked off the sideview mirror on the garage's door frame.

"Oh well, I could explain that. I turned out on Poplar and started down the hill through the curve, you know it. I had done that a thousand times. But I was so groggy, so woozy, I forgot to turn and drove smack into one of those big oak trees.

"BLAM!" he added, slapping his hands.

"Oh, Tom, were you hurt?" Claire asked, hanging on what Tom said.

"Blood everywhere, I banged my head on the steering wheel, broke my nose and cut my face pretty bad. And, I totaled the car.

"I just sat there not knowing what to do when a cop pulled up. He knew me, knew who I was, so he said 'Come with me' and stuck me in the back of his squad car with a towel over my bloody face.

"He took me to the police station and into an interrogation room. One of the other cops got out some iodine and bandages and patched me up as best he could. But I had blood all over my clothes.

"I heard the policeman who brought in me talking on the phone in the next room: 'Mr. Bentley, we have your son here at the station, you better come right over.'

"Can you imagine what the cops would have done nowadays? Things were different then. Because I was a Bentley, I got a pass, no charges, nothing on my license."

"Did your dad chew you out? He could be pretty blunt," Claire said.

"Not right then. I don't think it took him five minutes to get there, he must've run to his car. I could see the street out a window and his big Imperial screeched to a stop in front of the station, parked in front of a fire plug, and he ran up the steps. Dad told the cops thanks, helped me into his car and we drove home.

"We said not a word.

"I don't remember anything else from that night but I woke up in my bed the next morning. And there, in the bed beside me, he had put the broken mirror. My head hurt, I knew I was in trouble, I didn't want to get out of bed."

"So?"

"They came to me, I didn't have to get up. About that time my dad, my mom and both of my brothers came in my bedroom, brought in chairs and sat down around my bed.

I thought, 'Here it comes,' and it did. It was a firing squad.

"Dad glowered at me, as mad I ever saw him, red in the face, and said quietly, 'This has got to stop! I gave you some rope and now you hang yourself. If I ever catch you drinking again I will throw you out of this house bodily and fire you from the company.

"So help me God, I mean it!'

"I never heard my God-fearing dad swear before or after that moment. He went on: 'No son of mine is going to be a booze hound, you know better. You've had a rough time, you've had heartbreaks, but it ends here, *now*!' he shouted."

"And I caused it all," Claire said, putting down her fork.

"No, that's not true," Tom said firmly. "Like I said, I lost *my* self-control. Okay, you hurt me. But I bought the booze, I took the drinks. I drove drunk."

"So you stopped?"

"Yeah, dad sent me to this drying-out clinic in St. Louis to sober up. It worked. I saw how miserable some of the other fellows were. All I had lost was a car, some of them had major scrapes with the law. One hit a pedestrian and put some old lady in the hospital.

265

"Others lost wives, children, families and jobs, all for a drink—and I heard what my father had threatened, and I knew he'd do it.

"No, I didn't want that for me.

"I came home and joined A-A and did their twelve-step. Boy, it was tough to get up in those meetings and say, 'I'm Tom and I am an alcoholic.' But I did it.

"And, it was pretty hard for a Bentley to be anonymous in Randall, don't you know? I had to make the call once or twice but I quit. I was done.

"I watched one of Billy Graham's crusades on TV one night and he said something that hit me: 'God is in control. He may not take away trials or make detours for us, but He strengthens us through them.'

"That's the twelfth step: a spiritual awakening. That night I got down on my knees in my bedroom, my parents were out someplace, and I cried out, 'Jesus, help me! I don't want to live like this! The Bible says you can give me a hope and a future. Please help me, I want that!'"

"And?" Claire asked.

"God answers prayer. I have never been drunk since and scarcely had a drink. And maybe just to remind me of what God saved me from, the bark on that tree's still messed up after all these years. The scar jumps out at me every time I go down Poplar: Remember, Tom, remember!

"But you know what? Just a few weeks later Linda showed up. And from a career standpoint, I earned my CPA a year later, I turned it around. I stayed in A-A and helped several other guys drop the bottle."

"I'm happy for you," she said. "Did Linda know?"

"Yes, I told her."

266

The old couple sat quietly for a moment.

"May I ask you something?," Tom said. "Given the bad things, the difficulties that happened, was it a mistake? Should you have turned down the scholarship?"

Claire rested her cheek on her hand, took a deep breath and thought for a moment.

"No, I can't say that," Claire replied, staring off. "I know what you want me to say, but I can't.

"We haven't talked about the good things I did. People came through my court who had been seriously hurt and I brought them justice. I purposed to be fair and consistent, that got some notice. I had a reputation as an originalist. What does the law say? What's the case law, the precedent? Then let's do that, be fair!

"President Reagan appointed me to the Sixth Circuit in 1982 so I moved down to Cincinnati. The appeals court gave me the opportunity to handle some big-picture cases and make some big-picture decisions. I like to think I had a positive impact on this country."

Claire nervously shifted in her wheel chair.

"Did I miss you? Yes, of course. I've missed you, Tom, for sixty years, I truly have.

"Did I miss Randall? I think so. But it's like Gaylene's sermon: How do you know when you're blessed? And you know me, I always have been something of a loner.

"My life proved difficult and there were empty evenings, but I had the opportunity to do great things. I had the opportunity to help people who needed help—and bring justice to bad people who deserved it."

"I'm sure you did," Tom interrupted. "I can see you as a judge, you must have been a good one. You're thoughtful and studious. In high school you'd spend the afternoon thinking about whether we should go to a show at the Rialto."

"Yes, that's true," Claire answered.

"When President Bush had to replace Justice Marshall in 1991, my name came up on the shortlist sent to the President. I clearly remember getting the call.

"Me? On the Supreme Court? I could not have dreamed that! Just to be mentioned for an honor like that— no, I couldn't dream it.

"It didn't happen, of course," she added with a sigh. "When I heard Clarence Thomas made the list too I figured he would get the nod. He's a good man and a good judge. It disgusted me, the horrible things said about him but I'm glad he persevered."

Claire sat up angrily and leaned forward toward Tom.

"And you know what? I hate to think what would have been said about me in those hearings if the President had chosen me: Judge Dearborn—girlfriend of a dead mobster!

"Well, yes, I guess in a way I was. But I was innocent, I knew nothing of his shady dealings until I read that story in the paper.

"But would that have made any difference? No! What could they have made up based on hearsay, rumors, innuendos?

"Who else did she entertain—and how? What crooked deals did she pull?

268

"Did some of Bert's dirty money end up in her purse? Who did she give a slap on the wrist to in her court for a bigtime felony? Does she still work for the mob? Who else did she sleep with—and why?

"Don't you know they would've found someone, somewhere who vaguely, maybe, sort of, possibly, remembered something awful about me?

"Oh, they could have made me sound terrible!

"Tom, I could not cope, I would have broken down right there in front of the senators on national television and cried—or screamed —at them! Lies! Lies!

"I'm glad they chose him and not me," she added, sitting back. "I couldn't do it."

The pair sat and stared at each other. Tom looked into her blue-but-dull eyes. Claire looked at the friendly, oversize brown eyes magnified by Tom's glasses, above the gray moustache.

The moustache, when did he grow it? Was it something he did for Linda?

She liked it.

"We both made mistakes but we overcame them," Claire said with a heavy sigh. "We both lived good, upright lives and God forgave us when we did wrong; forgiveness. We did what was right as best we could, where we were."

They sat for a moment, looking at each other.

"I'm sorry it didn't work out," Tom answered.

"Me too," she added with a weak smile.

"Life doesn't turn out the way we think, what we just knew is going to happen. We were so young, so innocent, we were just kids," he said.

Tom paused.

"We never made it to Springfield, we never had our own home, we never lived our dream."

Claire smiled painfully.

"So what do we do now?" Tom asked. "Should we try again?"

He watched the eyebrows furrow, like they always did when she got serious and thought deeply.

"No."

She sighed.

"Can we just be friends? Can we just be two old friends who share some pleasant memories?" Claire answered.

"I guess so. Neither of us will be around much longer, we know that," Tom replied. Noisy Nancy came to mind.

He took his cane, stood up from the sofa and stepped over to Claire. He bent over and kissed her cheek for the first time in sixty years.

He smelled cinnamon again.

Claire reached up and squeezed his arm.

"Thank you," she said quietly.

She leaned her head on his arm for a moment, then looked up with her half smile.

"Good-bye," Tom answered as he walked toward the door.

His dinner sat on the sofa.

He turned into the hall, stopped, sighed deeply, then slowly shuffled back toward his room, his cane tapping along.

It was over.

Again.

Claire and Tom, the Glamour Couple of 1949, "an item" at Randall High so long ago, two really good kids, two crazy lovebirds who daydreamed of a shared life, teens who blended two families into one, were done.

Again.

Finished.

"It began with 'maybe' and ended with 'thank you,'" he thought.

He still had Tom Junior, he still had Judy, he had Chad and Hannah: "my kids." He once had Linda—and still had her beautiful memory—and maybe someday he would have Brenda again.

He would go on.

And what did Claire have?

He did not know and, frankly, he did not care; not his problem.

She had her chance, twice.

Someday Tony would come by and find B 9's door locked. But he had good people in his life until then.

Chapter 18
The Drive

The bad winter finally started to thaw. The sun came out for a few days, the snow melted, and Tom Junior finally took that promised day off to spend time with his dad on a drive.

Just the two buds, father and son, together again like those long-ago Scout campouts.

The countryside remained winter brown but the drive made for a treat. The only times Tom had been out of Hickory Bough since the move were a couple of doctor visits via the home's van. A doctor's appointment is never a treat.

Tom swung by, picked up his dad in a brand-new Lexus, and the pair headed out, away from Randall.

"You traded cars?" he asked.

"You bet, Pop, isn't this nice?" replied Tom Junior.

"I like to smell leather, but why does it have a TV in the dash?" the father asked.

"It's not a TV, it's a computer. It does route maps, controls the radio and A/C, all kinds of stuff."

Tom adjusted his glasses and peered at the highway map scrolling along as they drove.

"My oh my, what'll they think of next?" the father asked. The nifty gadget beat the drab countryside going by his window.

They wound through Mark Twain National Forest, crossed the state line, and after an hour or so stopped at a little burger joint in some out-of-the-way Arkansas hamlet for burgers and fries.

"Can you make a cherry Coke?" Tom asked the gum-chewing waitress as they ordered.

"What's that?" she replied.

"Nevermind," he said with a frown, "just bring me a Dr Pepper."

"Times have changed," he muttered to Tom Junior as the hired-help walked off to the kitchen. "Hey, they don't even have a jukebox!" he added, looking around.

"I think that's because everyone brings their own music nowadays on their phones," the son explained. Tom knew you could put music on a cell phone but he hadn't figured out how. Maybe Hannah could do it for him, she could handle all that technology stuff. Chad could too.

The little café might not be much but it provided a rare and enjoyable change from Hickory Bough's bland cuisine. Tom savored the fast food, with lots of ketchup poured over his crinkle-cut fries.

Tom Junior paid the check and the pair ambled back to the Lexus with toothpicks dangling from their lips. They headed on down a twisty road around Bull Shoals Lake. Dogwood blossoms sprouted here and there in the gray-brown forest.

Spring was coming.

They talked about all sorts of things: the company, Bentley Hardware did well last year; oldtimers at the warehouse, not many left Tom would know; baseball, particularly the Cardinals; the grandson's plans for college, probably Rolla for civil engineering, quite the math whiz; Hannah's four-point at Mizzou last fall and a new boyfriend from Neosho, haven't met him yet; the church called a new pastor, he's really pushing home groups; etc.

274

"So who's that woman you introduced us to a while back at Hickory Bough, the one in a wheelchair?" Tom Junior asked as he slowed to go around another curve.

"You mean Claire?"

"Yeah, I think that's her name."

"Oh, uh, we're just two old friends who share some pleasant memories."

Tom Junior chuckled.

"Oh, c'mon Pop! I think she meant more than *friend* to you sometime back there in the misty past," the son replied, stealing a wink. "I could tell by the way you looked at her."

Tom squirmed and twirled his cane.

"Oh well, yes, maybe, who knows? It's been a long time. She went her way and I went mine. Then your dear mother came along and made me very happy."

"So, would this Claire lady have made you very happy?" the son asked.

Tom didn't reply.

They drove on in silence.

"Well, I guess we need to head back, you want to go by the cemetery?" the son asked.

"I guess so, haven't been out there lately."

"Sure," Tom Junior replied, "I want to go by too."

He turned left and headed north. They crossed the border, passing the big MISSOURI WELCOMES YOU sign, over-sized for a little state highway. Out on the south side of Randall Tom Junior slowed, then turned through the big iron gate that proclaimed "Garden Of Peace, Gates Close At Sunset." They both knew the route well: Turn right at the tombstone with Jesus holding a lamb, then left at the big monument marked PETERS, then right again.

Tom Junior pulled to a stop in front of the gray marker:

Linda Kay Brown Bentley

1941-1980

Wife * Mother * Woman of God

The pair sat in silence for a moment, staring at the tombstone, as the engine idled.

"It's been so long, but sometimes it seems like yesterday," the father said with a sigh.

"I know," answered his son. "I still see her like a sixteen-year-old would. I didn't understand it then, I still don't.

"What was cancer? Why her? One of the brightest, happiest people I've ever known, and my sweet, loving, devoted mom.

"She always had been so perky and upbeat, then she got very sick—but she kept on smiling. We'd go to see her at the hospital, I knew she hurt but she always managed a weak little grin when we walked in her room.

"Then that morning you set my sister and me down in the kitchen and told us, 'Your mother left in the night.'

"I hated all those trips to the hospital, all those tubes running into her body. I cried during the funeral. Teen-age boys don't cry."

"I know," father said. "But like you said, she always brightened when Brenda and you came in her room. You were her greatest joys. She brought light into my life when I met her, just when I needed it, and to lose her with two children, just as they became adults? Awful.

276

"I'm so glad to still have you, it means a lot," Tom said, patting his son's leg.

"Your sister took it so hard, have your heard from her recently?" Tom asked.

"No."

They sat for a few minutes more until Tom Junior suggested, "Do you want to get out?"

"No, no, I don't think so," Tom answered, shaking his head. "Let's go on."

Tom Junior shifted back in drive and the Lexus slowly eased away. For the first time in the thirty years he had been coming to this spot, his eyes fell on a small mausoleum a few yards behind Linda's grave:

DEARBORN

Campbell Robert

1898-1980

Jewel Mae Laerdal

1901-1990

Claire Elaine

1931-

But seek ye first the kingdom of God

How could he have missed that? It shook him. Tom snapped his neck around to look back as they drove away.

"Something wrong?" Tom Junior asked.

"No."

They slowly wound their way between the tombstones and trees back to the gate. They headed along the curvy county road that took them back to Hickory Bough.

Tom had a great night's sleep with pleasant dreams about Ozark drives. He got up early the next morning, took his pills, got dressed and met Tony as he wheeled by.

"Ready for some breakfast, world traveler?" his friend called cheerfully.

"Sure, why not?" Tom replied and the two made their way down the hall. The conversation in the dining room seemed a bit livelier than usual, a change of pace made him perky. Tom looked out and noticed the sky had clouded over in the night. Oh well, he had sun yesterday.

"So what are we going to do today?" he asked Tony as he drained his coffee cup.

"I think the Cardinals have a preseason game with the Astros on the tube, let's catch that."

Tom hadn't seen Claire for a week or two and he thought, well, maybe, he might poke his head in to say hello.

Then again, why bother, maybe not.

The men happily jabbered baseball as they turned back into Tom's room. Tony started reminiscing about a game at old Busch Stadium years ago, a young father taking his little girl on a date with dad. He called the stadium "that ash tray by the arch" with usual sarcasm.

Tom laughed along with him as he sat down on his sofa. He and Linda had taken the kids on trips to St. Louis to Cardinals games, Six Flags and up in the arch. They did that Mississippi River cruise from Laclede's Landing once.

Yes, good times and great memories.

The spinning floor hit, blackness, the queasy stomach, tunnel vision. Tom stood up, then stumbled as he managed to grab a handle on the back of Tony's chair and twist his fall backwards so he fell across his bed.

The darkness cleared: Back in the war, shelling again. Word came down the enemy was moving in. Get your men outta' there, Bentley!

Tom got the platoon loaded into some trucks and Jeeps. He could hear light weapons in the distance now. He had his pot on and buckled its chin strap. He jumped in the passenger side of a Jeep and shouted, "Let's go!"

A sergeant turned the key.

Nothing.

The starter didn't even click. Maybe one of the locals had "borrowed" the battery in the night?

He and the sergeant, plus two privates in the back, jumped out and scrambled into a deuce-and-a-half idling next to them. Men already crammed the truck's back end but there were no arguments when someone got stepped on or pushed.

"C'mon, let's move! Go! Go!" Tom shouted.

The lieutenant looked back, sadly, as the big diesel growled off. Hours of work setting up a supply dump, stocked with valuable war matériel, now lost. But he had every man in his unit present and accounted for and that's what mattered.

Heck, the starving enemy probably needs the C rations worse than our guys, he thought.

They fell back several miles and Lt. Bentley watched as Air Force planes flew over to strafe the advancing enemy. Allied troops, Australia's K-Force, passed them, headed to the action. Ozzies are a tough bunch, he thought.

And friendly.

Tom remembered that night on a short leave when Malcolm and Dale, two fellow "left-tenants," befriended him and invited him to an Australian officer get-together. There were several cases of Four-X Beer to put away, "come over and have some stubbies and tucker, mate!" A portrait of King George hung on the wall next to the big blue flag with the Southern Cross.

He did, and it proved an enjoyable break of laughter with two other lonely young men, just like him, thousands of miles from home:

They were at university, Tom was in college.

They talked cricket, Tom talked baseball.

They missed Queensland, Tom missed Missouri.

"I want to pash the sheila," "I want to kiss Claire."

Several beers gave him a warm buzz. Hey, that felt really good! Life seemed better, at least for one evening.

Back to the situation at hand: He waited on orders by the side of the busy road as planes flew overhead. Clouds moved in, sprinkles started that soon turned into driving rain. At that point there wasn't much for a QM officer to do but get out of the way and try to stay dry.

He and his men would be busy soon enough.

Tom jumped in behind some big rocks, put on his rain gear and listened to the jets overhead. They stayed below the clouds and their booming roar echoed loudly across the hills. Shelling continued in the distance.

Time to kill, so he did what he always did when idle: He pulled out his wallet, opened it, and Claire looked up at him once again in black and white. She had mailed him a new photo but he knew the look well: the pouty smile, the hair over her right cheek, a beautiful reminder that there was someplace in the world where things were normal and people weren't shooting at each other.

He hoped Malcolm and Dale were okay.

Soon he would be with Claire all the time.

"Lord, please, make it soon."

Rain drops fell into his wallet and on the photo. He smudged off the water with his sleeve and stared on at the picture.

The mental fog slowly lifted, the dizziness eased, but Tom could still hear rain. He had been looking at Claire in the dream and as he came around his eyes focused and he realized he was still looking at Claire—the old one. The eyebrows were furrowed and she leaned toward him, her mouth agape.

"Tom, speak to me! Are you alright?" she pleaded.

"Uh, oh, where am I?" Tom groaned, grabbing his forehead looking around the room. The leaden Missouri skies outside his room really were dumping rain in buckets.

"You had one of your attacks, buddy," he heard Tony say. He looked around and saw his friend at the foot of the bed and Claire at his side. Josefina and a couple of orderlies huddled behind them.

"We have the ambulance on the way," Josefina said. "The blood pressure, it dropped very low."

Rain and rain.

Claire and Claire.

Boy, that was a weird one. But yes, he was safely at Hickory Bough, not hunkered down on some bombed-out Korean roadside.

"Uh, thanks everyone, I think I'm fine now," Tom said, taking off his glasses and rubbing his face.

"Are you sure you don't want to go to the emergency?" Josefina asked, worried.

"No, no, I'm fine. What could they do for me? Thanks everyone. You know this isn't the first time I've had one of these spells and probably won't be the last," Tom said with a chuckle, sitting up.

Claire sat there, horrified.

"What on earth happened to you?" she said, shaking his hand as she looked at him closely. "When I came in here you were pale-white, your eyes were rolled up, you were drooling all over your face. I thought you had died!"

"This is why I'm here," Tom replied.

"I have these from time to time, can't live alone anymore. I pass out, I fall, I hurt myself, welcome to Hickory Bough, Tom. It beats lying in the kitchen floor with a broken ankle. I know."

"Is there anything I can do for you?" Claire asked, her eyebrows furrowed in worry.

"No, I don't think so. I've had every medical test known to man—poked, probed, prodded, X-rayed, nuked, you name it—and the doctors say they can't find any one cause. They just give me more pills and say 'you're getting old.'

"I know that."

"If you're otherwise in good health, why didn't you move into one of those senior apartment complexes? What do they call them, independent living centers, assisted living?" she asked. "You're doing better than the rest of us."

"Because of Tom Junior and his family, they want to be close and there are no places like that in Randall," Tom replied. "Hickory Bough, sadly, is the best there is. What if I have one of these attacks and I don't fall on a bed? Bang! On the floor! My kids can be out here, or over at the hospital, in minutes," he answered.

"Would you like to go back to your room?" Josefina asked Claire.

"I guess so, if Tom thinks he's going to be okay," she replied with a quiver in her voice. "Are you *sure* you'll be fine? I need to know, I don't want you to be like this!"

Claire, frantic, had never looked at him that way before.

"Yes, it's over with, for now."

The nurse wheeled Claire out, who looked back, worried, over her shoulder as she went through the door. The orderlies went out behind them.

Tony waited until they were well down the hall.

"Hope you don't mind that I went and told your gal," he said.

"She's *not* my gal," Tom said bluntly.

"I rolled over there as fast as I could and got her after I pulled your emergency switch on the wall. Boy, everybody just scrambled, Bentley gets VIP service!

"Okay, I know you two are on the outs but there isn't anyone you needed here more than her."

"Whatever, I guess, thanks for the thought," Tom said, still dazed.

"Claire got really upset, I guess you hadn't said anything about your attacks," Tony added.

"What a scene, she was in here bawling her eyes out, yelling 'Jesus, help him! Oh God, please, no!' while Josefina and everybody scrambled to take care of you."

"Now that you mention it, I don't guess I had told her. Odd, I had been thinking some about going over to see her but I talked myself out of it.

"It's funny, I was dreaming while I was out, looking at Claire's picture in the war, in the rain, and I wake up to see, who?, Claire! And it's raining outside. Now that's a first," Tom said with a chuckle.

"Maybe the Lord's tryin' to tell you somethin'," Tony said. "You need her."

"Oh no, not you too!" Tom snapped.

"And what does that mean?" his buddy asked.

"Her dad used to say that: 'You-two-need-each-other-you-complement-each-other,'" Tom replied as he tucked his chin, in a false deep voice.

"Well, the guy was right, pal," Tom's friend replied. "Marry her!"

"*What*? Are you kidding me?" Tom responded with a mixture of surprise and indignation.

"Not on your life!" he shouted, waving his hand. "We're both eighty years old, and after what she's done to me? I'd move to get away from her if I could figure out how!"

"Just sayin' what's best for you," Tony replied with a shrug. "Take it or leave it."

"I'll leave it, thanks!

"Look, Tony, she had her chances!" Tom added, irritated, as he smacked the back of his hand.

"What's to keep her from rolling out the back door just as the music starts? Think *The Sound of Music*: 'They're gone!'"

"But changing the subject, what I really wish I could do is spot what causes those blackouts. Maybe I got too happy yesterday? Can you be too happy? I don't know. I haven't had one for several weeks."

"Best you take it easy for a while," Tony said as he headed out the door.

"Think I'll just lie here and read some."

Tom got up and dug out his iPad and started another book on the Civil War. Tony didn't show for lunch, Tom just had a salad, then wandered back to his friend's room to watch the game.

They were into the sixth inning when Clémence came in and cheerily announced "There you are, Mr. Tom!" as she handed him an envelope. "It's from your amour in C Hall."

"Merci, or however you say it," Tom replied with a grimace.

He took the envelope and, sure enough, it had the familiar, letter-perfect "Tom Bentley" on the front.

"Another love letter?" Tony asked. "You old rascal, you! Looks like you re-kindled the flame."

"Oh, gosh, no way," Tom said, opening the flap. He sniffed that enjoyable scent.

My dearest Tom,

What happened to you? I was scared and so worried this morning, are you better now? You have been in my prayers ever since, I can't get that horrible look on

285

your face, when I got there, out of my mind. It scared me terribly!

Please, please come by soon and let me know if there is anything I can do to help you.

Your friend,

Claire

"Well?" asked Tony.

"I think I need to give her my phone number, but it's nice to get these beautifully written notes," Tom said as he stuffed the letter back in the envelope. "She wants me to come by, she's all worried about me."

He could not help but notice that he had been elevated back to "dearest Tom."

"I can understand that. By golly, you really put on a show this time. Even the always-cool Josefina got all shook up," Tony said. "When did you perfect that eye roll thing? That spooked 'em out!"

"I don't have a clue, I wish these stupid doctors could give me one pill, or do an operation, and I wouldn't have to worry about those blackouts anymore. I guess they make more money stringing old geezers along instead of fixing them."

"Hey buddy, you don't know how blessed you are, at least you can walk," Tony replied grimly. "And whether you like it or not, Claire's a blessing to you. At least you have someone to worry about you."

"I doubt if she does. Okay, maybe you're right," Tom answered. "What did Gaylene talk about the other day, 'How do you know when you're blessed?'"

"Guess I missed that," Tony said, "maybe I need to get churched-up, start makin' her little clambakes."

"Sure, they can help us all."

Chapter 19
Better Not

Tom took it easy the rest of the day. The rain stopped and the sun came out right at sunset. The next day he was at the noon meal when the skies clouded up and it got dark. He turned on the TV weather station when he got back to his room to check the forecast.

Bad news, Limestone County had a severe storm watch with a big line of storms glowing red on radar out to the west, moving in from Kansas and Oklahoma.

Not good. Everyone in Randall, it seemed, knew someone injured or killed when that big funnel hit Joplin a year earlier.

Hickory Bough's nurses started scurrying around as the rain began.

The downpour got heavier and the sky took on a ghastly green-gray color shortly before Randall's tornado sirens screamed. Tom did as instructed and went in his bathroom and shut the door. He could hear the storm pounding outside, then the roar of hail on the roof for a few seconds. The lights blinked off and on but the power wasn't out long enough for the big generator outside his window to start.

The rain eased and he opened the door and looked around. All seemed normal, although he could hear a commotion down the hall. He grabbed his cane and set off to investigate. Water had run under the front doors as he crossed the dayroom and a janitor busily mopped up the mess.

Down C Hall the nurses and Mrs. Stevens nervously ran around—apparently right in front of Claire's room.

Claire?

Sorry, not his problem.

However, still, if something happened, well, maybe, he ought to go see, you know, just as a courtesy.

He hurried over and stuck his head in to see one of the big windows in her room had been hit by a hailstone and cracked.

"Should we move Judge Dearborn out of this suite?" Mrs. Stevens asked one of her staff.

No, came the answer, two other rooms had windows cracked as well and we're full. We have no place to move her or the others.

Claire said in her chair, stoic, through the hub-bub. She brightened when Tom walked in.

"Well, *you* missed the excitement this time," she chirped.

"Are you okay?" Tom asked.

"Oh, I'm fine. How about you? They got me in the bathroom like they told us, I heard a loud pop. They're more worried about it than me."

"Looks like," Tom agreed.

The janitor finished mopping and came in to inspect things. He scratched his chin, looked the glass over carefully and said he knew there was nothing to worry about. The window had tempered safety glass and it would be fine until he could get a glass company over from Springfield to replace it, take a day or two.

Should be no problem, ugly, but no problem.

"Excuse the mess, Judge Dearborn, I need to clean up some bits of glass on the carpet," he added.

Tom felt sorry for Claire because of the commotion in her room.

"Uh, say, a damsel in distress needs to have something to calm her nerves. What do you say I roll you into the dining room and let's enjoy a candlelight-and-crystal dinner without the candlelight and crystal?" Tom offered.

"That sounds fine," Claire replied. "I think things are getting back to normal but I guess I should clear out while they clean up. It is about meal time, isn't it?

The pair had the drill down by now: Tom handed her his cane, she put it across her armrests, he took hold of the chair's handles and off they went. They spotted a nurse in the hall and Claire told her she would eat in the dining room tonight.

"This is so exciting, how many weeks have I been here and I've never eaten in the dining room?" she said. "I need to get out more often!"

"Well, the thrill wears off quickly, let me tell you," Tom replied.

Tony sat at the guys' usual table and brightened when he saw the pair coming.

"Look here everybody, Tom has a hot date!" he called.

"Hello, Tony," Claire replied as Tom rolled her chair to a stop. "And how many stars is this establishment?"

"Michelin never made it here, they blew a tire," Tony replied.

The three of them laughed and Claire noted "the food is the same—it's the atmosphere," which provoked more laughter.

"And what's that wine you like, Moscato?" Tom asked. "I can have the sommelier check to see what years they have in the cellar."

"Excellent choice!" Tony called out. "The violinist will be here in a moment, requests?"

They were on a roll.

The trio jabbered through the meal and on, long after other residents finished.

"You would think they would have some sort of storm shelter or something in the building," Claire said in a serious tone, her eyebrows furrowed and her finger jabbing. "This just isn't safe! What if a tornado hits, it could blow the doors off the bathrooms. What do they do with the bedfast patients?"

It was the opinionated, we-should-do-this Claire at her best.

The men hemmed and hawed, they didn't know, surely Hickory Bough had procedures in place. After all, Mrs. Stevens has procedures for everything.

The next few days proved spring-perfect, chamber-of-commerce weather in the 70s with clear skies. The season's first crocus and daffodils popped up in the garden.

Nice day, maybe Claire would like to go outside?

She wasn't his problem but, hey, Tom Bentley's a gentleman, maybe she'd enjoy a break?

Claire didn't have to think about the offer, "Of course!"

Tom wheeled her outside and they spent time on the patio enjoying the new flowers and the chirping birds. The big thermometer's red arrow pointed midway between seventy and eighty.

"This makes me think of the gazebo," Tom said, smiling at Claire from a bench. "You liked to sit close to me there."

"Yes, I did," she replied. "But I think it's more like that Minneapolis hotel lobby—we can be seen."

"Here, if you can stand up I can fix things up a bit."

"That sounds wonderful you old romantic, are you sure you can handle it?" Claire asked.

"Let's try."

He had over committed.

It was all the old fellow could do to get her up, then help her twist around onto the bench, but he didn't let on. "Don't drop her! Don't drop her!" he told himself.

Claire sat down in something of a controlled fall and a loud "Oof!" as she grabbed the bench's armrest and panted for a moment.

"You don't know how good this feels, thank you," she said, fanning herself with her good hand. "Not to get too graphic but I haven't sat anywhere but that thing or a toilet in months. I feel like a new woman. This is wonderful!"

Tom laid his cane across the chair, sat down next to her and put his arm behind Claire, across the back of the bench. Surprised, she looked around at his hand and mumbled, "Oh my!"

"Just like old times, you little hottie!" Tom replied with a wink.

Claire laughed.

"Silly boy, you wild and crazy guy!" she snickered.

She laid her hand on his lap, he took it and squeezed it gently. She squeezed back.

"You don't know how special this is, I haven't felt this good in months, years!" Claire gushed.

They sat next to each other, quietly enjoying the warm afternoon as the birds sang in the trees and the bees buzzed around the flowers.

Spring had sprung. The old friends talked about their families, Easter, the weather. But most of all they enjoyed just being next to each other—again.

Maybe bygones could be bygones?

"What a beautiful afternoon, this is so nice," Claire said with a distant look. "This day makes me think of our senior class picnic at Hoot Owl Hollow, that big park, remember? The one over on Quartz Creek. I loved it."

"Yes, I remember that," Tom said, smiling, "Another bus ride, courtesy of Randall Public Schools."

"But in broad daylight!" Claire reminded him, laughing.

"I wore out my pocketknife carving our initials, TB+CD, on that big slab of limestone above the creek. I bet it's still there," Tom said.

"That was so sweet. I remember some of us girls sitting around the picnic tables, talking after lunch, you had disappeared. I figured you were off with the guys on the softball field but I couldn't see you over there. Then I spotted you up on that rock, what on earth is he doing? I came to see.

"There were lots of other kids' initials there—and you added ours!"

"I remember your surprise at what I'd done," Tom said, adding "*Oh, Tom!*" in falsetto.

"Well, we'll just have to buzz over and see if it's still there, won't we?" she said firmly.

"Taxi!"

They laughed as they sat and enjoyed the day.

"Tom, I truly hate to break this up but I better get back inside, I sunburn easily," Claire said, still looking up.

"Sure, we can come back out some other day. Just check your social calendar and let me know when you're free," Tom answered.

"I'll try to work you in!" Claire said with a snicker.

Getting her back in the wheelchair proved even harder than getting her out. Tom wondered if he would fall as he steadied her.

"I didn't know you had it in you," Claire said, looking up at him.

"I didn't know if I did either," the old man answered as he huffed and puffed. "Well, I better get you home early, I don't want to get in trouble with your dad!"

Claire giggled. "I don't think you *could* get in trouble with my dad."

He wheeled her through the dayroom, nurses in the horseshoe looked up as they passed, back to C 4, parked her inside her door in about the usual spot and set the brake.

"How's that?"

"You don't know how wonderful, I so enjoyed that!" she said, looking up at him.

The blue eyes sparkled.

Two days later Tom decided to check the weather on his iPad when he got back from lunch. Maybe they could go outside again?

The forecast wasn't good: Eighty percent this afternoon with storms, some possibly severe.

Better not.

"Oh well, spring in Missouri," he muttered to himself. After living his whole life here, he knew all the excitement of this spring had come and gone after the sirens blew the other day.

Some more rain and in a few weeks it would be hot and muggy again; summer.

The clear blue sky turned partly cloudy in the afternoon, then clouded over. He turned on his TV to find the familiar red crawler across the bottom of the screen listing counties under a severe weather watch. "Limestone" went by, he noted.

Oh well, here we go again, Tom thought.

But for whatever reason only a meteorologist could explain, a thunderstorm blossomed right over Randall. It hit suddenly, rain went by Tom's window sideways. The wind picked up and the sirens wailed again.

This time he would not go in his toilet, he headed out to check on Claire. There would be room for both in her bathroom if it came to that.

The big nurses' horseshoe in the dayroom had emptied as the staff ran to do whatever. He walked as fast as he could toward C 4 and turned in to see Claire staring, worried, at the cracked window.

"Oh, thanks for coming, it looks bad out there," she said as Tom tapped in. Suddenly the rain stopped but the wind picked up. Tom walked over to the windows and leaned over to look up at the sky, peering at ragged tails hanging from angry clouds, lit by constant lightning.

"I don't like this, we better get in the bathroom," he said and Claire nodded.

He stepped over to grab her wheelchair just as a gust hit the building and the cracked window popped and groaned.

"Wait! Let's get down on the floor—now!" he shouted over the roar outside. He took hold of Claire as she struggled up from her wheelchair. The old couple got behind her bed in a jerky dance, something between sitting down and a fall, as the wind howled. Tom put his arms around her and Claire wrapped her good arm around him.

BANG!

The cracked window broke and a thousand slivers flew out into the storm.

Their ears popped as wind as strong as a hurricane roared through her room and out the open window, taking anything and everything with it. The sound deafened them, like a hundred trains roaring by.

Claire moaned, Tom held her as tightly as he could. He could see debris—tree limbs, papers, a bicycle, some big piece of sheet metal—blow by outside. From inside, odds and ends—meal trays, furniture, televisions, clothes, magazines, bedpans, pictures—hurdled through Claire's door and out where the glass had been.

The torrent of air grabbed her empty wheelchair, spun it up, then dropped it on them.

Claire screamed.

Tom managed to grab the wheelchair and push it off.

"Oh, I'm hurt! I'm hurt! Help me! Help me!" she pleaded. "Please!"

"Hang on, this won't last long!" Tom said, hoping. He turned his head and looked back at her to see blood running over her face.

The wind suddenly dropped as a big piece of black plastic flew in the room, catching on the ragged window frame, flapping loudly.

Claire's suite had been sucked clean, even the covers and sheets on her bed were gone.

The power went off and emergency lights blinked on in the hall, but the room remained dark. Just then the lights came back on as he heard the emergency generator behind his room start up.

Chaos reigned in the hall. There were screams and cries from nearby rooms, nurses and orderlies ran back and forth. Tom went to stand up but a sharp pain caught his bad leg. He could barely get up on his knees.

"Let me help you," he said.

"No, no, I can't. Don't hurt yourself! Please get somebody, it hurts really bad," Claire said, wiping blood out of her eyes with her good hand.

"Just leave me, but get help!"

But Tom couldn't get up either. The pain was too much, he slumped back on the floor next to her.

"They're going to have to drag both of us out, I can't get up," he said, panting, reaching for her. "Hang on, I hear someone coming."

Just then Clémence poked her head in C 4.

"Oui, he's here!" she yelled down the hall.

"I told you so," Tony said as he backed to a stop behind the nurse. "I knew exactly where the ol' boy would be in this mess—and it wasn't pickin' daffodils."

"Help *me*! Help *us*!" Claire cried in pain.

"We have help on the way très vite!" the excited nurse shouted as she stooped down to look at the pair. She gasped at the blood covering Claire's face. She ran out in the hall to get a first aid kit. She came back in a moment just as there were more shouts in the hall.

They heard Mrs. Stevens yell "check this one!"

Two emergency medics dashed in the room, rolling a stretcher and lugging a big emergency kit.

"Take care of her, I'm okay for now," Tom said as he rolled back from Claire so the medics could reach her. Mrs. Stevens stepped in the doorway just as Clémence returned.

"Go on and check what else we have, we have these two covered," the wide-eyed manager ordered. Clémence scooted down the hall as other emergency teams sprinted by.

The technicians stanched the flow from a cut on Claire's scalp, then put a splint on her leg before lifting her onto the stretcher and wheeling her out.

"And how about you sir?" one of the technicians asked Tom. "Where does it hurt?"

"My left leg, I have a war wound, hurts really bad."

The technician pulled out a knife, said "sorry" and split Tom's pant leg from foot to belt loops. The ugly scar gave him pause.

"Oh! I don't know, we better splint it just in case," he added. Another tech brought in a second stretcher and they braced Tom's leg, then lifted the old gentleman and wheeled him out.

The day room had descended into a frenzy, accentuated by flashing red lights from ambulances and police cars outside. They rolled him through the front door and into the back of an ambulance beside a man he didn't recognize.

A medic hopped in behind him, shut the door and the ambulance started easing its way out of Hickory Bough's messy parking lot as its siren started. Tom flashed back to the last time he rode in an ambulance, that awful night he fell and broke his ankle.

They had a rough trip. Debris, big tree limbs and an overturned truck blocked the road. The driver cut through residential streets, then back out on the main street. Tom and the other fellow in the back were stoic, lying there as they rocked along. Tom's pain eased.

The Randall hospital's emergency room overflowed with people with all sorts of injuries. The crew unloaded the two men as a triage nurse came by to check them out.

"Excuse me, miss, where's the woman from Hickory Bough?" Tom asked. "She should have arrived just a few minutes ago."

"Sorry, can't talk about other patients," the nurse said curtly as she punched information in a laptop and walked on. Tom bit his lip and waited.

It took a while but a doctor finally looked him over, then had an X-ray taken of his leg and Tom spent much of the evening behind thin curtains, listening to the hub-bub just beyond them.

He prayed for Claire.

Where was she, was she okay? Where did she go? When would he know?

He stared up at too-bright fluorescent lights in the ceiling for ever so long. The ER doctor finally came back.

"It looks like you just have a bad bruise, did something fall on you?" the physician asked.

"Yes, a wheelchair."

"Well now, that's new one," the doctor said with a smile. "I think you'll be fine but let's put you in overnight for observation, just to be sure."

"Whatever. Listen, doc, I'm trying to find out about a woman they brought here from Hickory Bough, her name's Claire Dearborn."

"Sorry, can't release confidential information," the doctor said as he left.

Just then Tom Junior and Judy poked their heads through his curtain.

"There you are! Are you alright, Pop?" the son asked.

"Yeah, just a bad bruise but Claire's here too. See if you can find out something about her."

Judy nodded and said she would check. The father described the horrible scene to the son.

"Honestly, I was afraid we were gonna' get sucked out that window, I can't describe it," Tom said.

"From what I saw driving over here the nursing home got the worst of it," the son replied. "The funnel went right across the south end of town and there's not a whole lot out there besides you guys. There were some houses hit and some cars and trucks flipped around."

The usual paperwork started with waiting, and more waiting, and an orderly finally wheeled Tom into the hall and to a room. A nurse gave him a painkiller and the sore leg went numb.

Tom Junior stayed with him until Judy walked in.

"Claire's down the hall but she's asleep, they don't think it's that bad," she said. "She has a cut on her scalp and they gave her a couple stitches. She has some big bruises on her abdomen, they're concerned there might be internal injuries."

"Why don't you go down there in the morning?" Tom Junior suggested.

That sounded doable and besides, the painkiller made him dopey. His son gave him a hug and Judy bent over and kissed her beloved father-in-law on the forehead.

"I'm so happy it was nothing serious, we love you," Judy said with a pat on his arm. "I'll call Hannah in the car, and we'll let Chad know you're okay when we get home. We'll be back tomorrow."

"Thank you so much," the father replied as they left his room. He went to sleep as they walked out.

He woke at first light as a nurse came in to check on him.

"When do I get parole?" the old gentleman asked.

The nurse laughed.

"I'm not sure, your personal doctor is coming out shortly to check on you. I suspect you'll be released this morning, doesn't look serious," she replied.

"Excuse me, but I understand Claire Dearborn is down the hall?" Tom asked.

"Are you friends?"

"Yes, um, close," Tom replied.

The nurse looked at him intently.

"Well, I'm not supposed to do this but if I bring a wheelchair in maybe we can roll you down there, just to say hello?"

"You don't know how much I would appreciate that."

She came back in a moment with a chair and helped Tom into it. They rolled out his door and turned right. Claire was three doors down, her door stood open as they rolled in.

Claire had her best "I'm bored" expression as she watched TV but brightened when she saw Tom. A big bandage covered most of her head.

"It's my turn to roll around," he said with a smile. Claire clapped her hands and laughed. "I'm so glad to see you, are you okay?"

"Fine, and I was going to ask you the same thing," Tom answered.

"Lucky for me I keep my hair up nowadays. Can you see me flying out that window with my hair spinning around in a whirlpool? Whee!"

"That would look like something from *The Wizard of Oz*, 'I'll get you, my pretty!'" Tom replied as they both laughed at the gallows humor.

"Seriously, my hair cushioned the blow. All that blood looked worse than it is," she added. "I think I can do a comb-over!"

"Well, I can't comb-over anymore, there's nothing left to comb over," Tom replied.

They laughed again

Just then a middle-aged, blonde woman came in and Claire brightened.

"Marty! Oh Tom, this is my niece, Martha Dawson. Marty, this is an old high school friend of mine, Tom Bentley. Martha and her husband live in my parents' house out on Poplar."

There were pleased-to-meet-you's and polite chatter. He excused himself and rolled back into the hall and toward his room.

"Old high school friend" he muttered to himself. "Well, I guess I am."

He got back to his room and rolled up to the bed, set the chair's brake and looked around for his cane to stand up.

Nowhere.

Oh no, not that.

His beautiful pecan wood cane: gone.

Chapter 20
Answered Prayer

As promised, Tom Junior came by when the hospital released his father.

First: A cane.

They drove out on the bypass to shop. A dollar store had one, black, made of plastic, really a kid's toy. Not the same, but what to expect for a buck? Tom figured he could adjust. If his grandson couldn't make another one he'd get out his iPad and order something online. You can buy anything on that Internet, world-webby thing, whatever they call it, he thought.

Hickory Bough appeared to be in surprisingly good shape, given the previous afternoon. A disaster cleanup crew worked as janitors continued hustling around. Roofers roamed across the top of the building as a roaring tar pot by the driveway filled the air with stench.

Tom checked out B 9: Just as he left it. He decided to go down and see how bad Claire's room looked. Some of the disaster crew was finishing up there with Mrs. Stevens closely supervising.

"Welcome home, Tom!" the manager called out cheerfully as he walked in.

No, Hickory Bough wasn't home, but he nodded and said a polite "thanks." The busted window had been replaced and new curtains in a muted green plaid had been hung.

But the room and its furniture had been stripped bare.

Everything that said "Judge Claire Dearborn" had been sucked out—photos, mementos, the mounted gavel. The bed had been made. Surprisingly, her clothes-filled closet remained untouched.

Tornados can be strange, Tom thought.

"This is amazing, I had no idea you could clean up the mess so fast," Tom said, shaking his head.

The disaster cleanup supervisor turned to him.

"Let me tell you, you folks don't know how lucky everybody in this place is. When this window and the others down the hall popped, it relieved the pressure as the tornado went over. Had they not given way, the whole building might have exploded and collapsed. I don't want to think about that."

Tom leaned on his new cane, shocked. "How do you know when you're blessed?" he muttered.

"Is everything alright in your suite?" Mrs. Stevens asked.

"Far as I know, when will Claire return?"

"I haven't heard, maybe tomorrow."

Tom nodded and shuffled back to his room. Walking just wasn't the same without *his* cane. This plastic thing just did not feel right, but he had to have it, his leg still hurt despite a painkiller, and that catch that had been there for sixty years always bothered him.

Tony saw him coming down the hall.

"So did they cut anything off?" he chirped.

"Not that I know off, I just have a bad bruise, I guess, still sore," Tom answered. "They gave me some pain pills. Just what I need, more pills to take."

"And what about your gal?"

His gal?

No, Tony, she is not.

Well okay, maybe, sort of.

"Claire has a big cut on her scalp and several bad bruises on her stomach and leg, she's still there. Come in and I'll give you the gory details."

The friends visited for a while, then Tom turned on one of the cable news channels that showed video of storm damage in southern Missouri and northern Arkansas with a passing mention of "one nursing home sustained minor damage."

"Don't let the ol' lady Stevens hear that!" Tony chuckled.

Tom went to eat that night, read his iPad and Bible, took a shower and went to bed. He turned out the light and stared into the dark.

He missed Claire.

Was she okay?

When would she be back?

Would she be back?

Things had been rough for her at Hickory Bough, maybe she was gone for good. Maybe she would try to make it with her niece again out there at 1572 Poplar.

If so, he'd get Tom Junior to drive him out to say hello—and they could go by 902 Poplar for old times' sake.

That is, if the house were still there.

He whispered a prayer as he did every night in thanks for God's love, Brenda, "my kids" and more.

Then he added, "And Lord, I need Claire, and she needs me. Please fix this, please bring her back."

Restless sleep came on him quickly. A dream turned into a nightmare: A young Claire ran down a dark street screaming, "Help me! Help me!" He rushed toward her but he could never catch her. She ran faster than he did as he gimped along on his war-wound leg.

Or, maybe she didn't want his help.

Maybe she ran away from him.

He shaved and dressed for breakfast the next morning and met Tony at their table.

"Hey, noticed you have a new cane," his friend said as Tom tapped across the floor and sat down.

"Something happened to the other one in the storm, probably stuck in somebody's backyard, maybe some mongrel dog's chewing on it," Tom answered.

"Well, you're okay," Tony said. "Canes can be replaced, sharp old guys like you can't. We need you around this joint. It makes my life better to wake up in the mornin' and think, 'What mischief can Bentley and me get into today?'"

The pair laughed.

They headed back to their rooms to do whatever. Tom surfed around on his iPad, looking for canes, when Josefina stuck her head in his door and chirped, "Claire's back!"

Tom wheeled around quickly, he hadn't moved this fast since the sirens blared. He grabbed the cane and headed for C 4 as rapidly as he could tap down the hall. He came up on a stir outside her door as her neighbors and the staff welcomed her.

"Well, well, look who's here!" Clémence said, and the crowd parted as Tom shuffled in.

Claire had a big bandage on her head but otherwise looked fine. She brightened as Tom came through the door.

"Well hello, fellow survivor!"

"Yes, glad to see you're back and in one piece," Tom replied in an upbeat tone.

"I'm fine, just a couple quarts low on blood," she said as she patted her head. "And my side hurts. Good thing you can't see my tummy, purple and green."

"Did that hospital make you miss Chez Hickory Bough?" Tom asked.

"I'm amazed how normal my room looks," she answered. "But all my personal things got sucked out, not the same here. It makes me sad, I can replace some. They gave me a new wheelchair. Just as well, I harbor a grudge against that old one."

"Yes, my big loss was my cane."

"Oh no, it's gone? Didn't your grandson make it?"

"Yes, loved it, sucked out the window. Tom Junior helped me pick up this thing," he said, waving his new stick. "Doesn't feel right, I'm trying to find something on the web."

"Come in and let's visit," she said, waving "come here" to him as the others left.

He noticed the blue eyes twinkled.

Tom sat down on the sofa. Claire stared quietly at Tom.

"You saved my life," she said.

He shrugged.

309

"Oh well, possibly. Perhaps you could have made it into your bathroom and then you would not have gone to the hospital."

"But if you had not been here, how would I have gotten in there? I would have been stuck out here, by myself. Everything happened so quickly."

She continued to stare, eyebrows furrowed. Things were going around and around between her ears, he knew the look.

"Tom, my father was more right than he knew, I need you. I guess that silly, little third-grader knew what she was doing."

"I don't know what to say."

"Say nothing, you know it's true. Thank you."

"You're welcome."

Claire had changed.

She seemed friendlier, more perky, more outgoing than she had been. The second Claire sat in front of him.

Why the change? Was it a lonely night in a hospital room? He didn't know, but it answered one old man's prayer.

The pair happily recounted all that had happened to them, both agreeing they were just happy to be alive.

The chipper, friendly conversation transitioned from the storm to other things: Tell me about your niece and her husband. Tell me more about Tom Junior and Judy. What was it like to be a judge? Tell me about your grandchildren. What was it like to be in the Oval Office?

Claire finally asked, "Don't you have a daughter? You never talk about her."

Tom sighed.

"Yes, Brenda, the problem child, the opposite of Tom Junior."

He sighed again.

"Linda passed away when she was eighteen, just as she graduated from high school. She took it hard, she and her mother were very close. In an odd way, and I don't think she ever said this in so many words, she blamed me for Linda's passing, very strange."

"So does she live here?" Claire asked.

"No, I have no idea where she is."

Tom sat and thought for a moment.

"I guess you could say, what's the expression?, she 'flipped out,' I think that's how people put it nowadays. I haven't heard from her in twenty years. She and Tom Junior kept up with each other some, he would pass along that she had called or they had chatted online, but he hasn't heard from her in years. Last we knew she lived someplace in California."

"That's sad, I hope I can help somehow."

Tom shifted uneasily.

"She has a different personality, always edgy, aloof, blunt, definitely not a people person. Brenda was the different child even before Linda got sick, so different than her brother who always has been one of those supportive, 'sure, whatever you say' kind of people."

"Like his father?" Claire said, looking at him sideways and smiling.

"Well, I guess so, maybe like father-like son.

"But she certainly doesn't have her mother's perky, upbeat personality. If she thought something, she said it. That got her in trouble in school and elsewhere. Some teacher would critique a theme, say, and she'd throw the paper in the trash and tell the teacher off—and we'd get a call from the principal."

"And I'm sure you worry about her?"

"I pray for her all the time," Tom replied, shaking his head, "I don't know if she's dead or alive."

"It sounds like you've had some tough times," Claire added.

"I guess, but I've had a lot of good things happen too, just as you said you have, good and bad. Tom Junior and his family are beyond wonderful, his children are great. And Judy, you can't wish for a better daughter-in-law. Then I managed to save the company; good things."

"Save the company?" Claire asked.

"Yes, Bentley Hardware always has been a wholesale and franchise operation. We supplied hundreds of little mom-and-pop hardware stores for years, a good business back when. But in the '60s the big discount chains sprung up and wiped out a lot of them, then the big-box hardware stores opened in the cities and killed our franchises there.

"By the late 1980s we teetered on bankruptcy. I had to let good employees go, I hated that.

"Our problems hurt Randall's economy and I don't think the town ever recovered. Some of that is because of the big-box stores on the bypass, but a lot of it was our fault.

"My brothers finally cashed in their chips in the late '70s, gave me their shares in the company for a dollar, and bought this construction equipment outfit. They both

312

moved to Kansas City. I got stuck, I had to make a silk purse out of a sow's ear."

"So you did it?"

"Yes, I like to think so, but Tom Junior should get credit. He earned this hotshot marketing MBA at Mizzou and hit the ground running when I brought him in, did better than his boozy father. I love the kid.

"What could we do? We were telegraphers making buggy whips. There was no market for what we did anymore. So Tom Junior worked out a plan.

"We opened these upscale hardware places in high-income zip codes. They stock top-quality tools and have expert clerks roaming the aisles giving advice, seminars on gardening and do-it-yourself projects, that sort of thing.

"It worked. If a location is a good one, Saturday morning you'll see Escalades, Volvos and Beemers parked out front. We aren't as big but we're making money again. That creates jobs, I'm proud of that.

"I turned things over to Tom Junior in 2000 and retired. I traveled for fun, different than when I hopped hotel bars."

Claire nodded.

"I did a lot of travel too after I stepped down from the bench. I had several nice trips to Europe—but never went back to France," she said it with a wink.

Tom caught it.

"Understood.

"Likewise, I didn't keep booze at home, I went years without having a drink of any kind. Linda made it easy, teetotaler," he said. "Her great line was 'I hallucinate on Dr Pepper.' I'd go out with Tom Junior and Judy for a special occasion, an anniversary, the grandkids sitting there, and have a couple sips from a glass of wine.

"I learned when to stop, self-control is a gift of the Spirit.

"The little old ladies who gave tours of our house for Pioneer Days, remember that?, served mint juleps one year and I blew a gasket. They did it innocently but there are people who remember Tom Bentley's bad old days. The last thing I wanted was for people to hear I was going on toots again."

The old friends sat in silence for a few minutes, just smiling at each other, with only the usual dull TV roar to break the stillness.

Tom smiled at Claire, Claire smiled at Tom.

"We never got to Springfield, did we?" Claire said.

Tom smiled again, chuckled, and shook his head.

"No, we didn't."

"I wanted to more than you know, back then," she said. "That was the one time in my life I thought I might become a mother."

"Really?" Tom said with surprise, raising an eyebrow. "Don't be offended but, well, somehow I never saw that as something you wanted. You were all intellectual, career driven."

"Well, yes, I was," Claire said with a sigh. "I was the cold one, the smart one, the snooty rich kid, aloof, didn't think about a family. But I have a soft side, you know that.

"You were so normal—always smiling, everyone liked you, good ol' Tom, and that's one thing I saw in you that I admired," she added. "I guess people wondered what you saw in me, we were so different."

"Opposites attract," Tom said with a smile. "And also, you were a real looker."

"Thank you, I guess."

"You don't know how much I enjoyed walking around the square with you, holding hands, and having guys turn and stare. They weren't looking at me."

Claire blushed.

"They did?"

"Trust me, they did."

"Well, whatever, I'm a woman, I'm human. I saw older sisters of my acquaintances getting married straight out of high school, and a year or two later here they were, pushing strollers around the square with these cute, chubby babies. It all seemed so natural and sweet, they seemed so happy.

"I wanted that. You were my only hope of it happening, I guess I scared other guys off, but for some reason Tom Bentley liked me."

"If you haven't figured it out by now…." Tom answered.

"So that was part of the dream, at least for me: I thought maybe if we married during our freshman year in college, and then if we had our own little place over in Springfield, well, one thing leads to another, and we might have a baby of our own.

"Ha! I don't know why but I had the idea pop in my head on commencement night, when we were driving around town in my new car—what if, what if—the next time I wore a cap and gown I had a belly? Skinny Claire has a pea in her pod!"

The thought made both of them laugh.

"I bet she would have been as beautiful as her mother," Tom said, taking off his glasses and wiping his eyes as he chuckled.

"Oh! I thought he would be as handsome as his father!" Claire answered, slapping her leg and smiling.

"Blue eyes, a bushy head of blonde hair, she'd look like a dandelion with all that hair sticking up," Tom said.

"No, big brown eyes and always smiling—just like his popular daddy."

They both laughed again.

Tom leaned over and Claire held out her hand. He took it.

"Or best of all, brown eyes and blonde hair so everyone would know it belonged to us, our baby. The most beautiful baby ever, something we did together."

"But it didn't happen," Claire said with a sigh, looking down.

"Time went on, every month went by, my body clock stopped ticking, like all women. I did law school, then worked in an office, then on the bench. I found it all rewarding, I won all kinds of honors, I had a successful career, that made me very proud.

"And I showed up on the shortlist for the Supreme Court! Good golly, how many women can say that? But I had that unfulfilled dream. Did I miss something?"

Claire shook her head.

"I let my family down, my parents were proud of what I had become, but I let them down. I saw how happy they were around my brothers' kids, all six of them. They were Papa and Nana's dear grandchildren, they loved those kids as much as they loved my brothers and me.

"I don't know, maybe they loved them more. They had photos all over the house.

"And Christmas? Oh my! Christmas was a near riot for several years with little ones running around the house and toys everywhere. You had to watch your step! I came back for the holidays a few times but Aunt Claire became the odd-man out, the fifth wheel."

She sighed.

"None of them were mine.

"So think: What if Claire and Tom had kids? They adored you, think how big Christmas would have been with even more little ones running around? We would have had our own little brood, running back and forth up and down Poplar, between the grandparents' homes.

"Can you miss people who never were? Can you love children you never had?"

Claire sighed, then waved her hand.

"Oh, why bother! That all happened a long time ago. The magic is gone, the dream is gone, we'll both die soon. What difference does it make now?" she added angrily.

Tom grimaced.

"We are *not* over so the romance is not over, the dream is not over," he said firmly.

"You chased me in school, Claire Dearborn, now maybe I need to chase you!

"Look, we can make our lives magic again if we want—and I want! We can still make our dream come true!

317

"I know we can have something, we can make something, that people will look at and say, 'Now that's special! Isn't that a surprise? Those are two special people!'"

The blue eyes watered as she stared at Tom.

"Do you mean what I think you mean?"

Tom swallowed hard.

He looked out her new window for a moment, tapped his cane, then turned back to her.

"Yes.

"Claire, will you marry me?"

She lost it.

Claire bent over and bawled. Stunned, Tom fumbled in his pocket and handed her a tissue.

"Sorry, it's been used but it's all I have."

She dabbed at her nose with the wadded tissue.

"That's okay," she said as she sniffed.

"It happened so long ago, there on my parents' back porch, you brought up marriage the first time. No more hints, no more teasing, no more what-ifs—you meant it. And I told you, 'If you ask me, you know I will say yes.' And I meant it, I really wanted to marry you."

"Well?" Tom asked.

"But I talked us out of it. It wasn't going to happen like my well-thought-out plan, so I didn't want it *then*.

"You know what I did want? I wanted a blowout!

"I wanted a big church wedding with a huge reception at the club to show you off!" Claire said between sniffs. "I wanted to tell everyone, 'Look at me! That quiet girl, the introvert, the plain-Jane wallflower you never notice, look who I caught! Look who my husband is! Tom

318

Bentley! Randall's Mr. Nice Guy, the son of the tycoon who owns that big company, that war hero is *my* husband! Aren't you girls jealous? He's *mine*!'

"Claire…" Tom started, but she interrupted him.

"Ha! I wanted a wedding people would talk about for years, not just the two of us standing, holding hands, in the dingy living room of some old justice of the peace reading from a worn-out King James Bible, with his wife as the lone witness, holding a State of Oklahoma marriage license with the ink still wet."

"Claire…" Tom started again.

"I did want you, but my plans went all wrong. The result? I ended up without the fancy wedding *and* without the wonderful man. The wedding became more important than the marriage, so I lost both.

"What we want, and what we need, and what we get are not always the same thing."

She sniffed and wiped her nose again with Tom's wadded-up Kleenex.

Tom sat quietly. "Please, I'm not worthy," he whispered.

"Oh yes you *are*! You are a wonderful man!

"We should have driven over to Miami that afternoon," Claire continued. "I would not have had the wedding but I would have had the man. Our parents would have understood with you going off to war. Then we would have had more than pictures and letters. We could lie in our beds every night, thousands of miles apart, and feel our fingers.

"There's the ring: Yes, he's still here. Yes, she's still mine.

319

"And Tom, I would've been there for you at the station that night. Maybe I would be holding a toddler? We'll never know.

"But one snap decision, in one moment, changes lives and decades. I didn't think about all that when I accepted the scholarship, and thinking is what I'm good at. I let my emotions take over."

Claire stopped and wiped her eyes with her sleeve.

"You don't really see all that in me, do you?" Tom asked.

"Yes, I do, I don't deserve you!" she cried again. "I'm getting emotional and I get in trouble when I do that. Maybe I need to stop and think about this."

Tom shook his head.

"Look, Claire, you've been thinking about this for sixty years, this isn't emotion," Tom replied firmly. "You are being very logical."

The eyebrows furrowed.

"Well, you're right. You asked me, so I'll keep the promise I made back when, there on the porch."

Claire sighed and the watery blue eyes looked up at him.

"Yes, Tom, yes, let's do it.

"It may be some little, quick ceremony, like a justice of the peace in Miami, but at last I'll have you!"

Tom stood, then bent over the wheelchair's armrest, kissed her lips and smiled down at her.

"I know I'm not much of a prize anymore," Claire said.

"Ah, you forget! In my mind's eye I will always see you as you looked on prom night in that black gown with

320

waves of golden hair falling over your shoulders," Tom replied. "You were breathtaking. And I saw you a thousand nights in Korea when I looked at that picture your mother took."

Claire smiled as tears ran down her cheeks.

"I have a great family, my kids," Tom added, holding her good hand. "Now, I want to add you to the blessings I have."

"I hope so," she said, sniffing.

"I guess we need to work on the details," he said. "I guess I better get back to my room, we missed eating."

He bent over and they kissed again. Claire touched his cheek as she gazed into his eyes.

Tom took his cane and headed out, stopping at the door and looking back. Claire looked longingly at him with a nervous smile.

"I love you, Claire."

"Tom, I love you too."

He closed B 9's door when he got back, he didn't want Tony or anyone else barging in. He reached in his pocket and pulled out his phone to punch in Tom Junior's number. It rang a couple times and he heard the familiar "Hi, Pop!"

"Hey number-one son, I have a favor to ask. How much money do I have in my checking account?" Tom asked.

"Oh, gimme' a minute and I can look it up here on my computer, several thousand I think. You don't spend much these days," Tom Junior said. "But then I don't know what will be left of the hospital bill after your Medicare friends pay their part."

"Well, we can pull some extra out of the IRA, and I've got a fair amount of cash in my trading account. You still have a debit card for the account, right?"

"Sure, right here in my desk drawer, so what's up?"

"I want you to buy an engagement ring."

Silence.

Tom could faintly hear a musical beep-beep-beep from one of Chad's computer games in the background.

"You what?" Tom Junior gasped. "Ha! It's that Claire-something, I knew it!"

"Dearborn. Mind you, keep this top secret for now."

Tom heard a loud sigh on the other end.

"Uh, I have to ask: Pop, are you off your meds?"

Tom laughed.

"No, son, I have never been more alert. Get the biggest rock you can find for whatever money I have, I'd say she has a medium-sized finger, gold solitaire.

"Wait, hold the phone: Instead, go for something that really sparkles, lots of fire and pizzazz, even if the stone's smaller. I want to shock her, just leave her floored, speechless. I want something she can really show off."

Tom heard a commotion and could make out Judy talking to Tom Junior.

"He what?" he heard Judy gasp.

Tom heard rustling and Judy took the phone.

"Dad, listen: If you're going to do this then Tom and I better go buy it together or people will talk," his daughter-in-law said firmly. "I do not want my husband out buying engagement rings!"

322

"Whatever, maybe you better go over to Battlefield Mall in Springfield to keep it quiet. We want to keep this low key and simple," Tom said. "Thanks for the help, I love you both," and he hung up.

Tom Junior strolled into B 9 before noon the next day and found his father reading. He shut the door behind him.

"Hey, Pop!"

"How did it go?" Tom asked.

"Uh, I have only bought one of these things before in my life, as you know," Tom Junior said with a chuckle. He reached in his pocket and pulled out the little box and opened it. The solitaire's sparkle lit up the old man's face.

"A little over two carats, simple gold band, that pretty much cleaned out your account. But boy, look at that sparkle!"

"Will you look at that!" Tom agreed, his eyes wide.

"Looks like the Fourth of July. That's perfect, good job, thanks son. Of course, you'll be my best man?"

"It would be an honor, Pop, it would be an honor. I need to run back to the office but let's get together soon, I need to know more about my new mom. I hope I can keep my mouth shut at the office."

Tom stood up, took the ring and the two hugged as Tom Junior left.

"Good luck!"

Tom stuck the ring in his pocket and shuffled off toward C Hall. He found Claire asleep in her wheelchair, her Nook and reading glasses on her lap. He quietly closed

323

the door and tip-toed over to the sofa. He sat there for a while, just watching her.

Claire slowly came around and glanced at him.

"Oh, I didn't know you were here," she said as she yawned. "What are you doing?"

"Watching you, Goldilocks, you're so beautiful when you drool," he said with a big smile.

"Ha! You crazy man!" she said laughing as she wiped her mouth. "I can tell my married life will be more exciting."

"I have something else you should find exciting," Tom said. He scooted forward on the sofa as he found the ring box in his pocket, opened it up and held it out.

Claire's eyes got big and her jaw dropped.

"Tom! How did you? When?"

"Hey, you're not the only one who can pull surprises," Tom said with a wink. "Would you like to try it on?"

"I, I don't know what to say, of course! My left hand doesn't work very well but let's see what we can do. I may have to wear it on my right."

She put her glasses on and stiffly lifted her left arm up and dropped the hand in her lap. Tom took the ring out and pushed it onto her ring finger, a snug fit.

Claire held up the hand as high as she could and admired the diamond's fire.

"Oh, I never, I never thought I would see this day!" she said as she stared at her new ring. "Oh, I don't know what to say, I'm speechless."

"Good, that's just what I'd hoped for," Tom said. "Say nothing at all. I just want you to be happy."

But Claire took her glasses off and started crying.

"Tom, I don't know, maybe we shouldn't do this," she said, sniffing.

A third rejection? He sat up, shocked.

"Why?"

"I'm not Linda."

Tom leaned over and held his head in his hands.

"Look, Tom, please, I got to thinking last night after you left. Maybe I'm not the woman for you."

"I know you're not Linda," he said firmly. "Linda was Linda, Claire is Claire. I love you for who you are, just as I loved her for who she was. I loved her with all my heart, we had a happy marriage, she gave me two children. But she's gone, that's history.

"The question for you and me is, are we history—or are we the future?" he asked. "What does the Bible say? 'Forget the former things, do not dwell on the past.'"

Claire wiped her eyes on her sleeve.

"Okay, but sometimes I can be difficult."

"You think I don't know that?" Tom said, laughing.

"I'm just thinking this through. You say you want to make me happy and, well, I want to make you happy too," she said between sniffs.

"Sounds like a plan!" Tom replied, smiling.

Chapter 21
Something Small

Mrs. Stevens sat at her desk, monthly report time again. She tried to figure how to get the spreadsheet cells to add up to the number headquarters in St. Louis wanted. At least the tornado would be next month. Her office door opened and Claire wheeled in, carrying Tom's plastic cane as he pushed her.

Odd, residents rarely came to her. She went to them.

"Good afternoon!" she said pleasantly, turning from her computer screen to greet her visitors. "Have a seat, Tom," she added, waving toward an empty chair. He settled down, bracing himself on his cane after Claire handed it over. Claire set her brake.

Both sat there, smiling.

"And how may I help you?" the manager asked, puzzled by the interruption.

Tom cleared his throat.

"Mrs. Stevens, we want to get married," he replied.

She felt her jaw and her pencil drop at the same instant.

"You want to do *what?*" she asked, thinking she had misunderstood. Maybe they meant they wanted to leave Hickory Bough to go to some grandchild's wedding, a niece or nephew, or something. Sure, she could arrange that.

Claire leaned forward and in a low, firm voice replied, "Tom and I wish to be married. What is the home's procedure?"

This floored the manager.

Mrs. Stevens leaned back in her chair, she could not think of anything to say. She managed senior centers, rehabilitation departments, assisted living homes, retirement developments and, yes, nursing homes for twenty-plus years.

She thought she had seen it all: fights, drug abuse, attacks of insanity, prescription thefts, suicide, insubordinate employees, convulsions, fires, deaths—lots of deaths, even hanky-panky between old-geezer residents.

And yes, she thought to herself as she looked at this old couple, tornadoes.

But this—this!

Maybe the old pair had some kind of a joke in mind? But Tom and Claire weren't smiling. Both sat there solemnly, facing her.

Could these two in their eighties, one of whom could not walk, be serious?

She stuttered, "Well, I, uh, there might be, um, well, I, oh, I don't think we have a specific policy on that; rare."

Tom and Claire both shifted in their seats.

Hickory Bough's manager thought for a moment and added, "But I guess we could handle it as something small, a little reception, like a hundredth birthday party, we have done a few of those.

"We did one several years ago for that spinster, what was her name, Humphries? But no one came. Do you think anyone will come?"

Tom and Claire laughed loudly, to Mrs. Stevens' puzzlement.

He nodded, "Yes, we'll have some family, that would be fine. We've talked about it and we know it'll be a little thing, nothing major. I'll have my kids and Claire's niece and her family will come. Some extended family might drive in.

"A few of the residents who know us might like to attend. I know Tony wouldn't miss it," he added.

The thought of Hickory Bough's resident comedian loosened the stiff mood.

Mrs. Stevens covered her mouth, shook her head and chuckled.

"Look, I know this isn't any of my business, but are both of you *sure* you want to do this? Have you thought it through?" she asked.

"More than you can possibly know," Claire answered firmly, stiffly lifting her left hand and placing it on the front of Mrs. Stevens's desk, "You don't know, you don't know."

Her sparkling rock caught the manager's eye. The phone rang but she ignored it.

"Have you told anyone yet?" she asked.

"No," Tom said, "except my kids, Claire plans to call her niece today. We just decided this and we want to do everything right, so we came to you first."

"And who would you like to officiate?" the manager asked.

The couple answered in unison: "Gaylene."

Oh no, she feared that.

The manager deeply appreciated all Gaylene did for the residents but, well, she had a way of getting overly excited.

"Have you said anything to her?" Mrs. Stevens asked.

"No, not yet," Tom answered. "I'm sure she'll be willing."

"And when would you like to have the ceremony?"

"Maybe after Memorial Day, early June?" Claire asked. "I know you have a lot of visitors around the holiday so you could get that over with first."

"That sounds acceptable," Mrs. Stevens said, rubbing her temples. "I need to think about all this and get things firmed up. I guess we need to get you a license. I assume you both are of legal age?" she asked with a rare, sincere smile.

All three laughed.

"I don't know if the county can send someone out here, I always thought you had to go down to the courthouse but that would be a challenge for you, I know. It would be hard to get you up all those steps," the manager said.

"Yes, quite," Claire replied.

"Let me do some checking, I have a neighbor who works for the Limestone County Recorder of Deeds," Mrs. Stevens said. "I think that's where you have to go, we married in Illinois, it's different. Let me make a phone call, maybe they can have someone drive out."

"That'll be fine," Tom answered.

"I'll talk to the kitchen, we can work up a little reception thing," Mrs. Stevens said. "I'll let you know what I find out."

Tom and Claire nodded, thanked her and turned to leave.

The manager watched them go as she slowly shook her head.

"What are they thinking?" Mrs. Stevens muttered.

But golly, that big rock on her finger looked pretty serious.

She brightened. They said they wanted it to be simple with a small crowd—cake, punch and cookies should cover things—nothing major. Fine, the kitchen has those nice white table cloths in storage and they could set out some flowers. That should do it, and a cake from that bakery out on the bypass.

Tom and Claire crossed the dayroom, both sensing the manager's foreboding.

"That didn't go well," Tom told his fiancée.

"She worries a lot, maybe she has to," Claire answered, rolling Tom's cane around on her armrests. "I guess we better do what we can to keep this low key."

Mrs. Stevens seemed to have the right idea: Like a little birthday party with a couple-dozen people. The only difference would be Gaylene in her vestments, reading from her *Book of Common Prayer*.

Keep it simple.

"Do we need Gaylene?" Tom asked with a wink. "You're a judge, can't you marry yourself?"

Claire snorted and laughed. "It doesn't work that way!"

Things were rolling, the bigger question might be how long it would take to get organized.

"Timing is an issue we need to consider," Claire suggested. "Neither of us buys green bananas anymore."

More laughter.

"You're right! We need to make sure the newspaper gets the wedding announcement before the obituary," Tom added. "Maybe we can do a bridal registry at the drug store so our friends can help us stock up on walkers, fiber pills, oxygen tanks and diapers."

Claire enjoyed a good belly laugh.

"Excuse me, I do not need adult diapers—yet!" she replied, giggling.

It felt good to laugh after all they had been through in past weeks.

"I remember the first time you made me laugh, out there on the porch in the cold," she said, catching herself and looking fondly at Tom.

Claire sighed and looked back at her hand and stretched her fingers out, she couldn't take her eyes off the ring.

"It's really going to happen," she said distantly.

Mrs. Stevens called her neighbor, who talked to the county recorder who said yes, someone in the office could come out. There's a lady on the staff who lives out that way. Unusual, but we've done this. Just have a check for the $50 fee, Social Security cards and driver's licenses.

And yes, proof of age.

Chapter 22
That Won't Hurt Anything

The snowball started to roll.

The *Randall Ledger*'s cub reporter came by the recorder's office the next day, as she did every week, to get the list of marriage licenses for the paper's vital statistics section, always printed above the divorce list that she picked up from the court clerk down the hall.

Oh by the way, the clerk mentioned, we had an odd one. Some old couple out at Hickory Bough wants to get married. Both of them are eighty, imagine!

The tip made it back to the newsroom but the editor didn't have time to track the couple down and do a story. Deadlines don't wait. Instead, two sentences went in the paper's popular, but gossipy, bullet-pointed "Around The Square" column that filled the first column of the front page:

"* Spring has sprung and love blooms eternal. A Hickory Bough couple in their ninth decade contacted the Limestone County recorder's office for information on a marriage license."

Mrs. Stevens's copy of the *Ledger* had plopped on top of the mail in her in-box but she hadn't looked at it yet when the state editor at the *Springfield News-Leader* called. The Limestone County recorder tells us a couple of your residents want to get married, may I talk to them?

Hickory Bough's manager did not like newspaper reporters.

She remembered how badly the *Ledger* handled a story a couple years earlier when the county health inspector gave the home's kitchen a low rating after a routine check. A long, page-one feature revolved around a single dead cockroach found on the kitchen's loading dock. A lengthy side story described the diseases spread by roaches and how readers could prevent roach infestations in their homes.

Her phone rang for days.

Upset relatives, worried about elderly loved ones, called and yelled. She lost residents.

Headquarters was not amused.

The manager agreed to take a phone number and pass it along to the couple, figuring with their keep-it-simple plans the call wouldn't be returned. If the couple wishes to speak, she emphasized, then they will call you, it's not my responsibility.

She wrote down the number and walked over to Tom's suite, now pretty much empty every day. The manager then crossed to C Hall and, no surprise, Tom sat quietly looking out the window at the birds as his fiancée read her Nook.

The manager nodded to Claire, then whispered the topic as Tom took the note. He mumbled "that won't hurt anything," and decided to return the call. After all, they both had friends around the area who would be happy about the way things worked out.

"Be right back," he said to Claire, she smiled, and he shuffled out to the dayroom, dug around in his pocket for his phone, sat down and called the newspaper.

Yes, it's true.

He, Tom Bentley, a widower, had proposed to his high school sweetheart, retired federal Judge Claire Dearborn. They had reunited after six decades and looked forward to life together, however long that might be; not much to it.

Oh yes, chuckling, Tom noted they were the Randall High Class of 1949 Glamour Couple, then he went to the Korean War and his fiancée went east to law school. The reporter thanked him.

Well, so much for that. Tom thought it would get a paragraph or two, buried under the comics or crossword puzzle.

Hey, maybe they'd run it by the obits.

The next day's Springfield paper plopped at the front door to the biggest stir at Hickory Bough since the tornado. Right there, across the top of page one, splashed a big feature. Local TV had it too, quoting the paper.

Then a wire service picked up the article and hundreds of newspapers all over the country posted the story on their websites. It became the three-sentence, end-of-the-news closer on radio stations' hourly news reports, just before local weather and traffic.

Both Mrs. Stevens's office phone and Tom's cell phone rang incessantly. A video crew from a local television station came by for interviews.

Things were getting out of hand quickly.

A frazzled Mrs. Stevens said no, the video crew may not come in, she would have to talk to headquarters. Corporate's PR director in St. Louis will call, have a nice day.

Only he didn't.

335

The six o'clock news opened with a hard-hitting report, accompanied by video of Hickory Bough's big sign and its parking lot with an ambulance by the front door of how the "nursing home" had forced some old couple to get married.

Why?

Management had no comment! What are they hiding? Is this a cover-up?

Could this be sexual harassment?

Had the woman been improperly touched?

And what does this sort of thing say about our community?

The station's stern-looking investigative reporter, the one whose tie always hung loosened and whose shirtsleeves were eternally rolled up, ended the story by looking straight into the camera and shouting, "Action News Now wants to *know*!"

Tom Junior's voicemail got buried somewhere in Tom's phone and the worried son showed up at Hickory Bough's front door about the same time as Claire's niece rushed in.

"They did what?" Tom asked as his son described the TV story.

"Watch it yourself, it'll be on at ten o'clock!" the son replied. "You better go see Claire."

"Good idea."

The pair got up and headed for her room, traveling as fast at the old man could tap down the hall. The women were loudly discussing the story as they came in.

"What did you tell them, Tom?" his fiancée demanded as father and son rushed in her room.

"Nothing! I never talked to a TV station, I guess they called Mrs. Stevens, I don't know!" he answered with a shrug.

Should they call the station? What would people think? The conversation went around and around and finally Tom Junior noted, "They did not mention your names, it's not your problem. It's all about Hickory Bough.

"Who knows? Maybe someone else around here's getting married. Let Mrs. Stevens handle it!"

Well, Tom Junior was right.

Tom stayed up with Claire to watch the ten o'clock version—well past their normal bedtimes. The story ran again, now buried behind a wreck on Interstate 44, a shooting in Joplin and a car dealer's loud commercial: "Check me first, check me last! Either way, we deal fast!"

They watched, appalled.

"Good grief!" Claire said, shaking her head. "Who thinks up such silly stuff?"

"I don't know, sweetheart, but maybe you'll have your big wedding after all," Tom replied.

They hadn't set a date other than "soon." Would this kind of thing go on until then?

Claire rested her head on her palm and said, "Let's go to bed. This whole thing will work out and probably blow over tomorrow."

But it didn't.

Two other television news crews and a radio reporter waited at the front door when Mrs. Stevens arrived for work the next morning. They stuck microphones in her face and started shouting questions as the cameras rolled.

337

Flustered, she waved them off with an "I can't comment, someone will contact you!" She ran to her office, catching attention at the horseshoe. No one had ever seen Mrs. Stevens run.

She slammed her door and called the PR office, and as usual her call rolled to voicemail. Apparently the frantic tone in her voice brought the response she wanted and the communications staff called her back in minutes.

Nothing to worry about, the communications director assured her, just put a sign on the front door that says "Media" with his name and number.

"Thanks and have a good'un!"

Click.

The manager hung up and took a sheet of copy paper out of her printer and started to make the sign when her phone rang again.

Change in plans: Instead, put up a sign that says "Press briefing here, 4 p.m." and tape it to the door. Someone will come out from St. Louis and they'll handle this. Give him whatever he needs—but let him do the talking.

She noticed she had four more calls while she was on the phone to headquarters.

The manager wrote out the sign, took a piece of tape and stuck it to the window on Hickory's Bough's front entrance. More reporters had arrived and all started shouting questions through the door.

Mrs. Stevens shook her head "no," pointed to the sign and went back inside. She hustled over to Tom's suite, still empty, then to the dining room where she found him eating breakfast.

"I don't know what's going on, this is terrible!" she said as she came toward him at a trot, out of breath and wringing her hands. "Headquarters is sending someone out to handle things."

Tom nodded and added "keep us posted" as he drank his coffee.

Oh my, Mrs. Stevens thought, it's nearly nine o'clock and she hadn't had her coffee yet. Would the whole day be like this?

That afternoon a mature, distinguished, sixtyish gentleman, wearing a suit, came through the front door and walked over to Mrs. Stevens's office. He looked in, the manager sat there, her head resting in her hands, worried.

"Excuse me, are you Mrs. Stevens?" he asked cordially.

"Yes, how may I help you?"

"The question, ma'am, is how may I help *you*?" he answered with a slight bow.

"And you are?"

"I'm Bob Dearborn, vice president of crisis media for Wheatley, Davis & Harrison. We're a media relations, advertising and marketing conglomerate based in St. Louis. Your owner, Bird Creek Senior Living, is one of our clients."

"So you're here to handle this silly television... Wait, did you say your name is *Dearborn*?" Mrs. Stevens asked.

"Yes, ma'am, Judge Dearborn is my aunt," he said in a rich baritone.

"Well! Oh my, who would have thought, let's go see her."

Mrs. Stevens jumped up from her desk and the two walked briskly to Claire's suite where they found Claire and Tom finishing lunch. Claire brightened as they walked in.

"Bobby! So good to see you! How are things in Creve Coeur?" she called as she waved at the door.

"Fine, and I must say you're looking good Aunt Claire. How is the blushing bride?" Bob said as he bent over and gave her a two-armed bear hug.

"I'm beyond wonderful, see the ring?" she said, waving her hand.

"Oh Tom, this is my nephew, Bob Dearborn. He's with the PR firm that will take care of the media stuff," she said, turning to the sofa.

Tom stood up.

"He's what?"

Claire had pulled another one.

"And I assume you are the lucky gentleman who has won my dear aunt's hand?" Bob asked as he turned to shake with Tom.

"Yes, I am, thanks. And if you don't mind me saying it, you have your late grandfather's voice," Tom said, still stunned.

"Thank you, I've been told that, what an inspiration he was, Campbell was one fine man. I did radio for years."

Bob turned to Mrs. Stevens and asked, "Do you have a spare room, a conference room maybe?"

"Yes, there's one across the dayroom from my office."

340

"Fine, that will be our communications center. Let me set up. I have staffers on the way who'll arrive late this afternoon. We need Wi-Fi and several electrical outlets. Can your kitchen keep coffee, tea and water for us?" Bob asked. "A few light snacks, cookies and that sort of thing, would be nice too. We will be here late."

"Yes, I guess so."

"Good. I'll be back to you for details in an hour or so for the four o'clock presser. St. Louis released a media advisory while I drove so we may have a crowd. I ordered a security patrol to handle traffic, parking and to guard the door. We don't want just anyone in here wandering around, and for the most part I'd like to ask the three of you to stay out of the conference room, we'll be busy.

"Any questions?"

"So you've done this sort of thing before?" Tom asked.

"Oh yes, the big Mississippi flood of '93, some plane crashes, shootings, a bombing, a riot or two."

Tom shook his head.

Bob left with a bewildered Mrs. Stevens chasing right behind.

Tom turned and stared a hole in Claire.

"What?" she asked blankly.

"How do you do it?" he asked.

"Do what?" she answered innocently.

"You know what: a PR flack for a wedding! And this on top of that afternoon in chemistry, then the bus ride. What else? Let's see, there was the four-year-old song on The Malt Shop jukebox, which got weekly record changes, shall I go on?

"You know what I mean! There's a Claire I still do not know!

"Sometimes, I feel like that little old man in that movie *Up!*. I'm just hanging onto the balloon," Tom said.

"Are you saying I'm shaped like a balloon?" Claire asked with her half smile.

"Well, no," Tom said as he lost his seriousness to laughter.

"So are you complaining? Wasn't he an elderly widower? Maybe you have something in common with him."

"No, I guess I'm not."

They both laughed.

"You just have to make the most of what you have," she replied firmly. "I have a lot, and now I'll have you! This is just my way of assuring we have our quiet, simple little wedding."

Tom continued to stare at his fiancée.

"And by the way, I have to mention, what about the coincidence of you showing up at Hickory Bough just a few weeks after I moved here?" Tom asked, staring intently into her now-sparkling eyes.

"I'm not sure what you mean," Claire replied with a shrug. "Again, are you complaining?"

Tom sighed. Who knew what went on in that blonde-and-silver head?

Bob and Mrs. Stevens were back soon. The old couple slouched in Claire's room, both well into afternoon naps. Bob coughed loudly and both jerked awake.

"Yes?" Tom asked as he stretched.

342

"What do you two have planned?" Bob asked.

Claire had come around.

"Well, we're planning to have a simple little ceremony in a week or two here at Hickory Bough," Tom answered, rubbing his face. "Nothing elaborate, we just need you to chase off the reporters so we can get on with things."

"That's our plan," Claire added.

"That's not gonna' happen," Bob said firmly.

"We better talk," he added as he sat down next to Tom.

"This thing has exploded. I wore out Bluetooth coming down I-44. My cell phone has been buzzing in my pocket for two hours and my email in-box has a hundred messages. That doesn't count texts. I expect a hundred-plus people there in the parking lot at four o'clock."

Tom and Claire stared, slack jawed.

"But why?" his aunt asked. "We're just an old couple, two old coots. Who cares?"

"I don't know," her nephew replied. "June's coming up, the wedding month, and the media think this is some sort of sweet little feature, what's known as a 'bright' in the news biz."

"Some picked up the TV clip from last night and they're after a seamy angle: What's going on out at that perverted nursing home?"

"Excuse me!" Mrs. Stevens said, ignoring "perverted" to correct Bob with "we are a senior living solution!"

343

"Whatever. Anyway, the two of you are hot. Rush Limbaugh calls them the 'drive-by media.' Like it or not, the drive-bys are pulling in your driveway."

"Good golly, what should we do?" Tom asked.

"I'll do the best I can, I have a personal interest in this one," Bob said, winking at Aunt Claire. "This is a tidal wave, the best we can do is steer it. If we don't, the reputations of Hickory Bough and the two of you can be destroyed."

"Does headquarters know about this?" a more-nervous-than-usual Mrs. Stevens asked.

"That's why I'm here," Bob answered.

"I'm here to make you look good. This is a sweet, innocent, feel-good story and that's what I'll talk about. We want everyone involved to come out on top—all made possible by the great folks at Hickory Bough."

"It seems like covering good news would be a no-brainer," Tom said.

"No, it isn't," Bob answered. "Sharing positive information can be tricky. There's a reason why the evening news leads with fires, rapes and scandals. It's why people rubber-neck when they pass wrecks on the highway.

"Look, my grandfather had a gift of seeing the future, where things are going, what's going to happen? Let's do the same," Bob added.

"Don't think about stopping this, think about steering it the way you want it to go. Don't think about that plague of locusts out front, think about book deals, speaking engagements, late-night talk show appearances, maybe a movie deal," he added.

"How about Meryl Streep as Claire?"

Tom, Claire and Mrs. Stevens stared, speechless.

"Meryl Streep?" Claire said in awe.

"Think royalties.

"You two can have each other *and* make a lot of people feel good about life—and make some money in the process. Those are not bad things. And you can talk about how wonderful Hickory Bough is and how it all happened right here. People will start buying Hickory Bough T-shirts and coasters."

Mrs. Stevens smiled for the first time.

"Oh my," Claire said, shaking her head. "What have we done?"

"You haven't done a thing except be your sweet, lovable self, Aunt Claire," Bob said as stood up to kiss her cheek.

"I remember when my name came up for the Supreme Court seat," Claire volunteered. "Everything went nuts, reporters were everywhere, and I didn't even get the nomination."

"Same thing," her nephew replied. "Wasn't the White House press office there?"

"Yes, someone took care of all that."

"Well, that's my job," Bob said.

"So first things first, when's the date?"

"We want to do it sometime in June," Tom replied.

"June is a long time off, sooner the better. We want to have this quickly enough that it stays on the front burner."

"Well, this weekend is Memorial Day and a week from Friday is the first of June," Mrs. Stevens said.

"Perfect, a Friday will get us the best air time on the network morning shows, and the first of the month will let them segue into all sorts of wedding stories and interviews with psychologists and ministers. Can you be ready that soon?" Bob asked, turning to Mrs. Stevens.

"I guess we can," the manager said. "What about the two of you?"

"I just want to hurry up and get it over with," Tom said, "for the right reasons, of course. What do you think, dear?"

Claire nodded. "I guess so."

Just then Gaylene rolled into the room.

"Hello, everybody! I haven't seen you in such a long time!" she gushed, then looked around the room.

"Something's happening!"

"Mrs. Stevens, you better shut the door," Tom said wryly.

She did. Bob invited Gaylene to sit by him on Claire's bed.

"Gaylene, Tom and Claire and getting married," Mrs. Stevens explained.

"That is so wonderful!" Gaylene gushed.

"Now just a minute," Mrs. Stevens cautioned, "this gets complicated. There were stories in the paper and on television, a lot of people are interested in this. We've asked Bob Dearborn, here, Claire's nephew, to help answer reporters' questions.

"And Bob, this is the Rev. Gaylene Gillogly, she's the rector of an Episcopal church near here and the chaplain of Hickory Bough."

"This is so wonderful!" Gaylene said as she nodded.

"We need you to do two things," the manager continued. "First, Tom and Claire would like for you to do the ceremony and second, let Mr. Dearborn handle the reporters."

"Of course, it would be an honor! So that's why all those people are in the parking lot!" she said.

"Exactly," Bob replied. "May I suggest we set the wedding for 8:12 a.m. a week from Friday?"

"Uh, could you be more precise?" Tom said, which brought a chuckle from the group.

"Maybe. Maybe we can say 8:12:30," Bob explained. "We're going to offer a live video feed to the networks. Twelve minutes after the hour will give them time to do top-of-the-hour news and weather, then an intro to their stand-up here, and away we go. We should keep the ceremony to fourteen minutes so they can break at the bottom of the hour."

"Are you serious?" Tom asked with a frown.

"That's my job," Bob replied.

His companions stared at him.

"Maybe, maybe not, it all depends on what else is going on next week. If something blows up, or terrorists do something awful in the Mideast, all bets are off. But we need to be ready.

"Listen, I better get ready for the briefing," he added.

"Uh, can we eaves drop?" Tom asked.

"Sure, but stay out of sight."

At four o'clock sharp Bob walked out onto Hickory Bough's covered entryway to face a phalanx of reporters,

347

photographers, producers, light and sound people. Floodlights blinked on.

"Hey don Roberto, you rascal, what you doin' out here in the sticks?" someone called from the back of the pack to laughter.

"Well hello, guys! Glad to see everyone else made it past that wreck in Kirkwood.

"Anyway, I'm here in Randall to help tell a very happy, very sweet story about two wonderful old people, retired federal appeals court Judge Claire Dearborn and Korean War hero Tom Bentley" he answered. "It's a reminder of just how special life can be."

Holiday weekend or not, another Sunday afternoon rolled around and the senior network news managers gathered as usual forty stories up in Midtown Manhattan. What would the morning show have this week?

Ratings hadn't been what the head shed wanted, ABC's *Good Morning America* had ticked up again in the latest survey: Find eyeballs, they felt the pressure.

The dozen or so staff sat down around the table and shuffled a stack of story ideas as the executive producer went through her pile.

"Okay, what have we got, looks like a quiet week. We have the holiday tomorrow, lots of features in the can, breaking news on boating accidents and the like expected. What about the rest of the week?"

Someone noted the President would be at Camp David and Congress was in recess, nothing out of Washington.

348

The forecast? The long-range weather looked surprisingly quiet.

Sports? Not much, with luck maybe some pitcher will throw a no-hitter.

The exec sighed.

"We don't have much to work with, even the Kardashians aren't doing anything," someone noted, which brought laughter.

"What about the royal family? Any scandals, new babies, anything from London?"

Nope.

"C'mon folks, we need dirty laundry! Any Hollywood scandals, any hot gossip?" the exec asked.

Silence.

"Any new movies?"

Well no, the entertainment producer explained, another couple weeks before the studios wanted to plug summer releases.

She sighed.

"This could be tough. Wait, what about this wedding, the old geezers in Missouri? Now that's a bright. People like that kind of stuff; sweetness and light."

Good idea, there were nods around the table, everyone loves weddings and June's the wedding month; great kickoff for some follow-ups, some good ad pitches.

And, Wheatley-Davis out in St. Louis is handling it, they have a list of interviews and video coming.

"Wait, they have PR doing their *wedding*?" some staffer asked, incredulously. "Who *are* these people?"

There were shrugs and "I dunnos" around the table.

"Go with it, we need all the help we can get," the exec said. "Puff the wedding."

Everyone stood up and shuffled back to their cubicles, time to make some phone calls and get the story producers busy in the editing suites.

Chapter 23
The Four Seasons

The menu had soup and sandwiches for lunch. Tom finished his iced tea as Mrs. Stevens scurried into the dining room.

"Gaylene's here, she wants to talk to you," the manager said. "She's in your suite."

"Sure," he answered, and he tapped back down the hall.

Ever-fizzy Gaylene waved as he walked in.

"Well, Tom! This is all so exciting!" she said.

"I hope this hasn't got out of hand," he replied, "It's not what we planned."

"I love doing weddings!"

"Sure, what's up?"

"I had a nice visit with Claire and we have the service all set! She is such a wonderful lady!"

"I think so," Tom replied.

"We can go over it now!" the chaplain offered.

"No, whatever Claire wants is fine," Tom replied. "If it were me, I'd just have you ask, 'Well do'ya or don'cha?' and we'd sit down."

That puzzled Gaylene, who sat for a moment thinking.

"Oh, if only all the couples I marry were so agreeable!" Gaylene chirped.

"Well, just one more thing! Tom, I always conduct interviews with both people before I perform a wedding! I had a great conversation with Claire!"

"Sure, what do you need?"

"I want to discuss your spiritual walk, your relationship with Christ! The man should be the spiritual shepherd of his household! I want to make sure you're ready!"

Tom thought for a moment.

"Gaylene, look, bear in mind I'm a widower, a father and a grandfather. I've been active in church most of my life, I was a deacon for years. I think I have a good handle on things. I'd be happy to talk about all that sort of stuff. But if you don't mind, can you tell me about yourself? How did you get in the ministry?" Tom asked.

"Oh, of course! Speaking of spiritual shepherds, it's because of my wonderful father! He pastored a parish in Columbia, Missouri, where I grew up!"

"Oh, I didn't know that, Claire and I went to Mizzou," Tom said.

"That's so wonderful! My father did a lot of work with students at Missouri! He called students 'my special people!' I like to think of everyone at Hickory Bough as *my* special people!"

On she gushed about growing up in church, sitting in a pew every Sunday, admiring her father's preaching, and his devotion to his flock.

She described his college ministry, talking depressed students out of suicide, helping them overcome alcohol and drug issues, problem pregnancies, and other crises college students face.

"But he was *most* proud of his work helping students decide on future careers as they graduated, especially young coeds! He helped several talented young ladies get into law school through this foundation he heard about!" Gaylene said, babbling on.

Tom gulped.

No, could it be?

"Uh, and just where did these young women go to law school?" he asked, his voice shaking.

"Columbia in New York! It's very prestigious!"

No, no, this could not be.

How could Gaylene *not* have put two-and-two together after talking to Claire? He felt his face go red.

Gaylene's father had been the one who talked Claire into law school.

She gushed on about her time in seminary and how her husband "is such a special person!" so understanding of her pastoral responsibilities.

Tom looked away, he could not listen.

Darkness fell, the room began a wobbly spin, his stomach churned, tunnel vision came on as everything went black. He slumped across the sofa and fell in the floor.

Where was he?

This was no flashback but a full-on, ghastly nightmare: He ran down the Randall station's dark platform through blowing snow, frantically pushing through a crowd pointing and laughing at him.

He must find Claire, he ran on and on through the cold. Breathless, he stumbled into the waiting room.

"You gonna' be here long? I need to lock up!" the angry agent yelled. The words echoed around and around.

"You gonna' be here long? I need to lock up!

"You gonna' be here long? I need to lock up!"

Then the agent joined the hysterical laughter as a horrified Tom stumbled back into the cold night. Shrieks and screams filled his ears as a train pulled away in a swirl of snow.

He called: "Claire! Claire!" to no answer.

He ran on and on into a dark blizzard—calling, pleading—as the hysterical laughter continued.

The siren wailed as the ambulance tore through downtown Randall with its lights flashing. A groggy Tom looked around and blinked, at last focusing on a man's face above him.

"You comin' around, pal?" the emergency tech asked.

"I guess, where am I?"

"You're on the way to the hospital, you blacked out," the tech replied.

Tom looked around as the ambulance sped on. Not again, he was getting tired of these things.

"Wait, I can't go to the hospital, I'm getting married!"

The tech stared at him, his stethoscope swaying just above Tom's nose.

"Hold it, are you that old guy they've been talkin' about on the news?" the tech asked.

"Yeah, that's me."

The technician grimaced, thought for a moment, then pulled the radio off his belt and clicked the button.

"Randall Hospital, ten-seventy-six for VIP patient arrival, five minutes. I'm clear."

No confused crowd greeted him this time. Half the hospital's emergency room staff stood, lined up either side of the ambulance door. Orderlies took his gurney straight to a private room past other patients waiting for treatment. Two doctors and an entire staff of nurses and techs went right to work.

"Your blood pressure and vitals seem to be back to normal," an ER physician said after checking him over. "You have a little rug burn on your forehead. I think you should spend the night here so we can keep an eye on things."

"Doc, I can't do that, I need to get back to Hickory Bough," Tom pleaded.

"Yes, I know, everyone in America knows. But I want to make sure you live until Friday. Let us keep you, we'll make some calls."

Tom nodded.

Living until the ceremony sounded like a good idea.

The nurses put him in a wheelchair and took him down the hall to a room. They helped him into a gown and into bed, then wired him to a jillion heart and blood pressure monitors, an IV drip and who-knows-what-else. A blood pressure monitor groaned every few minutes as it squeezed his arm.

Hospitals depressed him, they made him think of Linda's last days.

Oh, sweet Linda.

He poked around for the TV remote amid the spaghetti bowl of tubes and wires, just then a wide-eyed Claire rolled in, pushed by an anxious Tom Junior with Judy trotting fast behind.

"Are you okay? Please, speak to me!" Claire called frantically as she waved to him.

"I'm fine, I'm fine, just another one of my attacks," he replied calmly.

"I hear you missed all the excitement, Pop," Tom Junior said, leaning on Claire's wheelchair handles as Judy bent over to kiss him.

"That's true, you did," Claire seconded, visibly upset.

"Really? What happened?" Tom asked.

"Oh my, Gaylene at her worst!" Claire answered. "She came running down the hall, screaming at the top of her lungs: 'TOM DIED! TOM DIED!' I could hear her down in my room and, oh!, I thought *I* was going to die. She could have yelled 'Fire!' and people would not have gone as crazy.

"How did this happen, sweetheart?"

Tom shook his head, he could not bear to tell Claire everything.

"Well, uh, she was in my room, we, uh, had our before-the-wedding talk, and I, uh, was on the sofa and, I sort of, well, passed out," he explained.

His visiting trio stood there looking at the old man with the same expression: "And?"

Tom coughed and tried to change the subject.

"Gaylene told me during our conversation that she had talked to you, any surprises?" he asked nonchalantly.

"No, just basic stuff about commitment, my spiritual walk, that sort of thing," Claire said.

"Nothing unusual?" Tom asked, probing.

"No, why?" Claire looked at him sideways.

356

Tom thought for a moment.

"Oh, just wondered. Sometimes odd stuff comes out in these kinds of things."

"Like what?" Claire asked, suspicious.

"Just depends," Tom answered innocently.

"I guess that's true, so when will you get out of here?"

"I want to go now but, as the doctor put it, 'I want to make sure you live until Friday.'"

"Now that sounds like a plan," Tom Junior said.

"Oh, my sweet darling, please! Take care of yourself!" Claire said as she reached through the wires, cords and the dripline to take his hand. "We're this close!"

"I'll be alright, trust me," Tom answered.

The four of them had a good conversation, Tom thanked his son and daughter-in-law for picking up Claire as the trio left. He knew it must have been a job to get her in and out of the car.

He ate very late, finishing right before the ten o'clock news. He flipped on the TV just in time to catch the station's standard "News Now!" video of throbbing music above running reporters, a flooded highway, a flying helicopter and a burning school, which dissolved into the anchor's throaty opening: "The eighty-year-old Randall man planning to wed Friday has a heart attack and now is in ICU! Here's our reporter at the scene!"

"No! My heart is fine, can't you people get anything straight?" he yelled at the TV as he threw a cup at the screen.

Enough!

He flipped off the TV, turned out the light and tried to go to sleep.

"Claire doesn't know, she has no idea," he mumbled into his pillow.

Should he say something?

The daughter of the man who tore them apart so long ago would marry them.

How could that be?

Some innocent, kind-hearted pastor, who—just like their parents—thought he was doing the right thing, tried his best to help some poor, confused coed.

No doubt he meant well.

Tom could be bitter, or he could forgive.

But forgiving would take work.

"Lord, help me with this. I would kill the guy if he's still alive, he has no idea how badly he messed up two lives."

No, he would try to forgive and try to forget.

"You're an optimist, Bentley, let's go ahead with life and let bygones be bygones. Think about the future," he thought.

"You can't change your history but you *can* change your future," Tom mumbled aloud.

Randall's lone taxi brought Tom back to Hickory Bough the next morning. He had to dig around in his pocket to pay the fare. Bob rushed out to meet him as Tom got out.

"Are you okay? Do we need to change anything?" he asked.

"Not that I know of, I have fainting spells from time to time, but far as I know we're good to go."

"The hospital's PR woman called, frantic, last night," Bob replied. "All the local stations did live remotes in front of the emergency room and the networks picked up the story this morning. If anything, you two are even bigger now: 'Will the groom make it?'"

"Good grief," Tom mumbled. "Why would people care about one old sick guy?"

The dayroom had descended into a chaos of sawing, hammering and workers' shouts.

Tom shuffled in and around stacks of fancy white folding chairs waiting to be set up. Saws squealed and hammers banged, taking apart the nurses' horseshoe at the back of the room, then the big pieces got pushed down the hallways. Meal carts had been pressed into service to hold files and computers.

Tom glanced at the conference room, which had a big, hand-lettered COMM STAFF ONLY sign taped to the door. Bob's assistants pecked at laptops, talked on phones, and collected pages spit out by a printer. A couple of video monitors played the cable news channels.

"You look busy," he added.

"This thing has gone nuts!" Bob huffed. "You have no idea. I love Aunt Claire, she's always been sweet, but if I had known, I would've stayed in St. Louis. Gimme' a plane crash any day!"

Josefina wheeled Claire toward the men, weaving through the confusion.

"Oh, you're back!" she called out to Tom. "Kiss me!"

The couple exchanged a peck as Mrs. Stevens came out.

"I'm so glad to see you back!" she said with unusually honest enthusiasm.

"Everyone, may I remind you we only have two days left?" Bob said emphatically. "At this point I think you should have a serious talk with the chaplain. This thing has to run like clockwork Friday and I want to make sure she understands that. We can't have her running down the hall screaming again."

Mrs. Stevens sighed. "Let me track her down. Can we meet in your room, Tom?"

"Sure."

The group weaved its way through the clutter.

Gaylene rolled into the room just as the others found seats on Tom's sofa, chair and bed.

"Good morning, everyone! Isn't this exciting!" she gushed.

"Gaylene, we need to visit with you about the service," Mrs. Stevens said. "Mr. Dearborn has some things to cover."

"Yes! Wonderful! Whatever I can do to help!" Gaylene gushed.

"Reverend, please understand what happens in the service will be on national television, millions will be watching, and that means we will be on a very tight, very precise, schedule. Don't screw it up," Bob said emphatically.

Gaylene stepped back and grabbed the cross on her necklace, shocked.

"I would never do anything to ruin this special day!" she replied firmly.

"I know," Tom interrupted, "At least not intentionally. I think what he means is stick to the script."

"What happens if I make a mistake?" she asked.

That caught Tom's attention.

He could not ever remember hearing Gaylene ask a question.

"Then we'll bring in Tony to finish the service," Tom answered.

Panic gripped Gaylene and her eyes bulged as the others stifled laughter. Horrified, she rushed out of the room.

The four of them waited a few seconds, then Claire exploded. She burst out laughing hysterically and the others followed.

"Why did you say that?" she asked.

"I dunno', just wanted to get her attention," Tom replied. "It shook her cage, I've never seen her so serious."

The dayroom sat ready by Thursday as the kitchen struggled to feed Hickory Bough's residents in and around the confusion. A rehearsal went smoothly with Gaylene zipping through her lines in just under twelve minutes by Bob's cell phone.

Perfect.

Afterward, Tom tapped his way out the front door, past the guards, to get a breath of fresh air. Satellite trucks lined the road with their dishes pointed to the sky.

"Good golly, what have we got ourselves into?" the prospective groom asked Bob.

361

"You're the story of the week," came the reply, "*the* story of the week. Two people in the autumn of their lives getting married in the spring. It caught fire, lots of recorders will be running in the morning, people love it."

"So much for small and simple," Tom mumbled.

Just then a dark shadow rolled across the men and Hickory Bough's overflowing parking lot as a low roar came from overhead. Surprised, Tom looked up.

A blimp.

"What the?" he asked, shaking his head and pointing with his cane.

"It's a blimp," Bob replied.

"I know that."

"We got lucky. The thing was on its way to Southern Hills in Tulsa, the U.S. Open is down there this weekend, so we pitched the insurance company that flies it to have it spend the night at Springfield. It'll circle us here before the service. The network covering the golf tournament doesn't need it until Saturday afternoon; plenty of time to float down I-44. It can provide great bumper shots for the TV networks—Hickory Bough, the green Ozarks and Randall's skyline, such as it is."

Tom stood dumbfounded. A stupid blimp—for a wedding?

"Can you get me a ride in that thing?" Tom asked, watching as it slowly growled off to the west.

"I'd like to ride in it myself but, hey, we're both kinda' busy tomorrow," Bob answered with a chuckle.

He went by Claire's room and they shared dinner. Claire picked at her tray.

"I'm not very hungry for once," she said, putting down her fork.

"Same here," her fiancé replied. "I hope we can pull this off."

"I guess we don't know how special all of this is to people. But I do wish they'd stop calling me 'the December bride,'" Claire added, laughing. "Can I at least be a 'November?'"

"I watched TV this afternoon, all interviews with psychologists and rabbis and such—all talking about us! Why is that wedding in Missouri such a big deal? What makes this old couple so special? They all said the same thing: it's sweet and loving."

Tom shook his head and wiped his mouth with a napkin. "It feels odd to sit and watch TV and hear them talk yourself.

"Well, you'll get that big wedding you wanted after all, darling. I hope you still want to show me off."

"Oh sweetheart, of course!" Claire replied. "I told Gaylene I want her to introduce us as Mr. and Mrs. Tom Bentley."

"Whatever works for you. Now, let me see the ring before I go."

Claire held up her hand to him after she reached in her pocket and pulled out a gold band.

"And I have a little something for you to go with it," she said with a wink. "Martha brought it by."

"Same here, Tom Junior's bringing yours in the morning."

Tom bent down to kiss Claire one last time before the big day. He hugged her, then held her as she reached up and took his arm."

"See you in the morning," he said with a smile. "And you better be there this time!"

"Count on it!" she replied with a wink.

He took his cane and tapped his way past the little platform covered in a white cloth placed where the horseshoe normally stood, a hundred-odd chairs, microphones, cameras and lights.

How different it all looked than that first day he and Tom Junior walked in last fall. Life has some surprises, for sure.

He decided to take one of his sleeping pills. Certainly this night would qualify as "only when you have to."

Tom Junior knocked on B 9's door at six Friday morning.

"It's the big day, ready to go, Pop?" he asked as he came in. They had some yogurt Tom Junior had stashed in the lightly used refrigerator. Tom shaved and laid out a tuxedo, the first he'd worn since that photo shoot of the Glamour Couple. Tom Junior helped him with the cufflinks, then put on his own tux.

The men were ready way early. Tony came by, wearing a loud paisley tie, and poked his head in Tom's room.

"Hey guys! Just to see me wearin' a tie is worth the price of admission!"

Everyone laughed and Tony rolled off down the hall.

The music started, provided by a string quartet and a flute. Claire mandated a flute.

One of Bob's helpers tapped on Tom's door. "Gentlemen, it's time."

Tom Junior held his father's arm so his dad could get along without his cane.

"Pray for me, son, pray for me," Tom said, nodding.

A loud commotion suddenly started out in the dayroom and the music stopped, followed by hushed talking. Bob rushed down the hall to them, wide-eyed.

"Guys, we have a problem," he said, out of breath. "Some woman claims she's your daughter, Mr. Bentley, but she doesn't have an invitation and she's not on our invitee list."

Tom stopped.

"What did she say her name is?" he asked.

"Brenda Bentley."

"Let her in!"

"Are you sure?" Bob answered.

"Yes, please, put her in the family section with my kids."

"As you wish," Bob replied, scowling, as he hurried off.

"Could it be?" Tom Junior asked. "Is she here?"

"Why don't you sneak down there and take a peek?" Tom suggested, grabbing the hallway handrail.

Tom Junior nodded and trotted to the end of the corridor and peered around the corner. He disappeared, then came back at a near run.

"Yes, it's her! You won't recognize her but it's Brenda," the son said, out of breath.

Tom shook his head.

"Praise the Lord! Maybe all of this craziness will be worth it," he said.

The floodlights came on.

"We better get moving, Pop," Tom Junior said.

The pair shuffled down the hall and stopped just short of the dayroom. Tom discreetly peeked around the corner and yes, there she was: His daughter and Hannah chatted at the end of a row in the Bentley section.

He had not seen her in two decades and, not surprisingly, she looked older. The fiftyish Brenda wore a T-shirt that read "Rhymes With Rich," torn bluejeans and flipflops, quite a contrast to the dressed-up crowd around her. Brenda glanced up, saw her father, and mouthed "Hello."

He nodded and smiled.

The organist began *Ode to Joy*, Gaylene, impressive in her priestly vestments and looking unusually solemn, walked in from C Hall and motioned for the audience to stand. Tom and Tom Junior moved onto the spots marked with taped X's on the floor in front of Gaylene, then turned toward the door.

The double doors swung open and there she was: Claire rolled in, pushed by her niece.

Tom's jaw dropped: She really did look pretty good in white.

His bride might be eighty but she still looked like a million bucks. Claire wore a lace-covered gown and carried a small bouquet in her good hand, her long hair wrapped in a proper bun on the back of her head. He noticed a little fluff in her hair to cover her cut.

Martha rolled her aunt into position and the music stopped. Gaylene's mic came on with a click.

"The Lord be with you," she said, stoically.

"And also with you."

"A reading from the letter of the Apostle Paul to the Philippians:

"Finally, brethren…" Gaylene said, and stopped.

The dramatic pause caught and the crowd burst into laughter. Tom and Claire couldn't help themselves and laughed along.

Gaylene stood erect without cracking a smile.

"… Whatever things are true, whatever things are noble, whatever things are just, whatever things are pure, whatever things are lovely, whatever things are of good report, if there is any virtue and if there is anything praiseworthy—think on these things.

"This is the word of the Lord."

"Thanks be to God."

She motioned for the audience to be seated. Claire stood up with considerable effort. It was all Martha could do to lift her from the wheelchair, even as Tom Junior reached around his dad to help. Claire held onto Marty as Tom stood with his own slow wobble.

Gaylene looked to Claire's niece and asked, "Who gives this woman in marriage?"

"Her family," Martha answered.

"Dearly beloved," Gaylene continued from *The Book of Common Prayer*, "We have come together in the presence of God to witness and bless the joining together of this man and this woman in Holy Matrimony.

"The union of husband and wife in heart, body, and mind is intended by God for their mutual joy... Therefore marriage is not to be entered into unadvisedly or lightly, but reverently, deliberately, and in accordance with the purposes for which it was instituted by God.

"Tom and Claire, are you ready to take your vows?"

They nodded.

"Claire, will you have Tom to be your husband; to live together in the covenant of marriage? Will you love him, comfort him, honor and keep him, in sickness and in health; and, forsaking all others, be faithful to him as long as you both shall live?"

"I will."

"And Tom, will you have Claire to be your wife; to live together in the covenant of marriage? Will you love her, comfort her, honor and keep her, in sickness and in health; and, forsaking all others, be faithful to her as long as you both shall live?

"I will."

Gaylene led the two through the exchange of rings, which proved tricky. Tom didn't want to push Claire's bad hand too hard, she shook and wobbled enough already.

Then a boy and girl with the Randall High jazz combo sang a beautiful duet of *Unforgettable* as Claire continued to wobble.

Could she make it?

Standing for ten minutes matched her outer limits. Tom smiled at Claire and she smiled back nervously as she whispered, "I'm trying." The eyebrows furrowed nervously.

Gaylene led the crowd in The Lord's Prayer, finishing with a loud "Amen."

"Just as there are four seasons in a year, there are seasons in our lives that we must pass through to arrive at the place God has prepared for us," Gaylene intoned solemnly. "Some of these seasons will be unbearably hot, some bitterly cold, and some dreadfully lonely.

"These seasons will involve difficult people, as well as trying circumstances. During these times, we likely will not be able to see any value in what we are going through.

"Tom and Claire, I believe God has used the difficult times in your lives to bring you to a place of harmony and peace, close to Him and with yourselves. May your union bless you as you work to bless others.

"Enjoy this day the Lord has made, be happy and rejoice.

"And now, under the authority granted me by God and the State of Missouri, it is my pleasure to proclaim you husband and wife."

In the half-second before the applause began, Tony shouted, "Kiss'er, Tommy!"

The crowd erupted in laughter and applause.

And he did.

And she did. The girl could still really kiss.

Tom hugged Claire as she threw her good arm around him, still holding her bouquet. Tears ran down her cheeks.

"Are we in Springfield?" she whispered to Tom over the applause.

"Yes!" he replied.

As they stood, Gaylene proclaimed, "Ladies and gentlemen, please join me in greeting Mr. and Mrs. Tom Bentley."

The string quartet and the flute played.

Just then, one of Bob's helpers at the back held up the "One Minute" sign.

Perfect.

Martha and Tom Junior helped Claire back in her wheelchair, Tom shifted and turned, took the chair's handles, and the couple headed down the aisle.

He couldn't help but glance at Brenda. He smiled at her and mouthed "Later!"

Tom expected bright sunshine out the door but the outside looked dark as Hickory Bough's front door opened. He realized a mob waited for them—reporters, cameramen, light people, sound engineers—clustered under Hickory Bough's covered entry way.

"Just be yourself," Bob whispered to Tom as he and Claire went by and stopped in front of a row of microphones.

"First let me say," Tom said after they had stopped, "that my wife—oh, that sounds nice—got her wish of a big wedding, thanks to all of you."

The questions started as the laughter died down: How does it feel to be married? What do you plan to do now? Are you taking a honeymoon?

"Mr. Bentley at your age, do you expect marriage to add years to your life?" one reporter asked.

"No, but I do expect it to add life to my years," Tom replied as he turned and winked at Claire. She blushed at the laughter.

An excited young woman reporter started her question, "Judge Dearborn…" and Claire interrupted her.

"Excuse me," Claire answered sweetly, "I am now Mrs. Tom Bentley."

"As a successful career woman, do you feel limited by having a husband?" the reporter responded.

"Not at all! Tom is a wonderful man, we complement each other. I'm sure both of us will be enriched. We are both better people as a team. I'm a better person with him, and I know he will say the same about me."

Tom nodded. "That's true."

"You've just been married, what are you doing next?" another reporter asked.

"We're goin' to Disneyland!" Tom said with a big smile.

Claire looked up at him. "We are?"

He enjoyed the banter but his heart was inside: Brenda. He cut things off.

"Well everyone, thank you for being here and making our day special but we, uh, have some people we need to see," Tom added. They waved at the cameras, then Tom haltingly got down on one knee next to the wheelchair so they could provide the cameras a lingering kiss.

Tom turned Claire's wheelchair and they went back through the door.

"You cut them short, what's up?" Bob asked as they rolled into the dayroom.

"I need to find my daughter," Tom said.

"Hi, Dad," Brenda said as she walked up. "I had to be here."

"So how did you hear about it?" her father asked.

"How could I *not* hear about it?" Brenda replied, "That's all everyone's talking about. It took a while for it to soak in. Hey, that's my Dad!

"I had to come meet my new mother."

Tom hugged his daughter and kissed her cheek.

"Darling, please meet Claire," as he put his arm around her and motioned down to his new wife.

"How do you do?" Claire said, offering up her good hand.

The women shook.

"She's not very pretty but I guess that's the best you can do at eighty," Brenda told her father.

Claire didn't blink.

"I hope we get to know each other well," Claire said pleasantly.

"She's mine 'til death us do part," Tom said.

"And that may not be very long," Brenda replied.

"Changing the subject, where have you been? How did you get here?" Tom asked.

"Abbeville, down in South Louisiana, for some time. Some of us have a commune, we raise organic fruits and vegetables and free-range chickens. I hitchhiked, got stuck in Fort Smith so it took longer than I expected. A trucker dropped me off out on the bypass. I walked from there," Brenda said.

"Uh, that's five or six miles, what time did you start?" Tom replied in obvious discomfort.

"About dawn," Brenda answered.

Tom shook his head.

"Sweetheart, you should have called, your brother could've picked you up."

"Probably not, he was in bed."

Tom was more than glad to have his daughter but it hurt to see her personality hadn't changed.

"Well, anyway, you're here so let's go have some cake!" Tom said in a chipper note.

"Is it gluten free?" Brenda asked.

"Honey, it doesn't matter," Claire said, taking her step-daughter's hand. "Just take one little bite, just come have some fun."

"Okay mom, if I can call you that, I guess I can make an exception if that's what you want," Brenda answered.

"Certainly, please do," Claire replied, keeping her forced smile.

Tom Junior came up and started chatting with his sister so Tom and Claire headed to the dining room.

"I see what you mean," Claire said quietly, shaking her head.

"I'm sorry," he answered.

"Not to worry, we have some in our family. She can be Tom and Claire's first project."

"Thanks for understanding," Tom replied.

"Brenda wants a mother, I can be one!" Claire said firmly.

"The last time I talked to her, that was twenty years ago, I simply asked her to call more often," Tom said as he pushed the wheelchair toward the dining room. "She went

373

off in a fit and chewed me out. 'Nothing I do is ever good enough for you!' She hung up on me, I haven't talked to her since, until this morning."

The milling crowd cheered as Tom and Claire came into the room and Randall High's jazz combo leaned into its signature number, *Take The A Train*. There were more lights and TV cameras, a balloon drop and confetti.

The usually bland room erupted in happy confusion.

The couple went around behind a long table and stopped behind a large cake. Tom sat down next to Claire. Mrs. Stevens raised her hands to quiet the crowd and the music stopped.

"This has been a big day for all of us and we are so happy Tom and Claire permitted all of us here at Hickory Bough to be a part of this special day in their lives!" the manager chirped.

"And thanks to Hickory Bough and its staff for all you've done. You made the day special," Tom added quickly.

Bob in the back of the room gave him a thumbs-up.

They cut the cake, shared slices and Mrs. Stevens handed them glasses of champagne.

Claire froze, then leaned toward Tom and whispered, "Is this a problem?"

"Cheers!" he answered, as they clinked glasses, crossed arms and drank the toast.

There were more toasts and applause, then the combo began Vera Lynn's *We'll Meet Again* to a loud "Ahhhh!" from the crowd.

What else could follow? *There! I've Said It Again*, as Tom looked at Claire and winked.

"Is this another one of your surprises?"

"Just a request for the band, that's all," Claire said, smiling. "It's almost time to get on the bus!"

"Is that fourteen-year-old planning something?" Tom asked.

"Maybe," Claire replied with a wink.

Both went into hysterical laughter. Tom spilled cake crumbs down the front of his tux.

The festivities wound down by late morning, and workers already were taking down the chairs and re-assembling the dayroom horseshoe. The wedding party changed clothes, then had sandwiches.

The afternoon flew by as Tom Junior, Judy and their children finished moving Tom out of B 9 and into C 4. Brenda pitched in.

"Who's that girl sitting next to me during the ceremony?" Brenda asked as she carried a box to Tom's new address.

"That's Hannah, your niece," the father replied.

"She really makes me think of mom," Brenda said fondly.

"Indeed, she does, and sharp as a tack."

"I'd like to get to know her, doesn't she have a brother?" Brenda asked.

"Chad, likewise, your nephew, great young man."

"So my dear, where are you spending the night?" Claire asked as Brenda dropped the box in a rapidly filling C 4.

"My brother invited me over, I guess I'll have to stay there," Brenda complained.

"He and Judy have a lovely home and they have a spare room, I know you'll enjoy seeing him and Judy again. Hanna and Chad need to get to know their aunt," Tom replied.

Gaylene says I always do the right thing, Tom thought. "Keep trying," he muttered to himself.

"Let's talk tomorrow about getting you back to Randall, we'd love to have you nearby," he told Brenda.

"It would be a lot of trouble but I have a mother again, so it might work," Brenda replied.

What that meant Tom wasn't sure, but regaining a lost daughter would make the day a double blessing.

Bob and his crew left in late afternoon. "Long drive back to St. Louis," he said as he stood at Hickory Bough's front door.

"Come give me a hug, Bobby," Claire said, "and thank-you for everything."

"My bill will provide ample thanks," the nephew teased.

"Whatever you want, every dollar was worth it," she replied with her half smile.

Chapter 24
Home Again

There were odds and ends to tend to as a very special, bright and happy June day dissolved into a beautiful evening. Gaylene came by B 9, back to her bouncy self, and Tom passed her an envelope with a generous gift wrapped by a thank-you note written in Claire's perfect handwriting.

Tom finally rolled Claire into her room, gave her a kiss on the cheek and promised "I'll be back soon."

"Sooner the better!" she said, her blue eyes sparking. "How about nine o'clock?"

"Eight-thirty?"

"Even better!"

He bent over and hugged her, took his plastic cane off her lap and tapped back down the hall, humming. What a lucky guy!

So here they were at last, the wedding night. It wasn't a tiny apartment in Springfield, or a motel on Miami's Highway 66.

A nursing home? Explain that to a twenty-year-old. What was the promise in the gazebo that night? "My home is in your arms."

True.

He asked Claire as they ate breakfast the morning after how she got ready for the night?

"I cried my eyes out," she answered. "I'm glad it was dark in here so you couldn't see my red, puffy eyes."

"I'm sorry, did I do something wrong?" a worried Tom asked.

"Oh no, honey, I was just happy. Despite the mess-ups and mistakes, I finally had my guy—and a big wedding too!" she answered as the blue eyes squinted happily at him.

"I was a happy bride too, Madame Claire!" Clémence told me as she helped me.

Tom showered and shaved, then put on the black silk pajamas Tom Junior and Judy had given him.

"You need something slinky, dad!" Judy told him, laughing. "Those old flannel things you wear won't do on your wedding night, Romeo!"

Opening the gift made Tom's face turn red as "my kids" snickered.

"It's too late for me to slink," he mumbled.

A dab of after shave, then he put his bathrobe and slippers on, and shuffled off to Claire's "suite" from his now-empty room.

Good-bye, B 9: no more loading dock, no more dumpster.

The darkened dayroom nearly had returned to normal with the horseshoe reassembled, even if all its files and computers weren't arranged.

Mrs. Stevens had seen to it that C 4's little sign had been updated to "Mrs. & Mrs. Bentley." He tapped on the closed door and heard that beautiful voice he loved coo "come in."

"Good evening, Mrs. Bentley," he said into the dark as he opened the door.

"Good evening, Mr. Bentley," Claire replied with a giggle.

He took the "Do Not Disturb" sign off the inside doorknob and put it on the hallway side as he closed the door.

He put down his cane, put his glasses and bathrobe on the nightstand, adjusted his slinky pajamas and pulled the covers back as he slipped in beside her.

"Claire *Bentley*," he whispered to her.

"No, no, Mrs. *Tom* Bentley!" Claire said warmly.

"As you wish."

"I didn't know if you wanted my hair up or down so I left it down," she whispered.

"Excellent, down for sure. If you'd had a Dorothy Hamill in high school we would not be here," Tom replied.

Claire got the giggles.

"Dorothy Hamill wasn't around then. See? I do know you, silly boy!" she said as she ran her finger down his nose. "I know what you like!"

"Do you still want to be my girl? You said that in one of those perfect little notes you wrote back when," Tom said.

"Yes, now I know that everything I thought I knew about you is true. You really are a wonderful guy—and you're *my* guy now.

She sighed.

"I'm sorry I don't look like I once did, I know you found me attractive then. I guess Brenda's right, 'she's not very pretty.'"

Tom groaned.

"Oh c'mon, Claire, believe me, really. I still see you in that black evening gown at the prom with your hair in golden waves. You were a stunner, and you'll always look like that to me."

"Thanks, I need to hear that."

Claire rolled toward him, he could make out a broad smile in the dim light. He put his arm under her neck and pulled her close. She rolled on top of him and they kissed passionately.

"That was wonderful, what's next?" she whispered, an inch from his face.

Tom sighed.

"My dear, I'm afraid that's all there is for a man my age," he whispered back.

Claire rolled over, slapped her forehead and laughed.

"Excuse me, but it's funny! So, I guess I'm about sixty years late?"

Tom sighed.

"Well, uh, maybe twenty," he answered, embarrassed.

"Whatever, we're finally together and that's what counts. It's the Lord's blessing that we're even here, that we lived this long. Thank you for loving me," she cooed.

"My pleasure, and sorry I can't, uh, how shall I say?, make you feel more loved."

Claire laughed again.

"Oh Tom, I love you, just the way you are!"

"Me too, I love you, darling."

They cuddled, enjoying each other's warmth.

"I really am home in your arms," she whispered.

"Me too."

Tom watched her eyes slowly close, once, twice, and Claire drifted to sleep.

It had been a long day, he felt sleep coming too.

He shifted and softly laid his head next to hers as he kissed her ear and nuzzled her cheek. The fine hair tickled his face, just as it did on that bus ride long ago. He listened to her slow breathing.

Life doesn't get any better than this, he thought.

What next?

Brenda.

Then all that other stuff: book deals, movies, speaking engagements? Crazy! But after a wedding like this—a blimp!—he could believe anything.

Could their dream include more than they imagined?

He didn't care about the money, he had plenty and Claire had more, lots more, but maybe they could do somebody, somewhere, some good? A special couple for some special reason and, thank God, they would find it.

For now, he'd just savor this moment, a moment they had both dreamed of so long ago.

Tom gently kissed her forehead as he listened to Claire's slow breathing, her head on his pillow, a mist of hair across his face.

Cinnamon.

They were in each other's arms.

They were home. The dream, at last, had begun.

Acknowledgements

I write.

Five decades ago this spring, I received my first remuneration for something I put on paper. It was a small scholarship for winning a Veterans of Foreign Wars patriotic speech contest for high school seniors, which I used to pay tuition that fall as I entered the University of Oklahoma.

Perhaps that prize triggered something in my mind. Perhaps I could make a living at this?

Since then, I've employed nearly every written medium known. My name went on newspaper stories, magazine articles, speeches, columns, video scripts, press releases, government filings, PowerPoints, church lay leader training manuals, web pages—even a technical paper on cattle breeding.

Every written medium but the big one: Novels.

The very real alter ego of my friend, Tony, first put the thought in my mind: Why not try fiction? Why not create a special gift for the novel-devouring love of my life?

Tony introduced me to his friends Tom and Claire, and they helped me find their delightful home town on one of those maps that also shows Yoknapatawpha County, Mississippi, and Lake Wobegon, Minnesota.

The year I've shared with Mr. and Mrs. Bentley has been a delight. Perhaps the lovestruck newlyweds will share more of their lives with me sometime. I hope so, we have become good friends. They taught me that even in our latter days, life can offer something surprising.

My very special thanks to Theresa Ward, Andrea Franco-Cook, Amy Merritt, Erin Pedigo, Matthew Hite, Evelyn Gravitt and Emily Cain for their help in telling a unique love story.

Paul Hart
February 2019

Made in the USA
Coppell, TX
29 July 2020

31877103R00225